"A compelling narra[tive]... [a]bout life's pain and hopeful about its possibilities.   —*Kirkus Reviews* (starred review)

"Emily Murdoch has written a painful, hopeful . . . book that charts the best and worst of humanity, especially family, with characters who worm their way into your heart."   —*Booklist* (starred review)

"Beautifully written. The deep bond between the sisters is almost physically palpable, as is their intense longing for love and acceptance; they will quickly endear themselves to readers."
—*School Library Journal* (starred review)

"Murdoch's debut is poetic and beautifully written. Carey and Nessa's story is memorable and deeply moving, and readers will find it very easy to fall in love with these girls."   —*Publishers Weekly*

"As a male, I'm often looking for titles that reluctant readers might enjoy. I can honestly say I now have a book to share that all teens will enjoy." —Russ Stamp, Information Services/Teen Specialist, Pikes Peak Library District-Penrose Library, Colorado Springs, Colorado

"It's one of the best books I've read so far in 2013 and one of my favorite books dealing with tough subjects. I gave it a theme song, I made it a graphic, I wrote it a raving review."   —Paperiot.com

"Unforgettable. . . . *If You Find Me* is a taut, gripping coming-of-age story. It is terrifying and uplifting all at once and made the more so because it is so believable. Emily Murdoch, please write more books."
—*Asheville Citizen-Times*

IF YOU
FIND ME

IF YOU
FIND ME

emily murdoch

St. Martin's Griffin
New York

IF YOU FIND ME. Copyright © 2013 by Emily Murdoch. All rights reserved. Printed in the United States of America. For information, address St. Martin's Press, 175 Fifth Avenue, New York, N.Y. 10010.

Quotations from *Pooh's Little Instruction Book*, inspired by A. A. Milne, with decorations by Ernest H. Shepard. Copyright © 1995 by the Trustees of the Pooh Properties, original text and compilation of illustrations. Used by permission of Dutton Children's Books, a division of Penguin Group (USA) Inc.

www.stmartins.com

The Library of Congress has cataloged the hardcover edition as follows:

Murdoch, Emily.
    If you find me / Emily Murdoch. — First edition.
        pages cm
    ISBN 978-1-250-02152-6 (hardcover)
    ISBN 978-1-250-02153-3 (e-book)
    1. Sisters—Fiction.   2. Foundlings—Fiction.   3. Abused children—Fiction.   4. Family secrets—Fiction.   5. Domestic fiction.   I. Title.
    PS3613.U69385I5 2013
    813'.6—dc23

                                                          2013002656

ISBN 978-1-250-03327-7 (trade paperback)

St. Martin's Griffin books may be purchased for educational, business, or promotional use. For information on bulk purchases, please contact Macmillan Corporate and Premium Sales Department at 1-800-221-7945, extension 5442, or write specialmarkets@macmillan.com.

First St. Martin's Griffin Trade Paperback Edition: April 2014

10 9 8 7 6 5 4 3 2 1

For the bright and the brave

IF YOU
FIND ME

SPRING AND FALL (1880)

to a young child

Margaret, are you grieving
Over Goldengrove unleaving?
Leaves, like the things of man, you
With your fresh thoughts care for, can you?
Ah! as the heart grows older
It will come to such sights colder
By and by, nor spare a sigh
Though worlds of wanwood leafmeal lie;
And yet you will weep and know why.
Now no matter, child, the name:
Sorrow's springs are the same.
Nor mouth had, no nor mind, expressed
What heart heard of, ghost guessed:
It is the blight man was born for,
It is Margaret you mourn for.

—GERARD MANLEY HOPKINS

Part I

THE END

Sometimes, if you stand on the bottom rail of a bridge and lean over to watch the river slipping slowly away beneath you, you will suddenly know everything there is to be known.

—WINNIE-THE-POOH, FROM *POOH'S LITTLE INSTRUCTION BOOK*

1

Mama says no matter how poor folks are, whether you're a have, a have-not, or break your mama's back on the cracks in between, the world gives away the best stuff on the cheap. Like, the way the white-hot mornin' light dances in diamonds across the surface of our creek. Or the creek itself, babblin' music all day long like Nessa when she was a baby. Happiness is free, Mama says, as sure as the blinkin' stars, the withered arms the trees throw down for our fires, the waterproofin' on our skin, and the tongues of wind curlin' the walnut leaves before slidin' down our ears.

It might just be the meth pipe talkin'. But I like how *free* sounds all poetic-like.

Beans ain't free, but they're on the cheap, and here in the Obed Wild and Scenic River National Park, dubbed "the Hundred Acre Wood," I must know close to one hundred ways to fix beans. From the dried, soaked-in-water variety to beans in the can—baked beans, garbanzo beans, kidney beans . . .

It don't sound important. It's just beans, after all, the cause of square farts, as my sister used to say with a giggle on the end. But when you're livin' in the woods like Jenessa and me, with no runnin' water or electricity, with Mama gone to town for long stretches of time, leavin' you in charge of feedin' a younger sister—nine years younger—with a stomach rumblin' like a California earthquake, inventin' new and interestin' ways to fix beans becomes very important indeed.

That's what I'm thinkin' as I fill the scratchy cookin' pot full of water from the chipped porcelain jug and turn on the dancin' blue flame of the Bunsen burner: how I can make the beans taste new tonight, along with wishin' we had butter for the last of the bread, which we don't, because butter don't keep well without refrigeration.

Sometimes, after a stint away, Mama will appear out of nowhere, clutchin' a greasy brown sack from the diner in town. Then, everythin' we eat is buttered thick as flies on a deer carcass, because it would break mine and Jenessa's hearts to waste those little squares of gold.

Mama says stealin' butter is free, as long as you don't get caught.

(She also says *g*'s are free, and I should remember to tack them onto the ends of my *ing* words, and stop using *ain't*, and talk proper like a lady and all. Just because she forgets don't mean I should. Just because she's backwoods don't mean me and Jenessa have to be.)

At least we have the bread. I'm glad Ness isn't here to see me scrape the fuzzy green circles off the bottom. If you scrape it carefully, you can't even taste the must, which, when I sniff it, smells like our forest floor after a wetter month.

Snap–swish!

I freeze, the rusty can opener one bite into the tin. *Nessa?* The crunch of leaves and twigs beneath careless feet and the unmistakable sound of branches singin' off the shiny material of a winter coat is too much noise for Jenessa to make, with her cloth coat and footsteps quiet as an Injun's. *Mama?* I scan the tree line for the lemon yellow zing of her spiffy store-bought ski jacket. But the only yellow in sight drips from the sun, fuzzyin' up the spaces between hundreds of shimmerin' leaves.

I reckon I know how a deer feels in crosshairs as my heart buh-bumps against my ribs and my eyes open at least as wide as the dinner plates stacked on the flat rock behind me. Movin' just my eyes, I see the shotgun only a superlooooong arm stretch away, and breathe a sigh of relief.

We're not expectin' anyone. I think of how I look: the threadbare clothin' hangin' loose as elephant wrinkles, my stringy hair limp as overcooked spaghetti soaked in corn oil overnight. In my defense, I've been stuck on the violin for days, workin' out a piece I've yet to perfect; "suspended in the zone," as Mama calls it, where I forget all about the outside parts. Although, here in the backwoods of Tennessee, it don't matter much. We've had maybe one or two lost hikers stumble upon our camp in all the years since Mama stowed us away in this broken-down camper in the sticks.

I listen harder. *Nothin'.* Maybe it's just tourists after all. I run my fingers through my hair, then rub the greasy feelin' off on the legs of my jeans.

The few times I seen myself in the fancy store mirrors, I didn't recognize myself. Who's that scruffy, skinny girl with the grasshopper knees? The only mirror we own is a small shard of glass I found in the leaves. In it, I can see one Cyclops eye at a time, or half the button of my nose. The *v* sittin' pretty in the middle of my top lip, or the peach fuzz on the tip of my earlobe.

"Seven years bad luck," Mama said after she'd seen the shard. And I ain't even the one who busted it. Luck ain't free. Seven years might as well be ten or twenty or forever, with luck bein' rare as butter, for Mama, my sister, and me.

Where's Nessa? I sink into a squat, my eyes sweepin' the ground for a broken branch to use as a club, just in case I can't get to the shotgun in time. After last night's storm, there are a few choice limbs to choose from. The crunchin' starts again, and I track the sound in the direction of the camper, prayin' Nessa don't come back early from her fairy hunt. *Better for strangers to move on without seein' either one of us.*

"Carey! Jenessa!"

Huh?

My breath breaks free in marshmeller puffs, and my heart beats heart-attack fast. It's a man, obviously, one whose voice I don't recognize, but how does he know our names? *Is he a friend of Mama's?*

"Girls? Joelle!"

Joelle is Mama, only she's not here to answer back. In fact, we haven't seen her in over a month, maybe two at this point. It's been a worry, the last few days. While we have enough beans to last a week or so, this is the first time Mama has been gone so long without word. Even Jenessa has started to worry, her face an open book, even if her mouth refuses to voice the words.

More than once, I've caught her lips countin' canned goods and propane tanks, and she don't need to say what she's thinkin', because I lug around the same worry: that we'll run out of necessities before Mama comes back—*if* she comes back—which is a dark-enough thought to tumble me into my own pit of silence.

My sister don't talk much. When she does, it's only to me, in moth-winged whispers, and only when we're alone. By the time Ness turned six, Mama had grown worried enough to disguise her youngest daughter as "Robin" for the day and whisk her off to the speech therapist in town, a smart-lookin' woman who diagnosed Jenessa with a condition called "selective mutism." Nothin' Mama said, threatened, or did could break Ness's resolve.

"Carey? Jenessa!"

I clap my hands over my ears and use my thinkin' to drown out the calls.

It's strange, hearin' a man's voice, when it's mostly been us females.

I used to wish I had a father, like the girls in my books, but wishin' don't make things so. I don't remember anythin' about my own father, except for one thing, and Mama laughed when I brought it up. As embarrassed as I was, I guess it *is* funny, how my one memory of my father is *underarms*. She said the scent of pine and oak moss I remember came from a brand of deodorant called Brut. And then she'd gotten annoyed because I didn't know what deodorant was, said I asked far too many questions, and her jug of moonshine was empty.

"It's okay, girls! Come on out!"

Why won't he just go away? What the heck is Mama thinkin'? I don't care how much money he promised her—I'm not gonna do those things no more. And I'll kill 'im, I swear, if he lays one finger on Jenessa.

All I have to do is stay hidin', and wait for him to leave. That's the plan, the only plan, until I catch a skip of pink dancin' through the brown and greenery, and the butter yellow head of a little girl lost in a fairy world.

Look up! Hide!

But it's too late—he sees her, too.

Nessa stumbles, her mouth open, and a gasp escapes. Her head whips left, then right. The man probably thinks she's searchin' for an escape route, but I know my little sister better than anyone, even God. Jenessa is tryin' to find *me*.

Makin' my own careless leaf sounds, I rise, my eyes on Nessa, who sees me immediately and flies across the forest into my arms. Our heads crank in the direction of new movement, this time in the form of a woman thin as chicken bones, her gait uneven as her heels sink into the soft forest floor.

Jenessa clings like a leech, her legs wrapped round my waist. The scent of her hair, sunbaked and sweaty, is so personal, it aches in my belly. Like a dog, I can smell her fear, or maybe it's mine. I shake it off fast as my face smoothes into stone and I collect myself, because I'm in charge.

Neither the man nor the woman moves. *Don't they know it's impolite to stare? Bein' city folk and all?* She looks over at him, her face unsure, and he nods at her before goin' back to starin' at us, his gaze unwaverin'.

"Carey and Jenessa, right?" she says.

I nod, then curse myself as my attempt at a "Yes, ma'am" comes out in a squeak. I stop, clear my throat, and try again.

"Yes, ma'am. I'm Carey, and this is my sister, Jenessa. If you're lookin' for Mama, she went into town for supplies. Can I help you with somethin'?"

Nessa squirms in my iron grip, and I command my arms to relax. At least I'm not shakin', which would be a dead giveaway for Nessa, but truth be told, I'm shakin' *inside.*

Maybe the church folk sent them. Maybe they met Mama in town, beggin' money for her next fix. Maybe they talked some Jesus into her, and came out to drop off some food.

"Are you Jehovah's Witnesses or somethin'?" I continue. "Because we're not interested in savin' by some guy in the sky."

The man's face breaks into a smile, which he covers with a cough. The woman frowns, swats at a mosquito. She looks mighty uncomfortable standin' in our woods, glancin' from me to Ness and then back again, shakin' her head. I smooth down my hair, releasin' my own musky scent of dust and sunbaked head. The woman's nutmeg brown hair, unsprung from her bun, makes me think of Nessa's after a hard play, with tendrils like garter snakes crawlin' down her neck and stickin' there. It's pretty hot for fall.

Even from here, I can tell the woman washed her hair this mornin'. It probably smells like fancy flowers, unlike the heels of soap we use to wash ours.

"There's a table over there, if you want to sit awhile," I say uninvitin'ly, hopin' she don't. But she nods and I take the lead, cartin' Nessa to the clearin' by the camper, past the fire pit poppin' and smokin' as the kindlin' catches on, past the canned goods locked in a rusty metal cabinet nailed to the trunk of a tree, and over to a battered metal foldin' table surrounded by mismatched chairs: two metal, one wicker, and two large stumps with cushions that used to cling like puffy skin to our old rockin' chair.

The man and woman sit, him in a metal chair, while she chooses the large stump with the cleanest cushion. I plunk Nessa in the wicker and keep the table between us and them. I stay standin', with plenty of room for a fast getaway if need be. But they both seem normal enough, not like kidnappers or drug dealers or crazy church folk. She looks important, in her store-bought tan suit. This fact makes me nervous more than anythin' else.

They watch quietly as I put my violin away in its case and then fill three tin cups with a stream of water from the jug. I want to tell them I boiled the water first, and that the creek is clean, but I don't. Dolin' out the cups, I cringe when I catch sight of my nails, ragged and uneven, a ribbon of dirt stretched beneath each.

Twice I step on Nessa's foot, and tears spring to her eyes. I pat her head—it'll have to do—then stand back, fold my arms, and wait.

"Wouldn't you like to sit?" the woman asks, her voice soft.

I glance at Nessa, squirmin' in her seat, shyly slurpin' her water, and shake my head no. The woman smiles at me before fumblin' through her briefcase. She slides out a manila folder thick with pages. The white label on the front, I can even read upside down. It says: "Blackburn, Carey and Jenessa."

"My name is Mrs. Haskell," she says.

She pauses, and I follow her gaze back to my sister, who pours a few drops of water into an old bottle cap. We all watch as Nessa leans down and sets it in front of a fat beetle laborin' through the sea of wanwood leafmeal.

I nod, not knowin' what to say. It's hard to keep my eyes on her when the man keeps starin' at me. I watch a tear slip down his clean-shaven cheek, surprised when he don't wipe it away. Puzzle pieces click-clack into old places and my stomach twists at the picture they're startin' to make.

He hasn't offered his name, and he isn't familiar to me. But in that instant, hittin' like a lightnin' bolt, I know who he is.

"It's called Brut. I can't smell it anymore without gettin' sick, thinkin' what he did to us."

The memory bridges ten years of space, and, just like that, I'm five again, and on the run, clutchin' my dolly to my chest like a life preserver. Mama, crazy-eyed and talkin' nonsense, backhandin' the questions from my lips until the salty-metal taste of tears and blood make me forget the questions in the first place.

"Do you know why we're here?"

Mrs. Haskell searches my face as my stomach contents begin their climb: beans, of course. Baked beans cold from the can, the sweet kind Nessa likes so much. I feel like a fortune-teller, knowin' her words are about to change the earth below and the sky above and rearrange everythin' we hold normal and dear.

I stare at her, expectin' the inevitable.

"We're here to take you home, Carey."

Home?

I wait for the ground to right itself, and once it does, I fling myself into the bushes and let the beans fly. Afterward, the anger licks my innards like a wildfire. I turn around, hands on my hips, and stare this woman down. She cringes when I wipe my mouth on the sleeve of my T-shirt.

"That's impossible, ma'am. We *are* home. We live here with our mama."

"Where is your mom, honey?"

I glare at her; no way I'm fallin' for the "honey" bit.

"Like I said, Mama went into town for supplies. We were runnin'—running—out of some stuff and—"

"How long has she been gone?"

I have to lie. Jenessa is almost hyperventilatin', on the verge of one of her nervous fits. She skitters over and stands next to me, reachin' for my hand and holdin' it so tight, my pulse punches through my fingernails.

"Mama left this mornin'. We're fixin' on seein' her before nightfall."

I give Ness's hand a hard squeeze.

"Your mother said she left over two months ago. We received her letter yesterday."

What?

The blood rushes from my head and my ears ring. I grasp onto a nearby branch for steadyin'. *I must have heard her wrong.* But she nods her head yes, her eyes full of *sorrys* I don't want to hear.

"Wha—what letter?"

Jenessa's tears tickle my arm like chiggers, and I want to scratch, but I can't let go of her hand. She sags against me, and again, I burn. *Look what they're doin' to my sister. Mama was right: Outsiders can't be trusted. All they do is ruin lives.*

Mrs. Haskell smiles an apologetic smile, a practiced smile, like we're not her first victims, nor her last. I wonder how many kids have stood before her like this, swayin' in their newly tiltin' worlds. Hundreds, I'd bet, goin' by her eyes.

However, I see a sadness there, too; a softness for us, a familiar bent of the head that comes from the things we're used to seein', like

the sun-dazzled canopies of the Hundred Acre Wood, or learnin' to
go without butter, or havin' Mama disappear for weeks on end.

She waits until I'm steady again. I hold on to her eyes, like a rock
in the roilin' river.

"Your mother wrote us last month, Carey. She said she could no
longer take care of you and your sister—"

"That's a lie! She'd never leave us!"

"She asked us to intervene," she continues, ignorin' my outburst.
"We would've been here sooner, but we couldn't find you girls. She
really had you hidden away pretty good."

"No!"

But it's a strangled cry, a hollow cry, floatin' away on the air like
dandelion fluff and wishes that don't come true. And then, as quick
as the emotion escapes, it freezes over. I stand up straight. I am ice,
slippery and cool, impenetrable and in control.

"You must have it wrong, ma'am. Mama wouldn't leave us
permanent-like. You must've misunderstood."

The three of us jump back, but not fast enough. Nessa's stomach
contents spatter Mrs. Haskell's fancy shoes. This, I can tell, is
somethin' she *ain't* used to. Mrs. Haskell throws up her hands, and
without thinkin', I fling my arms in front of my face.

"Oh, God, honey, no—"

"Just leave us alone," I snap. "I wish you'd never found us!"

Without a word, she knows another one of my secrets, and I
hate her for it. I hate them both.

Her eyes burn into my back as I lead Jenessa over to a pail. I dip
a clean rag into the water and dab at my sister's mouth, her eyes
glazed over and dartin' from me to them like a cornered rabbit. The
man walks away, his shoulders saggin'. He pulls a cigarette pack
from his coat pocket, the cellophane crinklin' like a butterscotch
wrapper.

Get a hold of yourself this instant, Carey Violet Blackburn! Fix this!

"You're scarin' my little sister," I say, my voice close to a hiss. "Look, Mama will be home tomorrow. Why don't you come back and we can discuss it then?"

I sound just like an adult. Pretty convincin', if you ask me.

"I'm sorry, Carey, but I can't do that. Under the laws of the state of Tennessee, I can't leave two minor children unattended in the woods."

I soak another rag in the water and hand it to Mrs. Haskell, lowerin' myself onto the rough bark of a downed tree. Then I pull Ness onto my lap, my arm around her waist, not even carin' about the acrid smell that replaces the sweet, sunbaked one from just an hour ago. Her body is limp, like a rag doll in my arms. She's already gone.

"Can I see the letter, ma'am?"

Mrs. Haskell picks her way over to the table, riffles through more papers, and returns with a sheet of my own notebook paper containin' a handful of lines that, even from a distance, I recognize as Mama's scratchy penmanship. I pluck the page from her fingers, turn from her, and begin readin'.

To Whom It May Concern,

I'm writing in regards to my daughters, Carey and Jenessa Blackburn . . .

It's as far as I get before the waterfall blinds me. I wipe my face with the back of my hand, pretendin' I don't care that everyone sees.

"Can I keep it, ma'am?"

Without waitin' for an answer, I fold the paper into smaller and smaller squares before shovin' it into my jeans pocket.

Mrs. Haskell nods. "That's just a copy. The original is in your

official records. We need it for the hearing, when your case goes
before the judge."

I jut my chin at the man on the bench, who's watchin' us, squin-
tin' through a latticework of cigarette smoke, his form spotlighted
by the wanin' sunlight.

"I know who he is, and we're not goin' with him."

"I have permission from Child Services to release you into his
custody."

"So we have no choice?"

Mrs. Haskell sits down next to me, lowerin' her voice.

"You have a choice, Carey. If you refuse to go with him, we can
place you in foster care. Two foster homes. Our families are pretty
full right now, and we can't find one that can take both of you at
present. In light of your sister's condition—"

"She's not retarded or nothin'. She just don't talk."

"Even so, her, um, issue requires special placement. We found a
home for Jenessa, but they're just not equipped to take two children
right now."

Nessa's thumb finds her mouth, and her hair, soaked with sweat,
falls in a curtain across her eyes. She makes no move to smooth it
away. She's hidin' in plain sight.

"I can't leave my sister alone with strangers."

"I don't think it's the best idea, either. We like to place children
with relatives whenever possible. Taking into account Jenessa's bond
with you, I think it would be detrimental to her emotional well-
being to separate the two of you. It's already going to be a big adjustment as it is."

I glare in the direction of the man on the bench, this man I don't
know and barely recognize. I think of runnin' away, like maybe we
should've done as soon as we saw them comin'. But we have no
money, no place to go. There's no car to pull the camper, since Mama

drove off with it, and we can't stay here. They know where we are now. They know everythin'.

I think of tellin' her what Mama told me about him, because there's no way she'd make us go with him, if she knew. But I look down at Ness, disappearin' before our eyes.

I can't leave my sister.

"How much time do we have?"

"Enough time to pack up your things. You'll need to pack a bag for your sister also."

She leaves us sittin' there, with the late-afternoon sun dapplin' the forest floor as if it's any other day. I watch her reach into the bin by the foldin' table, then walk back over. She hands me two of the shiny black garbage bags folded up like Mama's letter. I slip out from under Jenessa, balance her on the tree, and proceed to shake each bag into its full size. We all stop and watch the birds scatter into jagged flight at the unnatural sound of plastic slappin' the air.

"Just take the necessities. We'll send someone back to pack up the rest."

I nod, glad to turn my gaze toward the camper before my face melts again. How could Mama do this to us? How could she leave us to fend for ourselves—leave us at all—without explainin' or sa-yin' good-bye?

I hate her with the fury of gasoline set on fire. I burn for Jenessa, who deserves better than this, better than some screwed-up, drug-addicted mother, better than this chaos that always seems to find us, rubbin' off on us like some horrible rash.

Ness is my shadow as the camper door creaks on its hinges, this old piece-of-crap ve-hic-le we've called home for almost as long as I can remember—definitely as long as Ness can remember.

I glance around, absorb the mess, the clothes strewn about, the plates dribblin' crumbs or caked with dried bean glue, and begin to pack Ness's bag first. She sits on the cot, unmovin', not even jumpin' when I grab the nearest book, one of her Winnie-the-Poohs, and slam it down on a cockroach scuttlin' across the tiny stainless-steel sink; without runnin' water, it was as useless as a dollhouse sink, until I'd turned it into a place to store plates and cups. Mama never hooked the camper up to water because water sources meant campgrounds, sites out in the open, and judgmental strangers with pryin' eyes.

Almost everythin' of Nessa's is some shade of pink. I pack a pair of scuffed Mary Janes and her pale pink sneakers, her neon pink long-sleeve T-shirt, a dark pink-and-red-striped T-shirt, and another T-shirt with a peelin'-off Cinderella iron-on on the front. I pack her spare undershirt and underpants; "one on and one off," as Mama says when we complain. Ness's jeans look small and vulnerable stretched between my hands, and my heart wrenches.

When her bag is full, I use mine to gather up her rag doll, her one-armed teddy bear, and her stuffed dog. Her Pooh books. The brush and elastics. On top, I place my own pair of jeans (one on, one off), a newer T-shirt, two tank tops, my spare underpants, and the only shoes I own besides the ratty sneakers on my feet: a pair of cowboy boots from a garage sale in town, the toes stuffed with tissue paper to force a fit.

Not much fits me clotheswise, after a growth spurt last year. Now I'm glad, because it means more room for Jenessa's stuff. I don't need much room anyhow. I don't have toys from childhood or any stuffed animals. I left my childhood behind when Mama dragged us off in the middle of the night. My belongin's consist of a sketch pad I place on top of the pile, while I make a mental note not to forget my most prized possession: the violin that Mama taught me to play the year we moved to the Hundred Acre Wood.

Mama played in a symphony before she met my father. I grab the scrapbook crammed with clippin's from her performances and place it on top of the sketch pad, then draw the yellow plastic strings tight. The bag looks close to burstin' by the time I'm through. But it's good, because I bet the bag holds more than any suitcase would, if we had one.

Before I can call for her, Mrs. Haskell appears, and I hand her down the bag, which she struggles beneath. The man gets up to help, lockin' on my eyes while takin' the bag from her and slingin' it over his back. He does the same with the second bag.

"May I have one more bag, ma'am?"

Mrs. Haskell obliges. I fill it with our schoolbooks, with my Emily Dickinson, my Tagore, my Tennyson and Wordsworth, making the bag impossibly heavy. Lookin' at the man, I'd have giggled in different circumstances. He looks like a reverse sort of Santa Claus. A Santa Claus of garbage.

No one speaks as he plunks the lightest bag down in front of Mrs. Haskell.

I go back inside and gather Ness from the bed. Reachin' out, I pluck her thumb gently from her mouth. Her lips remain in an O shape, and the thumb pops right back in.

"You're gonna make your teeth crooked, you know it."

She stares right through me, droolin' a little, and I give her a hug before helpin' her stand up and walk to the door.

"How about a piggyback?"

I squat in front of her, and she slowly climbs on.

"Hold on tight, 'k?"

The sun is meltin', poolin' behind the trees, and still Mama don't come. I scan the Hundred Acre Wood, somehow expectin' her to show up with a greasy brown bag and save the day, but she don't.

The man takes the lead, with Mrs. Haskell strugglin' behind him, trippin' over roots and sinkin' into the mud, cursin' under her breath as Ness and I follow. It's a long ways to the road, and if we go the way they're headin', it'll be twice as long.

"This way, ma'am," I say, poppin' Nessa farther up my back and takin' the lead, refusin' to meet the man's eyes as he steps aside so we can pass.

I focus on the endless treetops scrapin' the sunset into gooey colors, the birds trillin' and fussin' at our departure. I close my eyes for a second, breathin' in deep to make serious memories, the kind that stick forever. I'd locked up the camper on my way out, but I don't know who has a key, since Ness and I don't, and we'd only ever locked up when we were inside.

Mama has a key, and the least she could've done, if she wasn't comin' back, would've been to leave it for us. And then I remember: the old hollow hickory, the one a few hundred feet past the clearin'. I'm eight years old, watchin' Mama slide a sweaty white string off her neck with a brass key danglin' from it, glintin' in the sunlight.

"This is our spare, and if you ever need it, it'll be right here in the tree. See?"

She places it into the hollow, where it disappears like a magic trick.

I feel safer, somehow, knowin' the key is there.

My secret.

If I ever need it, if Ness and I come back, it'll be there waitin' for us.

2

My head buzzes like bees around Pooh's honey pot, the farther we get from the camper.

I know they think we look funny. Talk funny. Mama's right: I have to remember my g's.

I, Carey Violet Blackburn, vow, from this second forward, no more dropped g's. No more ain'ts or don'ts. I'm going to do Mama and Jenessa right proud.

No one talks as we crunch our way through the forest. I try to follow what trails I can for their sake, but in these woods, there aren't enough feet to beat back the overgrowth on a continuous basis.

"Dammit!"

I turn and see the man help Mrs. Haskell to her feet, her panty hose ripped just below each knee, with one knee bloodied. She continues on, limping along as if one leg is longer than the other. I reckon she's broken off the heel of one of those fancy shoes.

Nessa shifts her weight, her twiggy arms linked around my neck. Against my back, she shakes like a leaf. Her thumb would calm her, but she needs to hold on with both hands.

"It's going to be okay, Ness," I chirp softly, summoning up some cheer. "You'll have a bed, a real bed—do you ever remember sleeping in a real bed?"

She shakes her head no against my shoulder.

"That's right. The bed in the camper is actually a cot. It's not the same. There are a lot of things you've never had—biscuits with Pooh honey, as much as you can eat. Ice cream—wait till you taste all the different kinds of ice cream—I reckon there must be two hundred different flavors, at least."

Nessa leans her head against my shoulder, lulled by my voice.

"There's this thing called TV—it's like your storybooks come to life, but on a screen, in a box that sits on a stand. You're going to love that. There are machines that keep food cold and wash clothes and do so many things that save city folk lots of time."

Nessa's breath is slow and even, tickling my ear. I whisper the rest, knowing sleep right now would be best for her.

"I don't remember most things, but some things you don't forget. And you know what else?"

Nessa shakes her head almost imperceptibly, and it's a good sign, her playing along.

"If you don't want to, you'll never have to eat another bean in your life."

The sun disappears and dusk covers the forest like the weathered tarp covering our firewood, casting the trees into unfamiliar shapes unless you're right on top of them.

"Is it much farther?"

Mrs. Haskell is huffing now, and the man walks behind her, as if to help her along if she needs it. Short of carrying her, there's not much he can do. I imagine him piggybacking her the rest of the way, and I crack a secret smile.

"Not much farther. Just over the hill," I say, stretching the truth a wee bit.

Mrs. Haskell stops in her tracks, glaring at me.

"It's not a big hill, ma'am. More like a hump, I swear."

She shakes her head, mutters under her breath, but at least we're back on the move.

An hour later, we reach the blacktopped turn off on the main road, a scenic overlook of the forest and the mountains beyond. It was here, years ago, that Mama clicked on the right-turn signal and pulled off the road, headlights bouncing down a dirt trail barely wide enough for the car and camper. I look back, trying to catch sight of where that dirt road used to be, but all that's left is the faint foot trail we've walked up.

Mrs. Haskell breathes a sigh of relief with paved ground beneath her shoes. She drops the garbage bag and stops to catch her breath, and as she does, tucks the loose hairs back into her bun. But it only makes it look worse, if you ask me, which no one does.

I know, because I'm a master at hairstyles, having practiced on Jenessa all these years—and believe me, fine hair is harder. A hairdressing magazine showed me how to braid, roll, pin up, part hair into all different dos. If Mrs. Haskell would just sit on the car bumper, I could work my magic in a jiffy.

At least I could if there weren't so many bats swooping after bugs.

Mrs. Haskell lets loose a high-pitched squeal and ducks, and I want to tell her the bats don't swoop that low, that it's an optical illusion, but she's already running. She wastes no time pulling a key ring from her briefcase and limping over to a Lexus, it says on the back, its silver paint glowing under the pumpkin moon just beginning its climb. She unlocks the driver's side and clicks the back door open for me and Jenessa.

"Let me."

His voice is tender, startling me with its nearness. He lifts Nessa from my back and carries her in his arms to the car, depositing her on the far side, her head leaning against the window glass.

"Thank you, sir."

I look down when I say it, but it seems like I should say something, so I do. Peering through my lashes, I watch him turn away and motion toward the back of the car.

"Could you kindly pop the trunk?"

Mrs. Haskell fiddles with something, and the trunk pops open. He deposits the garbage bags inside.

I slide in beside Nessa and pull the door shut with a *click*. Mrs. Haskell inserts a key into the slot beside the wheel, and different-colored lights flash on. The man slides into the seat next to her. As if making it final, Mrs. Haskell pushes a button, locking us all in, for better or for worse. She's barefoot, her wrecked shoes lying in the space between the two front seats.

"Put your seat belts on," she says.

I lean over and fasten Nessa's, and then my own—it only takes a minute to remember. The car lurches forward and the headlights sweep the forest I love, bringing it into focus one last time. My chest expands with an ache I can't swallow down. *If it weren't for Nessa . . .*

The lights of oncoming cars flash past, and in their strobe I study the back of the man's head, and his profile, too, when he turns to nod at the lowly chattering Mrs. Haskell.

Eventually, I get bored, though, listening to grown-up talk about the weather and the news and other such things I know nothing about. Tornadoes and hurricanes. People killed, nations I've never heard of fighting holy wars. I hold on to Nessa's hand as if it's for her sake, but it's for my own. The warmth of her palm against mine spins a familiar cocoon around us, and that's the last thing I remember before I, too, doze off.

———

The dashboard clock reads 10:15 as I blink my eyes, careful not to move anything else. At some point, Ness has slipped from the seat to curl like a Cheez Doodle on the floor mat. She isn't wearing her seat belt, but I don't have the heart to wake her.

"The girls don't seem much worse for wear and tear, considering how they were living," Mrs. Haskell says.

She clicks a stick and a light blinks as she passes a slow-moving truck strapped down with logs.

"To be honest, I wasn't sure what to expect. Your ex-wife's letter was routed to the wrong department, and I only received word of it weeks after the postmark."

The man grunts in answer, then looks over his shoulder. My eyes snap shut.

"Joelle carted the girls out into the middle of nowhere, all right," he says, his words careful, like he knows I might be listening. "At the same time, they were right here in Tennessee. Right under our noses the whole time."

"There's an APB out on her," Mrs. Haskell whispers. "It's procedure in cases such as these."

An APB? What's an APB?

"If she hides herself as well as she hid the girls, they'll never find her."

I'm surprised to hear the casual tone of his voice, although, what was I expecting? Anger? Remorse? For him to make pretend he loves me, wants me? If he wanted us, he wouldn't have beaten us, Mama and me. He'd at least sound sad for all the years we've been gone. But I can't tell what he's feeling. I can't read him like I could Mama.

"If they do find her," Mrs. Haskell continues, "you won't have a lot of say in how they handle it. She did take off with Carey as the noncustodial parent. In the state of Tennessee, that's kidnapping."

"Kidnapping?" I blurt the word, unable to stop myself. Then, as Nessa stirs, I lower my voice. "Are you saying he's gonna have Mama thrown in jail?"

He's the one who should be in jail.

The man sighs, his shoulders hard set. I watch the back of his head. He doesn't turn around.

"I'm not sure what they're going to do, honey, but your mom broke the law." Mrs. Haskell pauses to open her window a crack. "We'll have to see what happens when it happens."

Again, I feel the white heat fill me from my toenails to the tips of my ears. It should be *him* in trouble, not Mama. Not Mama, who'd tried to protect us from him. Heck, he hadn't even cared enough to look for us. He's only stuck with us now because of the letter.

I sit back in a huff, watching the cars zoom by, quite numerous now, as are the flecks of light thumbtacking the land in the distance. My emotions swirl like leaves caught in the breath of a dust devil, and the only thing I can seem to hold on to is the anger.

Why had Mama sent that letter? Didn't she know they'd call him, that they'd release us into his custody? Where else would we go? Didn't she care that they could separate us, stuff us into ill-fitting foster homes like the wrong puzzle pieces?

As if reading my mind, Mrs. Haskell's voice is strong, unwavering. "It's going to be okay, Carey. You'll see."

I answer her with my silence, understanding the full power of it for the first time. Words are weapons. Weapons are powerful. So are unsaid words. So are unused weapons.

"Are you hungry?" Mrs. Haskell hands me a bag of potato chips—sour cream and onion, which happens to be my favorite—as if she knows to take a thread from my old life and weave it into this new one.

I take the bag from her, saliva squirting at the back of my cheeks.

Closing my eyes, I savor the chips, trying to remember the last time I'd eaten the salty, crunchy goodness. *Heaven this minute lives in my mouth.* I have to pace myself, stop myself from gobbling down the whole bag in seconds. Mama brought us chips maybe three or four times. All too often, though, we couldn't afford extras.

Mrs. Haskell smiles over her shoulder. "Bet it's been a long time since you girls had chips. There's another bag in the glove box—do you like barbecue?"

I nod my head emphatically, under the potato spell.

She hands the second bag over, and for a few moments, the only sound in the car is the crinkle of the bag around my greasy hand and the sound of my chewing. Like I do with the first bag, I save half, a big half, for Nessa.

"You girls are too thin, but it doesn't surprise me, living the way you were. We'll have to get some meat on your bones, especially Jenessa's. We'll need her hitting those height and weight percentiles normal children grow through."

"She don't like beans much." Only they can't understand me with my mouth full of chips.

"Doesn't like what, hon?"

"*Beans*, ma'am. She got all kinds of sick and tired of 'em after Mama left. We ran out of the ravioli and Campbell's soup. All that was left was beans, and she don't like 'em anymore."

"*Doesn't* like them. That's the proper way to say that word, sweetie."

I know that. I forgot my vow. I blush redder than Jenessa's Crayola. "Yes, ma'am."

I catch them exchanging glances across the seats, and I see, what? Pity? Concern? It hadn't occurred to me that someone could feel sorry for us, let alone *pity* us. We were fine—we did right fine.

I took good care of Nessa—better than Mama. Better than they could, still.

Ness knows it, too. It was me who taught her her numbers and her ABC's, addition and subtraction, reading her books to her and then my own, and after we'd exhausted those, reading her favorites over again, only this time, having her read them to me. Pooh practice. I played her to sleep on my violin, ushering some culture into the woods, like Mama said.

"She loves butter," I add. "But she *doesn't* like peas. She loves birthday cake, too."

I smile when Mrs. Haskell smiles.

Of all the crazy things a little girl could love, Ness loves birthday cake. There'd only been a few—one on my ninth birthday, one on Nessa's third and fifth. Each time, Ness had lost it, squealing over the fluffy pink icing.

They look at each other again with that same sorry look, and my smile fades. *They have no right.*

"Well, when we get back to the motel, we'll get you and Jenessa a hot bath and dinner. Do you girls like hamburgers? French fries?"

My stomach rumbles before the sound of her words leaves the air.

"We like food, ma'am. I don't think we've ever eaten those things you mentioned."

This time, stopped at a light, Mrs. Haskell turns around in her seat and stares at me.

"Are you telling me your mother never took you into town? Not even to a restaurant?"

"She did. We went to town twice. Once to a speech therapist when Nessa stopped talking, and another time to the doctor when we both came down with the chicken pox."

"Twice? In ten *years?*"

"Yes, ma'am."

I hear the intake of breath from the man as Mrs. Haskell regards me with round, uncomprehending eyes.

"What, ma'am?" I say, fidgeting in my seat.

She's bugging me now. Not everyone can afford to eat out all fancy-like. Doesn't she know that?

"Where were you, then, all these years?"

What a ridiculous question. Really.

"In the woods. You were there . . ." I say, my words trailing off.

"Where did you get food and supplies?"

"Mama went into town for supplies every month. Canned goods keep, she said. We had a can opener," I add, my words tasting tinny and inadequate.

"My God. Who schooled you? Your mother?"

"I did. Mama brought us old schoolbooks. I'd learn them, and help Nessa learn hers."

Mrs. Haskell turns back around. The light is green, green means go, and I'm glad she has to pay attention to the road, instead of to me. Having strangers just stare at you is the oddest feeling. But it's more than that.

What had I said? Did I say something wrong?

My stomach sinking, I push aside the chips. Would my words hurt Mama later, after they found her?

I hope they don't find you—fly, Mama, fly! I'll watch over Nessa. We'll be right fine.

It's easy to look out for Nessa. She's my baby sister. She's my family, and family is everything.

I drift off again as the motion of the car—it's been a long time since I've been in a moving car—lulls me to sleep like a baby in its mama's arms. I wake just as we pull into a parking lot.

"This is it. The Social Services building."

The poles tower over the asphalt like chilly metal trees, haunting the area with pale yellow circles of light.

Ness is still asleep, thumb in mouth, T-shirt pushed up, exposing her belly button. I think of what Mrs. Haskell said, noticing for the first time the washboard rows of little-girl ribs. But we've always been skinny, as best I can remember. Mama is slim. So is the man.

I want to ask what we're doing here, as it's obvious the building is closed. I want to ask what's next, what happens next, but I swallow my questions in a lump and tend to Jenessa.

"Baby, we're here."

I push on her shoulder, but she's out cold. Gently, I sit her up, her head lolling against the seat. She grumbles. Her eyelids flutter.

"Nessa, wake up. We're here. You have to wake up."

Mrs. Haskell and the man exit the car, leaving me to it, and I'm glad. Nessa isn't used to strangers. Better she sticks to what she knows. Her eyes open reluctantly, and her thumb falls out as she blinks at me, surely trying to remember where she is and what we're doing in a car, of all places. I use my happy voice.

"Remember Mrs. Haskell came and got us? She drove us to where she works. That's why we've stopped." I lift her by the armpits back onto the seat. "Here, let me tie your shoes."

Ness yawns. I wait for the teary protest shouted from her eyes, because big girls tie their own shoes, but I don't get one. She sits silently as I plunk each small foot down on my thigh and tie the dirty white shoelaces, not too loose, not too tight, just like she likes them.

"Take my hand, okay?"

I slide out of the Lexus, tugging her with me. She inches across the seat, our arms taut. The cool air hits her skin, and she hesitates.

"It's okay, Ness. It's gonna be okay. You got me. I'm right here." I squeeze her hand in a show of solidarity. "C'mon."

I take her coat from the seat and stuff her arms in. Then I turn to Mrs. Haskell.

"She's just a little girl. She needs sleep—it's been a long day."

"I agree, Carey. Your father is bringing his truck around, and there's a motel right down the road. You girls will stay with me, and your father will be in the room next door. We'll finish up the paperwork tonight and appear before the judge in the morning."

Jenessa grips my hand something fierce. I must look skeptical, because Mrs. Haskell sighs, her forehead creasing.

"I think after all you've been through, this is a better idea than taking you girls to the group home for the night. It's another half hour away, it's late, and you need your sleep."

It could be worse, I reassure myself. *Could be left alone with more strangers. Or with him.*

I squat down to eye level and take hold of both of Nessa's hands.

"She's right. This way, we can get you some food and tuck you into bed before midnight."

Unconvinced, Ness pulls her hands from mine and folds her arms, her lower lip jutting out.

She wants to go home. She wants the woods. She thinks I'm in charge. But I'm not anymore.

"Ness, please?" I use her word. "I'm *exhaustified*, too. It's been a long day. I think it's a good idea."

She stares back at me, her dark eyes fringed in thick lashes, and I can almost see the cogs and wheels working behind them. To my relief, she finally nods. I get to my feet. Immediately, she takes my hand again.

I turn to Mrs. Haskell, ignoring the man where he leans against a pale blue truck, curlicues of cigarette smoke weaving around him.

"We'll go. But we ride with you."

"Fine," Mrs. Haskell says, motioning us back into the car. She turns to the man. "We'll follow behind you."

His gaze rests on me for a moment before he flicks his cigarette in a glowing arc. He walks over to where it lands and grinds it out with the toe of his boot.

"If you did that in the woods, you'd burn the whole place down," I say.

He shoots me a sheepish grin and picks it up, depositing the butt in a nearby trash receptacle.

"That better?" he asks, like it matters what I think.

I ignore him, leading Jenessa back to her seat in the car.

As if anything could be better.

Buckled in, I feel so small, as small as Jenessa, and just as helpless. The world is endless without the trees to fence it in, the sky huge enough to swallow us whole and spit out our bones dry as kindling.

Already, I want to go back, go backward. The keening rises like the song of a cicada, then two, then hundreds, until the whole world vibrates in a chorus of longing.

All we'd needed was more canned goods. More blankets. More buckshot.

We were doing right fine on our own.

3

Our motel room is huge, with two beds parked at the far end, boasting matching comforters and crisp white sheets. In the middle of the room is a round table with four chairs, and there's a television bolted up high in the corner, where the lime green wall meets the ceiling. The bathroom door is open. The tiles sparkle hard, like the sun straight on.

Mrs. Haskell smiles at Jenessa, a real smile, which Ness returns with a small one, and then she nods at the television.

"Wait till you see this, Jenessa."

Mrs. Haskell's index finger skims over a shiny plastic placard; then she picks up a rectangular thing—she calls it a "remote control"—pushes a button, and the television crackles to life. She pushes a few more buttons, and the screen flickers with images, coming to rest on a channel with the word *sprout* popping up at the bottom right-hand corner. Fat creatures with antennas on their heads giggle and waddle across a flowery field studded with bunnies.

Before I can control it, my eyes fill. *Teletubbies.* The jolt from the past is like a bucket of ice water dumped over my head. *I remember the Tubbies.* The fuzzy memory of a red Po doll fills my mind.

Jenessa's eyes widen until the whites show. Her bones turn to noodles and she sinks to the rug, only breaking contact with the screen to beam at me in amazement before locking back on the box on the wall.

Mrs. Haskell and I look at each other, her eyes bright. She clears her throat. I turn back to my sister.

"It's television, Ness. TV, for short. You like it?"

As if communicating from a dream, Nessa nods big, sweeping nods from ceiling to floor, while her eyes remain glued to the screen.

"Lift up your foot, okay?"

I untie and remove each sneaker, leaving her wiggling her toes.

"Ewwww," I tease. "Stink stank stunk, Miss Jenessa."

She giggles.

I unbutton her coat, smiling at the light pink T-shirt with the word *Diva* painted across it in silvery, glittery script. When I asked Mama what the word meant, she'd shrugged her shoulders, too high to reply. Ness loved the sparkles too much to care.

"Now your pants."

I expect her to protest, in front of Mrs. Haskell and all, but she doesn't, too mesmerized by the giggling Teletubbies making messy Tubby custard.

I lay her clothes neatly over one of the chairs, and take her in, my heart loving her so much, it could explode all over the room. Those blond curls, the knobby knees, the wonder on her face, the girlie white underwear boasting ruffles around the leg holes. Even as skinny as she is, she's a vision.

I make a vow right then and there that I'll allow no one to separate us. Whatever I have to endure with the man, I'll endure, as long as we stay together.

I reach down and scoop her up in my arms and settle her on the bed against two fluffy pillows. Mrs. Haskell turns the television angle to one Nessa can watch without straining. This is her first experience of a bed, and a sigh escapes her lips. It's the height of luxury for both of us.

"You can borrow this, if you'd like," Mrs. Haskell offers, nodding that it's all right to take the T-shirt, her eyes bobcat large and blinking through the thick glasses she pushes up her nose.

For the first time, I notice Mrs. Haskell's little suitcase, plucked from her trunk. She tosses me the T-shirt and I catch it, light purple, with the word *Chicago* stamped across the chest in curving script.

I know Chicago. It's in Illinois, USA.

"Did you used to live there?" I ask by way of thanks.

"I've heard Chicago is lovely, but I've never been. It's a musical group I listened to in college."

I brush past her into the bathroom to change. I've never heard of that *Chicago*. The only music I know comes from my violin. My stomach clenches as I think about it—about all the things I *don't* know, a mile-long list I'm sure will only grow longer as the days pass.

I reappear from the bathroom with my sneakers and clothes in hand, the T-shirt hanging to my knees. I watch Mrs. Haskell smile as Nessa giggles, her little-girl hands reaching toward the cooing baby's face in the middle of the sun setting over the Teletubbies' world, just before lines of names roll down the screen.

Nessa pops her thumb in her mouth, her eyelids heavy. I climb in beside her, sliding the blankets out from under her legs to set them billowing over us in a cloud. She moves her leg over until it's touching mine.

Neither of us can stay awake long enough to eat, but even better than food is how the white-star night flickers and dies like it doesn't belong here, in the midst of such largess. I imagine being free of it forever, of the sights, sounds, and smells seared into my memory.

But deep down, I know better.

I don't want to wake up from this dream I'm having, of a feather-soft bed, fluffy covers, and Nessa not half on top of me, the two of us crammed onto the narrow cot where we shared our body heat each night. The fit was easy when she was a baby. But babies never stay babies.

I hear his voice and instantly remember who he is, what happened, where we are. The man and Mrs. Haskell talk quietly. I inhale the strange aroma, note the trails of steam rising from white cups they both sip from at the table, a jumble of papers spread out between them.

"So, we go before the judge at noon, and then what?"

"We submit the paperwork to the court, and the judge releases the girls into your custody. It should be a short hearing, all told."

"And then they come home with me."

"Right. We'll need to get them evaluated by a pediatrician, a court-appointed psychologist, and test them academically, so we know where we're at. We'll need them enrolled in school as soon as possible. I feel the longer we wait, the harder it'll be. As their social worker, I'll be here for support throughout the process."

Through slits, I watch the man rake his fingers through his hair. Even I know we have mountains ahead of us. Mrs. Haskell smiles, unruffled.

"No doubt there will be an adjustment period for the girls, Mr. Benskin. For all of you. I won't lie to you."

The man strokes the stubble on his chin with faraway eyes. I don't want him catching me, but I can't look away. I watch his lips as he speaks.

"Did you discuss any of this with Carey? She's spent a long time in those woods. I don't know what Joelle filled her head with, but she's not taking too warmly to me."

I wouldn't have thought he cared what I felt. I let the knowledge settle, sinking like stones to the bottom of the creek, only this time, the creek is my stomach.

"She's agreed to go with you. Not without some hesitance, I admit, but she knows it's best for Jenessa."

The man nods.

"Please don't take it personally. Her reluctance is understandable. Since you're not, in the usual sense—" Mrs. Haskell stops. But not the man.

"Her father. I know." He sighs, deep and wide like Ness does sometimes. "I'm her father, but I'm a complete stranger to both these girls."

"I assure you, they'll have the services of the state of Tennessee at their disposal. We'll get them back in school and all caught up in no time. We'll help them adjust. Like I said, kids are resilient."

"And reporters? Won't they be all over this story?"

"I'm processing them as Carey and Jenessa Blackburn. That's the name they've been using, anyway, and your wife's maiden name is more likely to go under the radar, especially for Carey. I suggest we continue to use that name to enroll them in school."

My father nods weakly. I can *feel* what he's feeling. I've worn his face many times myself.

Hoping Mama will come back in time. Hoping I can protect Ness if an intruder enters our woods, or a hungry bear, or a hungry bear with cubs in tow, even worse. Hoping I can love Ness enough to grow her up healthy and normal, whatever that means. Hoping I can fill her growing mind and heart when I can't fill her stomach . . . hoping she'll forgive me for the white-star night, and keep on forgiving me every time I can't fix things. Like now.

"You're going to need buckets of patience, Mr. Benskin. Jenessa's muteness will take time to sort out, and Carey comes with her own set of issues, no doubt. There's no telling what these children have been through."

My father begins picking at the edge of his cup. When he looks at her, I can tell his eyes are locked on something in the past—something that seared deeply and left the worst kind of scar: the inside kind. Mrs. Haskell's eyes grow soft. She's good at that, and I can tell it comes from someplace true.

"The girls are their own family unit. You have to remember that. They're all each other had. It may be best to honor that, for starters. Carey is very mature for her age. Thank God, for Jenessa's sake. As long as the decisions aren't the big ones, I'd let Carey take the lead—at least until the girls warm up to you. It might help Jenessa adjust better, too, if Carey remains in charge."

The man's jaw is set, and his cheek muscle twitches. I don't know what it means, or what he's feeling; whether he agrees with Mrs. Haskell or resents her advice. I just don't know. I don't know him.

Abruptly, he pushes his chair back and towers above her.

"I'd better go get the girls some breakfast. They're going to be hungry as bears when they wake up."

"That's a wonderful idea. We're going to have to get them up soon. Court is in a few hours."

I wait until he's taken Mrs. Haskell's order and the door wooshes shut before I make the appropriate waking noises, stretching my arms toward the ceiling. Next to me, Jenessa sprawls on her back, her sweet curls falling over her face. She sleeps like a rock, like little kids do. Carefully, I smooth a curly tendril out of the corner of her mouth. I see no reason to wake her until the food arrives. Plus, it gives me alone time to talk with Mrs. Haskell.

"Good morning, Carey."

Mrs. Haskell's hair is flat and she's wearing the glasses again, in lieu of what I now know are contact lenses. It's astounding, not just that people actually put tiny circles of plastic on their eyes but that they actually work.

"This is for you."

She holds out a yellow brush in a crinkly plastic wrapper, small enough to brush Nessa's Barbie's hair, and a little tube of something. I look at it and mouth the word: *Crest*.

With her eyes matter-of-fact, she makes pretend I shouldn't already know what it is. I'm grateful for that.

"That's a *toothbrush*, and the tube is filled with *toothpaste*. You put a little on the brush and scrub your teeth with it."

"Oh yeah. I remember now."

My cheeks burn as the fuzzy memory returns, of Mama's hand moving back and forth in front of my face, my lips curled back as I stood on a little white stool and leaned over the bathroom sink.

"That's mighty convenient, in a tube and all. Ness and I used baking soda and tree bark. Mama said the soda would make our teeth cleaner *and* whiter."

"Baking soda is a good substitute, if you don't have toothpaste. Your mom was right."

I nod, relieved. Relieved not to be *that* backward.

As I brush my teeth at the bathroom sink, I hear Jenessa waking up, groaning in that low way of hers, which is as close to talking words as a stranger will get. Mrs. Haskell makes her way to the bed, and I concentrate on the brushing. I make a face at the toothpaste taste, studying myself in the mirror. I can't stop looking.

"It's okay, Jenessa. Carey's right there in the bathroom, brushing her teeth."

I hear the bed shifting and the pad of bare feet. Jenessa stands in the doorway, her lower lip trembling.

"I'm not going anywhere, baby," I say, my mouth full of white bubbles. "And, look at this! It's your lucky day."

I peel the plastic from the pale pink toothbrush sitting on the ledge of the sink and hold it out to her after squeezing a small ribbon of Crest onto it. Jenessa takes the brush, sniffing at the toothpaste. Her tongue darts out like a lizard's, testing it.

"It's *toothpaste*, to clean your teeth. That's what the people here use. Watch."

In slow, exaggerated motions, I scrub my teeth back and forth, back and forth.

If I was expecting her to decline or argue, she doesn't. She stands on tiptoes next to me and gives it a careful try, smiling at the bubbly film on her lips and then up at me, like a modern girl trying new things. I watch her watch herself in the mirror, as mesmerized by her reflection as I am by mine.

By the time the man comes back, we're seated at the table. I get up to open the door when he knocks, taking two bags from the bunch he's juggling.

Soon, the food lies unpacked on the table, and my stomach rumbles at the feast spread out before us. I don't know the names for all of it, but the scent alone is stunning.

Mrs. Haskell names the food as she fills our plates: french-toast fingers, maple syrup to dip them in. Scrambled eggs. Bacon. Hash browns. Fried apples. Some of it I do know: ketchup, apple juice, and butter—real butter. I drop a few squares on my scrambled eggs and even more on Nessa's, until her eggs rise like an island floating in a pale yellow sea.

I've never seen Nessa eat with such abandon, sticky syrup dripping down her chin, and bacon—heavenly, hot, salty bacon—three helpings inhaled in as many minutes.

"Slow down, Ness. You'll get sick if you eat that fast."

The grown-ups eye each other and then look to me. I get up and remove Jenessa's plate, holding it high above her head.

"You're going to throw up if you don't slow down!"

She kicks at the rungs of her chair, her hands in fists.

"You know we don't kick. It isn't civilized. Remember?"

Her legs still. She puts her fork down obediently, her eyes welling.

"If I give you this plate back, you'd better eat like a human being, not a grizzly. You hear?"

Jenessa picks up her fork and nods, her curls bouncing. I kiss her head and return the plate. She resumes her breakfast cheerfully, her legs swinging rhythmically under the table.

Mrs. Haskell smiles at me. I bet she's thinking of the puke from yesterday.

"Ness has a clean dress she can wear to the hearin'—hearing—but it's wrinkled," I say.

Mrs. Haskell holds out her hand. "Let's see it."

Reluctantly, I leave my breakfast and saunter over to one of the garbage bags, rummaging through it until I find the pastel pink dress and a pair of white socks with ruffles at the ankles, dingy white, but clean. I also pull out the scuffed Mary Janes, a little tight on her, but okay for an hour or two of wearing.

Mrs. Haskell grabs a metal triangle topped with a hook from her suitcase. I follow her into the bathroom, and she closes the door behind us. She pushes aside the shower curtain and turns on the water full force.

"This is a hanger," she says, catching me eyeing it. "For hanging up clothes."

Closing the curtain, she works Nessa's dress onto the hanger, where it hangs neatly from the bar above.

"The steam from the hot water should do the trick. I'm glad you thought to bring a dress. What do we have for you to wear?"

No way I'm wearing a dress, even if I had one, which, thank God, I don't.

"I have the jeans I washed in the creek, and a newer blue T-shirt. That's all I have that's clean."

I study the wallpaper, the little bunches of cherries on a cream background so real, I want to lick them. Pretending it doesn't matter is just that: pretending. The truth is, up until yesterday, it hadn't mattered what clothes I did or didn't have.

"I can wear my boots instead of the sneakers," I offer.

Mrs. Haskell smiles warmly. "I think that's a good choice."

Fifteen minutes later, she calls me into the bathroom, the dress in hand. It's practically wrinkle-free. I'm grateful Jenessa will look like a real little girl, not like some backwoods orphan thrown away like trash.

"Can you leave the water going?"

Mrs. Haskell nods her approval, reaches in to adjust the knobs, then leaves the bathroom.

I find Ness in front of the television, where a little bear is grinning as he's snuggled by his mama. I practically have to carry her to make her come with me.

Stripped naked, we stand under the man-made waterfall, and the steam enfolds us as I soap her down. I use the little bottle of yellow stuff to wash our hair squeaky-clean, like Mrs. Haskell instructed me to do. Another memory surfaces: one of washing indoors, bubbles everywhere, and Mama's face, smiling and relaxed, looking like a whole different Mama.

Jenessa is seal-slippery against me, splashing like a baby, and afterward, I wrap her in a fluffy peach towel that brushes the ground.

I haven't seen her smile so much in a long time. Having gotten over the events of last night, now it's like a game to her, a wonderful adventure full of tastes and sights and sounds she never dreamed existed, let alone imagined could be hers for the claiming.

I take the underclothes Mrs. Haskell hands in through the cracked door, crisp and new in crackly packages—I reckon it's no wonder the man took so long getting back with breakfast. With my own towel wrapped around me and tucked in above my chest, I help Ness step into the underwear, bright white and smelling like store-bought, a smell that crinkles her nose in curiosity.

"Arms up." I slip the new undershirt over her head. She fingers the tiny pink flower at the neckline. "You're as clean as the whistle of the Tennessee warbler," I tell her before sending her out to Mrs. Haskell.

Wiping the steam from the mirror, I stare at myself, relieved I don't look as much like the toothbrushing stranger from an hour ago. I still have the same honey blond hair, poker straight. A nose that matches Nessa's, mostly. But it's the eyes that hold me captive, empty of concentric creek ripples and breezy tree branches playing the sky like my bow plays my violin.

Who am I now? Who was I before? Am I the same girl?

Licking a tear from the corner of my mouth, and like so many times in the past, I pray to the one who knows: Saint Joseph.

Years ago, I dubbed Saint Joseph the Patron Saint of Beans. It came from a story in one of the rummage sale books Mama brought back from town. Saint Joseph once saved the whole of Sicily, Italy, by bringing forth a plentiful harvest of fava beans.

Nessa insists she loves fava beans, even though she's never had any. Maybe that's why. We ate most kinds of beans in the woods. We'd have starved to death without them.

Saint Joseph, if you're still listening, please look out for us? We're not in the woods anymore, and I'm not sure that's a good thing. Please keep us safe, and help me keep Nessa safe. Help me remember the e-s in "don't", not to drop my g's, and not to say ain't.

Most of all, please look out for Mama? No matter what she did.

On beans I pray.

4

"All rise."

I help Jenessa to her feet as the judge swooshes out of the court-room through a private door Mrs. Haskell said leads to his chambers, which is like his personal office–slash–dressing room. I don't know what the *slash* means. All I can come up with is the slash I make when I gut a squirrel.

"Well, that's that," Mrs. Haskell says, smiling.

The whole thing unfolded in a mixture of mumbo jumbo, cleared throats, and shuffling papers, with a few important facts set in stone:

1. It's true. When Mama took me away like she did, she broke the law.
2. The man *had* been the one with legal custody, like Mrs. Haskell said. I hadn't fully believed it until I heard the judge say it all official-like.
3. We belong to the man now.
4. Mrs. Haskell would send the court a monthly report, and there'd be weekly check-ins with her to monitor our progress.
5. We wouldn't be going to foster homes . . . or back to the woods.

And that was that.

Out in the hallway, Mrs. Haskell turns to me with misty eyes. I can feel it sure as fava beans that she really does care about us.

"Can I give you a hug, Carey?"

I shrug, awkward as a long-legged fawn as I let her enfold me in her arms.

"You girls are going to be just fine," she whispers, giving me an extra squeeze.

Standing back, she riffles through her purse and pulls out a square of stiff creamy paper.

"This is my card, with my office address and phone. If you have any problems or questions or need anything, don't hesitate to call me."

I watch her smooth Nessa's curls off her forehead, my sister's hair haloed in sun slanting through the high windows.

"You girls take good care of each other, you hear? Like you did in the woods. You did a good job, Carey. A damn good job."

I duck my head and smile, unmoored by the flood of unexpected emotion.

"You'll be okay, you know."

I take a deep breath and find her eyes, green like Mama's, but sharp and clear. She motions with her head in the man's direction, and I nod with reluctance, the smile fading. I don't see as we have much choice.

Mrs. Haskell grins at Nessa, who hops on one foot across the sparkling tiles, from white square to white square, avoiding the speckled ones. She presses the card into my hand.

"Don't forget, Carey. Anytime. And look on the back."

I turn the card over and see written numbers.

"That's my home number. Use it if you need it."

We all watch Mrs. Haskell's back zip down the hallway, as she waves over her shoulder without turning around. And then it's just us, the three of us, sharing the same DNA, although we may as well be strangers from different planets.

"Take your sister's hand, Carey. You girls stay on the steps, and I'll bring the truck around."

I obey, taking Jenessa's warm hand in my cool one as we follow a few paces behind. My legs tremble after all the sitting, but Nessa seems fine. She rubs her stomach in small circles, her face pleading.

"You're hungry already?"

She hops up and down, wagging her head.

"How about a nice bowl of baked beans with ketchup?"

She stamps her foot.

"Kidding! We'll have to see what he says, but I'm sure we'll get something good."

She skips down the hall, dragging me along.

I know what she's saying, like I always do, even without the words. I'm dying to try the *handburger*, too, and the milk shake, which I remember to be something like drinkable ice cream. I don't remember the handburger though, or the *fries*. Handburgers must be something you eat with your hands, not much different than in the woods. And french fries, well, French means France, so it must be something fried from France.

We may be backward in some ways, but Ness and me, we know our countries. We must have taken apart and put together Ness's wooden puzzle of the world a few hundred times.

I do know what pizza is—it's the favorite food of a little girl in one of Jenessa's books, made of bread, white cheese, and tomato sauce, baked and served in triangles. And we had funnel cake once; Mama brought it back to the camper as a surprise, full of the laughter and smiles that meant her meth connection had come through.

The man pulls around the front of the courthouse, waving us

over from the driver's seat. I help Jenessa up to the cab, sitting her between us, the lap belt stretched across us.

"You girls hungry?"

Jenessa bounces up and down, smiling, with all her teeth showing.

"She wants to know if we can have handburgers and milk shakes and french fries?"

The man—*our father, now that it's official*—smiles at us; a full-on smile, one of the first.

"You bet you can. They have the best ones at the Come Right Inn, but it'll take us about a half hour to get there. Can you two wait that long?"

Jenessa sighs loudly, her dimples swallowed up in a scowl. My father tries not to smile, and I appreciate that; no one likes a spoiled little girl. I think of the bulge of her belly after breakfast and marvel at how, once again, her stomach appears concave. But I don't think she's being cute at all.

I elbow Nessa.

"We can wait, sir."

"Good. It's worth the wait."

Outvoted, Jenessa rests her head on my shoulder. I look out the window over her head, watching the scenery flash by. It all looks so unfamiliar, and I feel naked without the cover of our lofty trees. Even the sun feels hotter in the absence of the Hundred Acre Wood's canopy of a million shimmering leaves.

Nessa stares out the front windshield, taking it all in. New is amazing to her. She can't fathom it being anything else. But I can. Although, it's good she's seeing it as exciting, because it could've been the opposite, after all those years tucked away in our Hundred Acre Wood. She could've stayed like she was yesterday. She really scared me yesterday.

And I'm still worried. I can't help it. Silent and sweet may not be the best combination amongst town folk. Out in civilization. Out in the real world.

The truck is silent except for the whistle of air through my father's cracked window.

I tug at one of Nessa's curls, and she flicks me off like a fly.

I'm not the main attraction anymore.

Feeling wicked, I do it again.

I know about cameras. Our mother had one, an old Brownie, but we never had any film to put in it. Ness kept bugs in it, like a cage. Fat beetles and even a butterfly once, always set free after five or ten minutes. I'm wishing I had that camera now as I giggle at the sight of Nessa grappling with the handburger near as big as her head, ketchup like Mama's lipstick smeared around her mouth.

Civilization is almost worth it for the food alone, I reckon. The fries are right good with lots of salt, and the burger runs with "medium-rare juices" down our collective chins.

"Slow down, Ness. Chew your food," I tell her, my eyes scanning the walls for the bathroom entrance, just in case our little wolf regurgitates.

I'm momentarily distracted by a chubby toddler in a high chair, clacking a spoon against the table and smacking his lips. *I remember Ness at that age, easily. Mama propped her up on a stack of yellowing newspapers, a rope around her waist tying her to the back of a chair.*

I take the handburger from Ness's hand, cut it in half, and place the smaller half on her plate. She flaps her hands in protest, then immediately goes back to eating.

"Mrs. Haskell said we need to be careful, sir. Ness needs to be built up slowly."

My father regards me silently, and for a second, as fast as the flash of a camera bulb, I see pride. Pride in me. Something unfolds in my chest: a winged, fluttering warmth. It's almost too much to bear.

I turn back to my sister. She's eating with her eyes closed, chewing slowly. I take a few bites of my own burger, dunk a few more fries in ketchup. I'm already full up.

"You need to build yourself back up, too, Carey," he says with a softness that only makes it worse. The warmth flutters behind my eyes. *No.* I blink it back.

"Yes, sir."

I take another bite of my handburger, then another.

"It's only forty minutes or so to the house from here. Everything's already set up for you two. I'm sure whatever comes up, we'll work it out," he tells me.

I glance at him and hold it this time, both of us measuring, wondering, worrying about this new life.

"Those are some gorgeous girls you have there," the woman with the toddler calls out to my father, smiling at Nessa and me.

"Thank you. How old is your boy?"

"Fourteen months. Already he's eating us out of house and home."

Their words float back and forth over our heads as I watch Jenessa eat her last fry and slurp her milk shake clean.

As for me, I've eaten almost half my burger. A pink-cheeked girl whisks off the remains (my father calls her a "waitress") along with most of my fries, returning minutes later with a spongy white box I reckon is made from the same material as my father's and Mrs. Haskell's steaming cups of (what I now know to be) coffee. She winks.

"There you go. If you don't want it, I'm sure your dog will love it."

I slurp the dregs of my milk shake, and she shakes her head *uh uh*. I stop, my ears burning. *Don't act backwoods.* I want to ask the man, my father, for another glass, but the thought of asking, of the connection it implies, is so uncomfortable, I don't.

The waitress hands my dad a slip of paper on a little black tray, and a pen.

"I'll take it whenever you're ready."

He raises his hand in answer, and she waits while he scribbles on the paper, then hands it back to her.

"You girls ready?"

Jenessa looks to me for an answer, and I nod. I dip my napkin in my water glass, lean across the table, and scrub my sister's mouth. She scrunches up her face and swats my hand away.

"We're ready, sir."

"Then let's go *home*."

Home. Four letters heavier than twenty thousand elephants. It's like he's saying a word bursting with a bunch of other words not yet ready for saying. His expression shifts, reminding me of the twists of colored glass in Nessa's kaleidoscope.

"Let's go."

Nessa takes the lead, smiling back at the patrons we pass, who can't take their eyes off her. I bring up the rear with our "Styrofoam" boxes. But Nessa's steps grow heavy, her feet dragging as she ducks beneath our father's arm, which holds the door wide. Her peachy complexion takes on a greenish tinge, like the time I made her try chickpeas.

I don't waste a second as I shove her toward the bushes lining the walkway to the parking lot. She stumbles and I catch her by the forearm. I have a moment to drop the food boxes and grab her hair into a ponytail before her lunch lands in the grass.

My father watches, dumbfounded.

"She's all right, sir. You saw I tried to slow her down. She's just not used to having—"

"Real food, I know," my father says, finishing for me, his eyes flashing. *Anger.* It's a face I know better than any other.

"Please don't be angry with her, sir. Please?"

"Angry? Why would I be angry? Poor thing. So hungry. I should've ordered her something lighter. Like a grilled cheese. It's my fault, not hers."

I rub Nessa's back in small circles.

"How about you? Your stomach okay?"

He reaches out to pat me on the shoulder, and I flinch. I don't mean to keep doing that, but I can't seem to stop myself. His hand freezes midway, then drops to his side.

"Yes, sir," I mumble. Truth is, my stomach's not so great, either.

Nessa's crying now, either because she threw up, which she hates, or because she lost all that tasty food.

"Don't cry, baby. You can have the rest of my handburger later."

My father goes back into the restaurant and returns with a roll of paper towels. I know paper towels. He hands me a Styrofoam cup filled with water.

"Do you need any help?"

I shake my head no, so used to caring for Jenessa, it's like caring for myself. I pour water on a handful of paper towels and swab off her mouth, then her chin.

"Breathe through your nose and stick out your tongue."

She obeys, and I wipe her tongue, too. But her normally sweet breath still reeks.

I rip off a fresh sheet and dry her tears as she hiccups and sniffles, her eyes droopy and red by the end.

"She's flat tuckered out, sir," I say.

We watch her. She's weaving where she stands, her face pinched. I tuck her under my arm and pull her close.

This time, I sit in the middle and Ness sits by the window, where I can quickly lean over and roll down the glass if need be.

I barely breathe, although I'm aware of every breath she takes. *He* takes. I try not to touch arms, his tan one leaning on his leg when he's not shifting gears, the hairs honeyed up by the sun. His hands are large and work-roughened, but his fingernails are clean. The radio's on low. I remember radios. The haunting strains of a violin piece I can play by heart—Violin Concerto in E Minor by Mendelssohn—rise through the cab and cradle us all.

His words are casual but careful, like when something's a big deal but you don't want to sound like it is.

"That's a violin case you got there," he says, nodding his head toward the backseat.

"Yes, sir."

"Do you play?"

I wait for Jenessa to shift position, her head finding my lap, her breathing slow and even.

"Yes, sir."

"Joelle taught you, did she?"

I nod, not sure if it's a good or a bad thing.

"Your mama made those strings sing like a bird."

I think of Mama playing, my head stuffed with years of sound. Thing is, the violin reminds me too much of Mama now. It reminds me of the worst parts . . . the hungry parts, and not just for food. And the white-star night . . . I'm not sure I ever want to play again.

I watch the cars whiz past, everyone in a hurry, all those different lives. A daughter and father pop up in the car beside us, the girl's head resting solidly on the man's shoulder. Each vehicle is like its own bubble world hurtling toward realities so unknowable, yet so personal, it hurts to look at them.

Even if I were to like him, which I'm not saying I do—I can't, after what he did to Mama and me—still, I'm thankful not to feel so afraid.

"Is she okay now?"

He ducks his head in Ness's direction. She's a warm thing carved into my lap.

"Yes, sir."

"I don't know how to ask this, but—"

I wait, not knowing what to say.

"Do you know who her father is, Carey?"

I squirm, my face burning.

"Mama called her a 'trick baby, a one-hit wonder' . . ." My voice trails off.

His face turns red, and I look away, like you do at other people's private things.

"Your mama still doing those drugs?"

"Yes, sir."

He sighs a long sigh, the kind that comes from the belly.

"Did you girls get to eat every day?"

I sneak a look at him. His eyes remain glued to the road, like our words are no big deal.

"No, sir," I reply truthfully. "Nessa cried when I killed the rabbits and birds, and it took a miracle to get her to eat them. The canned goods had to stretch. Mama didn't always come back when she said she would, and those times I gave my share to Nessa. When you found us, we were running right low. Ness wouldn't eat any more beans. Even with her stomach rumblin'—rumbling—like an earthquake."

"It's an awful lot of changes, from that to this, isn't it?"

"Yes, sir."

"You'll never want for food when you're with me, okay? That's my solemn promise. So eat all you want."

I don't tell him I couldn't have gorged if I'd tried, my stomach stuffed full of butterflies and grown-up worries. I also don't tell him I ache something fierce for the river, the trees, the flecks of robin's egg blue playing hide-and-seek through the heavy boughs. That's the kind of filling I crave.

I jerk forward at the downward shift of gears. The truck slows as he turns onto an old road crisscrossed with tar patches.

"This road will take us to the farm. I think you'll like it there. There's plenty of room for you girls to run around. Just like your woods."

The road soon turns into dirt, bumpy and loud.

"We're in Tennessee, USA?"

"Yes, ma'am. Just farther west from where you girls were living."

The strangest noise, a baying whoop, grows in volume. Ness sits up, excited, searching for the thing making the noise. She climbs into my lap to see better, staring out the windshield, the light soft but not yet dusk.

Woooooooo! Woo woo woo woo!

She turns to me, but I don't have an answer.

Wooooooo! Wooooooooo!

Nessa bounces, her face splitting into a huge grin as we catch sight of an animal we know from her picture books.

"That's my hound dog, Shorty. Got ears like radar. He probably heard the truck coming before we'd even left the blacktop."

I press back into the seat, holding Ness tighter.

"He's a bluetick coonhound. What, don't you like dogs?"

"I don't know, sir. We've never seen one outside of Ness's picture books."

His eyes widen in disbelief. I wish I'd just said yes.

"He's right big," I say, my voice quivering. "Why do you call him Shorty?"

His eyes crinkle with affection.

"Because he's short one leg."

I look harder, and it's true: The hound is missing his left hind leg, yet he runs alongside the truck like no one's business.

"I found him as a stray, skinny as you and Jenessa, snapped up in a bear trap. Doc Samuels couldn't save his leg, so it had to go. But he learned real fast how to make it work—see how he slides the one leg underneath him?"

I watch Shorty use his back leg like he was born that way, positioned under the center of his body, more than compensating for the lack.

"Smart critter," I agree, my eyes on Jenessa, who leans in toward me when my father isn't looking, her breath curling into my ear.

"My dog," she whispers, too low for our father to hear. "Mine," she adds, no changing her mind.

I squeeze her tight and smile into her hair, the bubble moment lasting all of about two seconds before the weathered farmhouse rushes into view, larger than any house I've ever seen, clad in a cheerful coat of yellow paint. There's a porch that wraps around the house and lots of rocking chairs, but that's not what causes my jaw to drop.

On the stairs is a pretty woman in an apron, her raven hair woven into a braid that snakes over her shoulder and hangs clear down to her elbow. Next to her is a girl, face dark as a thunderstorm, arms crossed over her chest, her mind made up, like Jenessa with Shorty.

Nessa's eyes are wide enough to pop out.

"Maybe I should've said something sooner, but I didn't want to scare you girls. That's my wife, Melissa, and her daughter—my stepdaughter—Delaney."

Jenessa and I look at each other and then go back to staring at the strange figures. I can't even pray to Saint Joseph, because I have no idea what to say, or what good a saint of beans could do for us now. My throat feels clogged with a bean the size of a baseball. My father opens the door and jumps to the ground, stretching his legs after all those hours crammed in with us.

This is a fine wrinkle all right. Jenessa turns to me, her eyes full of question marks. I shrug; even I know I'm out of my league. The keening ache washes over me again like creek water soothing a stone, and that fast, I'm pining for the crunch of leaves beneath my feet, the smoky campfire, the world I know with my eyes tight shut, and even the beans.

5

I make a big deal out of smoothing down Nessa's dress, then comb her curls with my fingers. *Steady now.* I draw myself up taller. The girl's eyes bore through the windshield like lasers.

I know, as I've always known, that I'm Ness's filter. She'll take my lead on things, mimicking my reactions, comfortable when I'm comfortable, confident when I'm confident. That's what little kids do when they trust people.

I remember those large eyes staring up at me when she was just over a year old. I was feeding her a bottle, more water than formula. Mama had been gone over three weeks at the time, but Ness hadn't minded because she had me. It'd felt like she was *my* baby, my arms a love-worn hammock rocking her endlessly, while she cooed and shined as if I were Saint Joseph himself.

If I'm okay, she's okay. It's the same thing I have to do now.

"Are you ready?"

Ness nods, sopping up confidence as if through osmosis. (And yes, I know what osmosis is. I'd devoured the eleventh-grade science books Mama brought back like osmosis, itself.)

I jump out first, then catch Nessa under the arms and swing her to the gravel. She takes my hand, damp with sweat, which stops her cold. She checks my face.

"It'll be okay. We have each other, right?"

She shrinks against me when we reach the walkway to the porch. I hold Delaney's gaze, and the girl's eyes narrow and the corner of her mouth twitches as she takes in Jenessa's eternal pink-ness and my own drab clothes, the T-shirt threadbare in places, my jeans forever dingy from creek washing. I hitch up my jeans to lessen the sag. It's like her eyes leave fingerprints all over me.

My hair won't stay behind my ears, and I wish I had a bobby pin, or a barrette. I tuck it back, hair that skims my waist since we lost our only pair of scissors. Taking a deep, shaky breath, I exhale. *I'm in charge.* Only I can't get myself to believe it anymore.

"How do you do, ma'am. I'm Carey, and this is my sister, Jen-essa."

I extend my hand, dried ketchup on my fingers, but if she no-tices, she doesn't let on. She holds my hand in both of hers, smiling down at us.

"It's wonderful to meet you, Carey. And you, too, Jenessa. I'm Melissa."

Ness peeks out from around my body, clutching the belt loops of my jeans. If she tugs any harder, they may fall down into a heap on the driveway.

"You girls must be tired after your trip. I have dinner warming in the oven, and Delaney will take you up to your rooms."

She doesn't seem to notice the way her daughter scowls at us. Under Delaney's gaze, my neck heats up, then my cheeks. Delaney smiles for the first time as she notices.

"I'll go get the girls' things."

My father lopes off to the truck, and I think of the garbage bags and cringe. We're out of our element, like fish flapping round a bird's nest, and I can see this fact doesn't escape Delaney. She looks *glad.*

I clomp up the steps, stopping by the door to remove my boots and then Nessa's shoes. I line them up neatly to the right of the welcome mat, then look to Melissa.

"That's very thoughtful of you, Carey. Wasn't that thoughtful, Delly?"

Delaney shrugs, using her heels to slip off one sneaker and then the other, picking them up and taking them with her.

We enter the house, Nessa's eyes like saucers, flitting from the crackling fire *inside* to the couches draped in crocheted blankets, like the kind our gran knit. Nessa's eyes linger on the china figurines on the mantel, not knowing they aren't toys. I know, because Gran had some of her own. Just in case, I make a mental note to lay down some ground rules that'll keep Nessa out of trouble during our stay.

"Get out of here, you mangy mutt!"

Shorty, padding along behind us, cowers on the stairs as if Delaney's words were smacks. Nessa gasps in delight and lets go of my hand, walking over to the dog, her arm extended. Shorty sniffs her fingers, his tail sweeping the wood. Nessa plunks down next to him and throws her arms around him like a long-lost friend. She smiles widely as the dog licks her cheek.

"Good thing baths are on the agenda. Doesn't she know better than to let a dog lick her face?" Delaney watches Jenessa with disgusted fascination. This time, I shrug.

Delaney turns to her mother. "What, now *she* can't talk, either?"

"Delly, please."

Nessa rests her cheek on Shorty's head, gives him one last squeeze, then scrambles to her feet. I hold out my hand and she takes it, and we ascend the stairs together. Delaney sighs loudly, like we're so much trouble. I bite my tongue, my own patience just about exhausted.

"Just take us to our rooms, please," I say, daring her to hear what I'm not saying, too.

On the second floor, the wood shines hard as glass. A long, thin strip of blood-red carpet with tangled vines embroidered along the borders stretches down the length of the hallway. Delaney stops at the first two doors, opposite each other, motioning toward one and then the other.

"These two are yours."

She leaves us standing there, watching her hair swish across her back until she disappears behind the last door at the hallway's end.

I look at Jenessa, who stares down the way we came. To my surprise, she whistles—I didn't know she knew how—and Shorty barrels up the stairs and down the hall, his front legs sliding on the slick surface. We smile at each other when he slows down and proceeds via the rug, his bright eyes trained on Nessa.

Tentatively, I reach out and pat his head, noting his fur, soft as velvet. But it isn't my attention he wants. Nessa plops on the rug, giggling. She scratches up and down his back, sending his front leg paddling.

Shorty shadows us from one room to the other. My room, and we know it's my room by the things in it, is like nothing I've ever seen. There's a bed—a real bed—and it's *huge*. Nessa fingers the stitches of the patchwork quilt, a scarlet background with different-colored patches flecked with wildflowers and little suns. It's one of the most beautiful things I've ever seen, and I, too, have to touch it to believe it.

There's a shelf on the long wall, already crowded with books, and a china figurine resembling the one downstairs perches in the middle of a white doily on the bureau.

On the opposite wall is a sampler behind glass, framed in dark wood: *Home is where the heart is.*

"Now let's go see your room."

I lead her into what seems like another world.

ONLY PRINCESSES ALLOWED! announces the plaque on the wall, and Nessa claps her hands in delight. The place is done up in pink and white, with buttercup yellow walls. She, too, has a wall shelf crowded with books, and her own patchwork quilt of pale pink behind squares of butterflies. Her arms reach up toward a little curio shelf high on the wall, where a china dog stands guard over a china girl, the figures cleverly out of reach of a six-year-old's less than nimble fingers.

"We'll take them down later so you can see, but these kind of dolls aren't toys, Ness. They're made out of something like glass— remember when I dropped that mason jar and it shattered all over the camper floor?"

Ness nods slowly, transfixed. She isn't hearing a word I'm saying.

"How do you think they knew about the pink? I'll leave my door open, okay? I'll be right across the hall if you need me."

But when I leave to go to my room, she's right there with me, clambering up on my bed and bouncing up and down in her bare feet.

There's a door on the short wall. Inside, it smells like cedar, wiggling loose another memory I haven't accessed in years: the cedar chest Mama kept her keepsakes in before the woods. Her recital photographs, of an angular young girl with what Mama called a "shag" haircut; her snapped violin strings, which she compulsively collected; a scrapbook of newspaper clippings; letters from Gran mixed up with ancient cards from my father.

This closet is empty. I set the hangers swinging, their tinkly skeletons bumping one another from a metal bar that stretches from end to end.

"Nessa, look! A whole little room just for clothes—I reckon it's bigger than the camper!"

I turn to her. My sister sits propped like a life-size doll against the headboard, snoring softly. Shorty, curled up flush against her body, eyes me.

"It's okay, boy. I don't mind."

His eyes close. It's been another long day.

Gently, I take a crocheted blanket, the only object in the closet, from the top shelf. Nessa's feet are dirty again, but it's honest dirt, as Mama would say. She smells sweaty, but it's a sweet sweat. I cover her with the blanket, hoping it's okay to use it. My sister's never been good at sticking to plans or schedules.

"Shouldn't she be taking a bath first, before you put her to bed? Her feet are filthy."

"Only because the woods got into her shoes. She took a shower this morning."

Delaney stands in the doorway, her hands on her hips. "This isn't her room."

"It is if she wants it to be." We've been sharing all our lives. "I don't mind if she wants to stay here with me."

"My mother won't like having Shorty on the bed. That mutt's lucky he gets to sleep inside the house in the first place."

Delaney moves aside as my father lumbers through, dropping one of the garbage bags on the floor against the wall.

"I put the others in Jenessa's room," he says softly, smiling at the sight of Nessa and Shorty snoring together. "I saw lots of pink, and Pooh books. I guessed that was Jenessa's bag."

"Thank you, sir."

Delaney takes in the garbage bag, her lips pressed into a thin line.

"She'll be fine until tomorrow. The bath can wait," my father adds, giving Delaney a hard look. "And I'm sure Melissa won't mind about Shorty."

"What's wrong with her, anyway?" Delaney glances from Nessa to me, her eyes hard.

I make sure my words bite back.

"There's nothing wrong with her. She's sleeping. She's tired."

"No. Why she can't *talk*, I mean." Delaney scrutinizes my face, as if expecting me to lie.

"She can if she wants to. She just doesn't want to, most of the time."

"My mom'll have something to say about that."

"Don't you have homework to do, Del?" my father says, but it's more a command than a question.

I worry, imagining Nessa being made to talk and the hissy fit she'd throw if she was pushed into it. There's no making her do something she doesn't want to do, especially when she's right. They're her words. It's up to her to use them. Or not.

Delaney ignores him.

"Why do you call your own father 'sir'?"

She's getting on my nerves, but at least she's forgotten about the garbage bags.

"Mama says it's a sign of respect to call grown men 'sir,' and women 'ma'am.'"

Delaney scoffs, like I'm the last person who'd know, coming from where I do.

"Well, I call them by their names—Mom and Dad. They're family, not strangers."

To her, maybe.

Inside, I hurt in that empty-puzzle-piece way. It's obvious she thinks he's her father, not mine, even though we share the same blood. Maybe she's right. I wonder if she knows he used to beat Mama and me, and if he's ever beaten her. Only, it's not the sort of thing you ask a person, especially a stranger.

"I guess we're stepsisters. That's what my mom said. Although I don't know if I want to be stepsisters with a retarded girl."

"She's not retarded."

My voice betrays nothing, even though the white heat, jagged as lightning, jumps through my veins. I know girls like Delaney from a few of my books. Bullies, who like to tease. Mean-spirited girls who laugh when other girls trip or cry.

"Excuse us, please," I say.

She plants her feet and narrows her eyes. *Hawk eyes*, I think. *Untrustworthy. Preying on the small and the weak.*

"I said, please leave!"

Delaney snaps her beak closed and flounces out the door. I sink onto the bed, sag there on the edge, trying to catch up with my new life. In the woods, a person has all day and night to process things. Out here, it's different. There's no time.

"She's not so bad once you get to know her," my father offers, sticking his head in as he passes.

I wonder how much he's heard.

"It's been hard on her, too, all these years. It's my fault really, so get mad at me, not her, okay? Door open, or shut?"

"Shut, sir."

I exhale. Blink back the wetness that threatens to spill. My stomach drops at least as far as we've traveled away from our woods. *What if I can't do this? What happens then?*

Shorty utters a low whine and slips out from under Nessa's arm, crawling toward me on his belly until he's pushed his body up against mine. He rests his graying head on my knee with a sigh and gives my skin a tentative taste. I bend forward and sniff. He smells like soap, like something with jasmine, which reminds me of Mrs. Haskell's hair.

The tears flow, hot as the creek in summertime. I don't know beans about civilized living. My mind feels crowded, like a room with too much furniture, until chair arms and couch legs poke me, cushions and pillows conspire to smother me. There's no room to move. *To think.*

I turn to the window, the glass dark and fogged with our collective breath. In my mind I hear my trees whistling in the wind and my heart melts into a puddle because I'm no longer there to whistle back. One missing mama and a dwindling supply of canned goods is a molehill compared to this.

I lean over and wrap my arms around Shorty, a kindred spirit if ever there was one. Us, two creatures plucked from the wild. One lost leg. One lost girl. I scrutinize my jeans, zeroing in on the jagged hole below the knee where I'd snagged on barbed wire coming back (empty-handed) from fishing. No wonder Delaney snickered at us. We look exactly like what we are: poor kids.

"Come in," I reply to the knock on the door. I sit up and quickly dry my tears.

"Now what?" I groan, seeing Delaney's face in the doorway.

"Catch," she says, tossing me a crocheted blanket. "I didn't think you'd want to wake your sister by pulling down the covers. You can use this one for yourself."

"Thanks."

She stares at the garbage bag, her expression different this time.

"What's this?" she says, toeing the violin case leaning against the bag.

"A violin."

I almost choke on the *v* word with the planet-size history curled up inside it, a history that could break me if I let it, spilling out my middle like Gran's jam cake when you first cut into it.

We exchange glances.

"Can you play it?"

I take her in: her perfect, shiny dirty-blond hair, her embroidered jeans speckled with twinkling jewels, her socks so white, there's no doubt creek washing wasn't involved.

"I've been playing since I was four. Mama—my mother—taught me. She was a concert violinist."

"That's what my dad said. He said your mother could've been famous if she hadn't gotten mixed up in—"

"I'm really tired," I say, and this time, Delaney blushes. "I still have to settle me and Nessa in—"

"Oh. Okay." She pauses. Then: "Do you need any help?"

I think of our stuff, right fitting to be stuffed in garbage bags when a person really thinks about it.

"Uh, thanks, but I got it."

She clicks the door shut and I'm alone in a foreign land, this kingdom called New Bedroom, so clean, it makes my brain hurt. As I sort through my things, I'm careful not to spill the bag onto the rug. I twirl the stem of a stray leaf between my fingers, then press it against my cheek. *Home.* Shorty hoists himself over to Nessa and goes back to sleep.

"Good dog," I say, and he opens one eye to let me know he knows.

The door clicked shut with a sticky sound. I sniff. Paint. *They actually painted for us.*

It's easy to unpack. Soon, my few items shiver together on hangers, while the lower closet shelf remains forlorn and mostly empty, except for Mama's scrapbook and my sketch pad. I place the violin case on the toppest shelf, wishing no one knew about it.

I cringe as I hang my coat on one of the hooks and catch sight of it in the full-length mirror on the inside of the door. It's a navy blue winter coat patched at the elbows, the color worn out in places, no different from my jeans. I'd found the coat in the woods, the material reeking of wet leaves and cat pee, the latter a scent I couldn't erase no matter how many times I'd washed it in the creek.

"*Don't pay it no nevermind,*" *Mama says, her eyes harsh. "You got yourself a coat, a right warm one, just like I prayed for."*

I wish she'd prayed for a store-bought coat, spankin' new, with the faux-fur linin' fluffed, not matted, and all the buttons still on it. Not four out of six.

"But you have a coat. A store-bought one with a zipper."

"Watch your tongue, girl. I'm the ah-dult. I'm the one takin' care of you girls."

I don't say it, but she's not, not neither one. At least she sure don't act like it.

"Be grateful for what you got, Carey," *she says, knowin' me so well that even hidin' my eyes don't help. "That coat hits right to your knees. We have no fancy airs to put on here. Warm is warm, no matter how it looks."*

Or smells, I thought, resigned.

But she was right. When winter set in, when Jenessa and I wore socks for mittens, we both had coats so we could play in the snow instead of remaining cooped up in the camper. We slept in the coats, too, so we didn't shiver all night and wake each other up.

I glance at Jenessa, breathing through her mouth, and Shorty, his ears squared as if awaiting further instructions, determined to make us a package deal. I don't mind at all.

"Stay here. I'll be right back."

I leave the door cracked and pad over to Nessa's room. I unpack her toys and clothes, clothes that hold the scent of wood smoke from the fire I built the night before last. Her own coat came from the Salvation Army, a pale pink cloth of some sort, reaching to her waist. I gather it up and breathe it in, but the ache only pounds harder.

Soon, the closet shelves are lined with her puzzle boxes and games, both Scrabble and Chutes and Ladders. A smudge-nosed, naked Barbie doll sits demurely, her legs dangling over the shelf's edge. I line up her sneakers on the floor below, and set her stuffed dog and one-armed teddy in the child-size rocking chair. *They'll look nice on the bed once they're cleaned.*

I fill an empty shelf across from her bed with her Pooh books, unable to count how many times I've read each book to her, the stories worn into my heart as much as hers.

Her socks, underpants, and undershirts go into the bureau drawers. When I'm through, I fold the garbage bags into squares, my mind returning again to Mama's letter like a tongue to a loose baby tooth. I can feel the paper in my pocket, close as skin when I move. I stuff the bags in the bottom bureau drawer, then go back to my room, closing the door behind me.

There's a clock on the little table next to my bed that says eight-thirty in spelled-out numbers. A person doesn't even have to know how to tell time—it tells it for you.

I marvel at the light switches; none worked in our camper, but they work here right fine. I flick the switch downward, and the room goes dark except for a beautiful cream-colored rectangle of porcelain plugged into an outlet. It looks like a sculpture, and I crouch down on the floor to see. Carved into its surface is a beautiful angel assisting two chubby children across a bridge. The angel's wingspan reminds me of an owl's, or an eagle's, it's so glorious.

I curl up next to Nessa, Shorty on one side and me on the other, making a Jenessa *samwich*. The blanket Delaney gave me is clean, downy, and warm. It smells like flowers. I feel like a flower.

My eyelids slip shut, lulled by the inhale and exhale of Shorty's breath. First I say a prayer for Mama, though, that she, too, is safe and warm, her belly full up. And then I let go, a feeling so foreign after all those nights alone in the woods, a shotgun nestled in the crook of my arm. I let go like I haven't since the white-star night, or perhaps since Jenessa was a baby. Ever since then, I've been a world of tired, clear down to my dusty bones.

I fumble for my shotgun, but it isn't there; my heart races as the shadows in the Hundred Acre Wood morph into hulking giants over twenty feet tall. *Who, who?* echoes through the leaves, and an owl blinks down, and I answer, *It's only me.* It *is* only me. Jenessa is gone. Frantic, I search the camper, the campsite, the curving shore of the roiling Obed River.

Who, who?

I don't know!

I fall out of bed, landing hard on my side.

"Smooth," says Delaney, smirking from the doorway. "My mom said to wake you for breakfast. Since you slept through dinner and all."

She wrinkles her nose. "You slept with that fleabag in the bed all night? Gross!"

Technically, I don't know what *gross* is, but her facial expression does a more than adequate job of conveying the meaning. She marches into the room and yanks Shorty by the collar. The dog whimpers, pressing hard against Nessa, his body a deadweight.

"Let him be," I order, my voice still rough with sleep. "We'll bring him down ourselves."

"Whatever. You better bounce. If my mom went through the trouble of cooking for you, the least you can do is eat it when it's hot."

Bounce?

I push up from the floor, ignoring her, and gently shake Jenessa's shoulder.

"Rise and shine, baby. It's a new day."

Delaney sniggers, an ugly sound I vow never to make. I shuffle Ness into a sitting position, propped against the headboard like she'd started out the night before.

Draped over the rocking chair are yesterday's jeans. My cheeks burn as Delaney leans in the doorway, watching as I pull them on. I'm not changing my T-shirt in front of her, no matter what she thinks.

"You're flat as a board. Don't they have boobs in the woods?"

"People like you, you mean?"

"Touché," she says with a sharp smile, instead of the anger I'd expected. I wrap myself in the crocheted blanket. Shorty opens one eye, like he knows what comes next.

"Let's go outside, boy," I say.

Shorty unfolds himself from my sister and carefully jumps down. We watch him stretch.

"He's arthritic, the old mutt. I thought you said you never had a dog before?"

"Doesn't take a genius to know he'd need to go out in the morning."

"Want me to stay and help Jenessa get dressed?"

I search her eyes, digging deep. I see no trickery, no malice.

"Suit yourself. She's hard in the morning, though. Make sure she doesn't go back to sleep. If she does, take the blanket from her. Tell her to put on clean socks, underpants, and an undershirt— they're in the top drawer of the bureau in her room, and her jeans and shirts are in the closet—and make sure she brushes her teeth. You have to watch her, or she'll skip it."

Delaney looks surprised that something like fresh underwear and clean teeth would matter to us. I roll my eyes and follow Shorty down the hallway.

It's true: We may not have had much. Not a fancy house, expensive clothes, or stuff to show off. But I've always made sure we're clean. Clean is free.

Mama once said teeth were like parents—you only got one set. Being poor was no reason to take them for granted. Me and Ness, we'd bathed in the large metal tub year-round, the sun helping to warm the water in the wintertime, although in the wintertime, we'd been lucky to brave the water once a week. But the rest of the time, we'd bathed twice a week, and that didn't count all the times we swam in the river. Mama said a person makes do with what they've got, and that's what we'd done.

Shorty waits for me at the bottom of the stairs, eyeing me as I peck my way down, steeling myself to deal with my father and Melissa and all the noise of the civilized world. But my father is nowhere in sight. My stomach rumbles and growls at the scents drifting from the kitchen.

Bacon, again.

A griddle spits. A woman hums to herself. Like a ghost, I tiptoe past, grabbing Shorty by the collar and leading him out the front door. The hound lopes off, scattering a flock of birds into the ether, puffs of dirt kicking out behind his flying paws. I suck in the late-October air, nippy but bearable with the blanket around my shoulders. I wish I had a robe like Delaney's, though, all thick and warm and shiverproof.

Delaney doesn't sleep in T-shirts. Last night, she slept in a long-sleeved, button-down top with matching pants, the cream-colored material shiny and etched with curled-up cats. Just by looking at her, I know she wears bras, like Mama, not undershirts, like me.

I glance down at my chest. I'm washboard skinny, just like Jenessa, which makes me skinny up there, too.

Shorty returns with a stick in his mouth, panting and smiling, and then trots off with it. When I hear a cow bellowing in the distance, I remember what my father said on the ride yesterday. Cows and goats, an old horse, a mule and donkeys. A farm. Not as a living, but as a place with plenty of room to wander.

I jump when his deep voice sneaks up behind me. "I see you're up."

I feel shy as I turn to face him. He holds a mug in his hand, a beat-up pair of work gloves peeking from the pocket of his sheepskin coat.

"Shorty needed out. Jenessa is getting dressed, and then she'll be down."

"I take it you girls rested well?"

I'm embarrassed to tell him how well. Two pillows apiece; a real mattress, not two old blankets sewn together and stuffed with yellowed newspaper to cushion a cot too small for two growing girls. Real blankets keeping us warm, no need to sleep in our winter coats . . . I think of Delaney snickering, and nod my head instead.

"Good. We didn't have the heart to wake you, the two of you out cold like that."

Warm. I raise my eyes from his boots. I practically know them by heart at this point.

"Thank you, sir, for the hospitality."

I don't know what else to say. He nods toward the distance.

"I see you made a new friend."

I think of Delaney, thinking how wrong he is. But when I follow his gaze, I see Shorty playing fetch with himself. Silly dog.

"I'm mighty grateful to that old hound," I say, thinking of my sister.

"Have you had your breakfast?"

I shake my head no, and think of Nessa. I feel a pang, knowing she hasn't eaten yet, either. Worse, I've left her with Delaney.

"I'd better see to Jenessa," I say, my shoulders hunched against the chill air, fighting the urge to glance back over my shoulder as I shuffle toward the house. I feel his eyes on me, trying to know me the way we're trying to know him; voice, walk, words—both spoken and unspoken.

I think of yesterday. Mrs. Haskell was right. Ness and me need to stick together. She'll need my help to decode this new world, with all the things she's never seen before, like inside tubs, flameless lights that don't reek of kerosene, meat from the store bundled in shiny, see-through packages. I'm sure she'll like it better than creek-caught trout and gamy squirrels and pigeons.

I hate myself for thinking it, but the bed and food are worth the risk of being here. At least it's worth giving it a shot. I wish I had my shotgun, though. But, when I made one final sweep of the camper, I forgot I'd left it on the tree stump. I didn't know how to explain my need for it, so I didn't ask Mrs. Haskell or my father to let me go back for it.

One thing I keep going over like a well-worn photograph is the first sighting of Melissa on the porch steps. Oozing smiles and griddle-warm welcomes, her voice soft and sincere—so different from Mama's cigarette-roughened bark and irritated, clipped sentences.

I can't imagine someone like Melissa letting my father hurt us. Maybe in the past he was just angry at Mama. Maybe he'd found her smoking the meth or drinking the moonshine. Maybe I had the rash, the one my sister always had until I stepped in and made Nessa like my own baby, changing and cleaning her regularly.

It's easy to get angry at Mama. She often forgot about us completely—like not coming home for weeks on end, or forgetting to hug us or wash our clothes. I didn't mind picking up the slack, because I'd have done anything for Nessa. But there were the times Mama got all fired-up mean, leaving angry welts from the switch all down our behinds and backs.

My breath comes faster as I think of the men she brought home from town, starting when I was eight years old. Their dirty, sandpaper hands rubbed me raw in the most secret, velvety of places. I saw them give her money, and the next day, there'd be warm pop or chocolate or, the one time, Jenessa's new Salvation Army coat and sneakers.

I was lucky I turned red early. There were no more hands after I turned red. That alone was worth the cramps and the mess of it.

I think of this man, this father, compared to the version in my mind. I'd hated him for hurting us, for making it so we had to leave, for not giving a damn about us. But maybe it was Mama who hurt us. Maybe she had it all mixed up.

Mama said possums don't change their tails.

It sure rang true, for Mama.

6

"There you are, Carey. Come have some breakfast."

"Thank you, ma'am."

Melissa beams at me, and she really means it; it's obvious in the way her face opens wide as the sky. I relax into it just a little, but her kindness is also a sort of free fall, pushing me off balance. *I have to stay strong, for Nessa. I can't let anything interfere.* I hide away the yearning like a squirrel hides its nuts in a rotting hickory stump.

Melissa guides me with a reassuring hand to an empty chair around a large table in a nook off the kitchen.

Nessa sits in her chair, wearing a pair of jeans and a T-shirt. She's mesmerized by the food, watching Delaney cut pancakes into mouth-size bites.

"Ness can cut her own food," I snap, more harshly than I mean to.

Delaney throws up her hands, turning to Melissa to confirm it—I'm impossible. She collapses into a chair across from us, glaring at me.

"No need for all the drama, Delly. Carey knows her sister best."

"Fine. I was only trying to help."

Melissa watches me, and so does Nessa.

"Sorry, ma'am, but she don't—she *doesn't*—need babying. It's bad enough she doesn't talk. The world is tough on the weak and the helpless."

"Why does she talk like that? She better not talk like that in school, Mom, or I'll be the laughingstock of the sophomore class! She's better off saying nothing, like Jenessa."

Melissa ignores her and turns to me.

"Those are wise words, Carey, and I understand your concerns. But everybody needs a little help now and again. Jenessa and Delaney are sisters now. You need to let them get used to each other."

"Really, Mother? That's it? You're going to let her speak to me that way and get away with it? You told me to be nice to her. Maybe you should tell her to be nice to *me*."

"Let it be, Delly."

I know I snapped at Delaney. I know I reverted to woods talk, and I need to get better at catching the words before I say them. I need to talk this new-world talk, not stick out like a sore thumb.

"Sorry, Delaney," I mumble, my eyes on my plate. "I worry about Jenessa, that's all. I'm not used to having anyone help."

I pick up my fork and spear two pancakes off the pile.

"At least tell me you can speak like a normal person? You sound, like, eighty or something."

"I was quoting Mama. I can talk right fine."

"'Right fine'? Mom!"

I lean over and grab the syrup, pouring some onto Nessa's chopped pancakes. I shake my head no when Ness stuffs a large uncut section into her mouth, getting syrup on the tip of her nose.

"Smaller bites, Ness. You know what happens."

I see a sadness fill Melissa's eyes, and I look away. *There's no room for pity. Feeling sorry for yourself does no one no good.*

"Make her work on talking normal, Mom. Because it's just going to make school harder if she acts all weird and stuff."

Melissa gives Delaney a long, hard look.

"What?" Delaney pouts. "I'm just sayin'." She puts down her fork. "May I be excused? Kara invited me over to try out their new trampoline."

"That sounds like fun, Delly."

Delaney sighs, looking from her mother to me. "You can come, too, if you want."

Melissa beams at Delaney, but I hear the uninvitation the loudest.

"Thank you kindly, but I'd better stay here with Jenessa. She needs a bath, for starters."

"She sure does," Delaney says under her breath as she gets up, pecking Melissa on the cheek. We hear the clopping of her feet as she runs upstairs. I relax against the back of my chair. Luckily, Nessa's too busy chewing to pay attention to grown folk jawing.

"Ma'am, Ness is in need of some meat on her bones, but she's not too good at stopping. I'd suggest removing the rest of the pancakes from the table. She'll sneak food when folk aren't looking."

"Thank you, Carey." Melissa gets up and grabs the platter, whisking it off into the kitchen. "I'll keep that in mind."

Ness looks at me, her eyes pleading.

"One more, and that's it," I say, handing over one of my own pancakes. She dances in her seat, acting as if I've offered her the world. I stand up to pour the syrup, but Melissa waves me back to my own breakfast. She pours the syrup for Nessa and tucks a paper napkin down the front of my sister's shirt.

Afterward, she pretends to read a newspaper, but I can feel her eyes on us. I concentrate on my plate, taking my own advice to eat slowly, not to overdo it, especially with the bacon. It's so hard, because it all tastes so good. I want to dance in my seat, too. I had no idea food could taste so good, but my stomach feels about the size of Mama's drawstring deerskin change purse.

I'm collecting mine and Nessa's plates and utensils to take to the sink when my father walks in, a cloud of cold trailing behind him. It smells like our woods in the early-winter mornings, with the copper kettle singing over the campfire, me playing my violin with socks on my hands, messing up just to make Ness giggle.

"My girls," he says, his voice husky, and Melissa smiles along with Jenessa. I keep my head down, chewing hard.

I remember Delaney's words, and borrow them.

"May I be excused?"

"You may," Melissa says, approval in her voice. "I'm thinking you girls will want to get cleaned up. I'll run a bubble bath for Jenessa and help her wash, if that's okay with you, Carey?"

I hesitate as a mental snapshot of Nessa's back fills my mind. There's no hiding it forever, I reckon, although I wish I could. I choke out a response.

"Thank you, ma'am."

I'm glad I can wash myself. I'm feeling grimy, and excited about washing with water that's actually hot. Funny how fast a body gets used to modern conveniences. The metal washtub seems like so long ago, like bathing beside herds of dinosaurs.

"Have you ever used a shower before?"

Looking down at my feet, I turn crimson.

"Once, in the motel. The hot and cold water blend together."

"That's right. Upstairs, the hot water is the left handle, and the cold is the right. When the temperature's right, turn the knob in the middle and the water will come out from the showerhead above."

"Thank you, ma'am." I glance at Nessa, and it's impossible not to smile at her syrup nose. "Melissa is going to give you a bath. Mind her, okay?"

Nessa nods and grabs onto one of Melissa's hands, holding it in her two sticky ones. My heart lurches, because it's always been me and her . . . but that's not normal. Not for most people in the world, and I want Nessa to be normal. I want her to stand on her own two feet, to have other people she can really, truly depend on. She's not a baby anymore. She deserves a real mama, a mama like Melissa.

Sorry, Mama.

Melissa leads her away by the hand, and I rinse off our plates in the sink, fascinated by the blue-colored squirt soap and the sponge, which is soft on one side and bark-rough on the other.

"This is a dishwasher," my father says, walking up beside me. He opens a door and pulls out the top and bottom racks, which roll out on little wheels.

"You don't have to wash them by hand. You rinse them in the sink, then stack them on the racks. Cups and glasses on top, plates and pots on the bottom. The machine does the washing for us."

"With electricity?"

"Smart girl."

He walks back and forth from the table, handing me plates and cups, which I rinse under a stream of hot water and stack as he instructed. He whistles a song I don't know, but a corner or two of the melody sounds familiar.

I fumble a dish and he rescues it midair. I flinch, before I realize he's only passing it back to me. I concentrate on loading the utensils. If he noticed, he doesn't say.

"Slippery suckers, aren't they?" he says, his words gruff.

I nod at his boots, and then the last dish is stacked, the last fork rinsed and placed.

"See?"

He takes a light blue box from a shelf in the cupboard and pours what look like colored crystals into a small compartment built into the door, then clicks it shut. I watch as he turns a dial above the

door to *Normal Wash.* I jump back as the machine comes to life.
We both smile.

"Go on up and take your shower. We have a two o'clock appoint-
ment with Mrs. Haskell. Her regular office is about twenty miles
from here. She has tests for you girls, to get you ready for school."

I nod when my voice fails me. *School, like the girls in my books.*
My stomach churns as I pass Melissa, who's on her knees next to
the tub in the first-floor bathroom, squinching her eyes shut as
Nessa splashes bubbles all over the floor.

I think of Nessa's back and make a beeline up the stairs and
straight into the bathroom connected to my new room, closing the
door behind me with my foot. I make it to the toilet just in time as
the pancakes and bacon thrust up and out, landing with a plunk
and my own splash into the toilet water.

I don't want to go to school. The woods are my school.

I think of the motel, and teaching Ness how to use a toilet after
she'd pulled a handful of leaves from her coat pocket and motioned
toward the trees out past the parking lot. Tears stung my eyes, seeing her joy in not having to trek out into the darkness of strange,
cold places. She flushed the toilet with a grin, watching the contents spin and spin and then, like magic, disappear.

Again, her eyes shouted. *Again!*

I run my shower, the water lacking the fishy creek smell I'd
grown used to and even liked after a while. Cupping my hands under the stream, I splash water onto my face. Once I double-check
that I'm locked in, I strip naked, squaring off with the full-length
mirror on the back of the shower door. I've never seen my whole self
all at once before.

I see lots of angles connected to bones. I turn around and
strain over my shoulder, my eyes tracing the white lines left by

the switch, and the two purplish-red circular scars from Mama's cigarettes, just below my left shoulder. All that's fresh is a bruise on my upper arm, where I'd slipped down some rocks while chasing a quail.

I stand under the stream of hot water. I could stand here forever. The peachy-pink bottle on the shelf squirts liquid soap onto a puffy scrubby thing hanging from the showerhead. The shampoo has black letters written on it: *Scrub hair.* And another bottle, called conditioner, has more black words: *After shampoo, put on hair. Wait a few minutes. Rinse off.*

So I do both, lingering in the heat and steam until I'm clean from the inside out. I think of Saint Joseph and thank him for all of it—plentiful amounts of food, the miracle of electricity, inside flush toilets, clean, running water, bubbles for Jenessa, heat and blankets and the thick, plush towel that wraps around my body nearly twice, hanging down to my bony ankles.

There's a soft rap on the door, and Melissa's voice floats like a ghost through the wood.

"Your sister is squeaky-clean. She's picking out some clothes. We have half an hour, okay?"

"Yes, ma'am."

"There's a brush and a comb for you, Carey, in the top drawer."

"Thank you, ma'am."

I hear her pass, and I turn to the sink, opening the drawer below the basin. Looking inside, I find an antique silver brush and comb set with my initials engraved into the metal: C. V. B.

Carey Violet Blackburn, named after my gran.

"Let me comb your hair, cookie."

"Okay, Gran."

"Come sit here on the footstool. That's a good child. A cookie for my cookie, when we're through."

"I love you, Gran."

"And I love you, cookie girl."

Gran had a set just like this. Jenessa, a real girlie girl, is going to go nuts when she sees it.

I think of the old horse brush we'd been using the past few years and the comb with more gaps than teeth left. I'd wither and die if Delaney or Melissa saw them. Not wasting a minute, I stride into my bedroom and pull out the brush and comb hidden under my T-shirts and bury the items at the bottom of the bin in the bathroom. I go to Jenessa's room, grab the two garbage bags from the bottom drawer of her bureau, and arrange them on top of the brush and comb, for good measure.

I stand there, staring at the garbage. Once again, the heat creeps up my neck and into my cheeks.

"You're a square peg," Mama says, none too kindly, "bent on shovin' yourself into a knothole."

Like silver brushes would make me fit.

"Fake it through until you make it true," Mama also said, for all of the one month she went into town for meetings. She'd been one of many who looked old before their years.

"For the first time, I wasn't the only woman missin' teeth!" she says, her cackle leechin' into a long, hackin' cough.

"Was it a good meetin'?"

"We chain-smoked, drank free tea, and exchanged hard-knock tales, if that's what you mean. I even made me a new meth connection."

I vow to follow Mama's slogan, which sounds very smart to me. Jenessa will have to do the same. Fake it through until we make it true. Be modern girls, normal girls, girls with a second chance.

"Fifteen minutes!" says Melissa with another rap on the door. I hear a softer, lower rap, and I know she has Nessa in tow.

I brush my hair down my back, pulling it over my shoulder to brush the furry ends. I fold my towel in half, sad to see it go, and hang it neatly over the bar on the bathroom wall.

If I don't want to use a length of rope for a belt, then I only have one viable pair of jeans, the ones I've been wearing three days now. Melissa's already washed our other clothes, but I haven't been able to part with these jeans, not even for a twelve-minute wash cycle, and even if the clothesline is viewable from my bedroom window.

I sniff the material, the familiar wood smoke filling my nose. But then again, I don't want to stink. Unsure, I pour a handful of baby powder into my hand and rub it into the crotch, inside, where no one can see.

My only other T-shirt has a peace sign on the front, like the sixties, Mama said, although I don't know what that means. *Sixty apples? Sixty elephants? Sixty peace signs?*

On further thought, I grab up my undershirts in a big ball and throw those in the garbage, too. They tower on top of the rest, but I don't care. I pull on a tank top instead and pull my T-shirt over that, which smells okay—like pine scent and fake sunshine. "Fabric softener," Melissa called it. I pull on clean socks and exit my room with my cowboy boots in tow, careful not to jostle mud onto the clean floor.

In the hallway, I applaud Ness in her pink-and-yellow T-shirt with an orange puppet on the front. Mama called the puppet "Elmo." On her feet are blue Keds, an old pair of Delaney's, Melissa says. They fit perfectly, and almost look new. My sister's blond curls shine, gathered off her forehead with a pink ribbon Melissa tied into a bow at one side.

"You look beautiful," I say, my eyes welling.

Jenessa runs over and hugs my legs, and we stand there for a moment, clutching each other. I take her hand and follow Melissa downstairs.

"Thanks, Mel. The girls looks great," my father says, grinning. "Everyone ready?"

He reaches out and touches one of Jenessa's curls. She burrows her head into his hand, and my father blinks, his voice gruff.

"You're a little lovebug, aren't you?"

Ness breaks away and runs out the door when she sees Shorty chewing a bone on the front porch. He abandons it for her, and she hugs him close, her face buried in his fur.

"I still can't get over it. Two peas in a pod, those two," my father says, shaking his head.

"The only animals we had were for dinner," I tell him, and he stares at me, his grin receding like the mountains during some of the worst storms, the ones where the roof leaked into rusty metal pots while we huddled together on the cot for warmth, our toes and lips blue.

Jenessa reappears and tugs on my father's hand, pulling him out the door. I note the emotions that play across his face—happiness, sadness, shock, regret—before he tears his eyes from mine.

Gravel crunches under the tires as we bounce down the driveway. Nessa kneels backward on the seat, waving at Melissa on the porch until we can no longer see her.

"Turn around, Ness, so I can do the seat belt."

First, I plop each of her feet on my thigh and tie her shoes—the laces are always coming loose—making bunny ears with the laces.

"Where did you learn to do that?" my father asks, astonishment in his voice.

"You," I say quietly as another memory slips into place, like a puzzle piece that knows where it belongs even before I do.

I see myself, a little girl from another world, riding in the truck with her daddy.

"Oh no. My soos are bwoken."

I pout, wavin' my feet in the air from my car seat in the back.

"*Want me to make you bunny ears?*"

"*Bunny eawrs! Bunny eawrs!*"

My father keeps his eyes on the road, his knuckles yellow-white as he grips the wheel.

Mama's voice scratches through my mind, too.

"*That son of a bitch left us to fend for ourselves.*"

"*But you said we left him.*"

Her swift backhand knocks me off my feet.

"*Don't you sass me.*"

"*Sorry, Mama.*"

My nine-year-old voice is tinier than a chipmunk's chirp as I clutch my cheek, tears stingin' my eyes.

"*Damn right we left him. I had to save my girl.*"

"*I know, Mama.*"

"*And don't you be tellin' no strangers our b'ness. Family b'ness don't leave this family.*"

I nod vigorously, her viselike grip dentin' my upper arm.

"*If you see anyone in these woods,*" she says, lettin' go only to cup my face so tightly, my eyes bug out, "*hide. Don't let yourself be seen, girl, and whatever you do, don't give your name.*"

"*What would happen, Mama?*" I ask, my face achin'.

Nessa wails, wantin' me to go to her. But Mama won't let go.

"*They'll take you away from me and make you live with him. And then I won't be there to protect you.*"

"*Yes, ma'am.*"

"*Now go see to your sister, before I slap that cryin' right outta her.*"

The Children's Services parking lot teems with cars, thick as ants on spilled beans. My father has to circle around back to find an empty parking space.

"Take your sister's hand," he says as we jump out.

I lift our arms into a V, sister fingers entwined. "I've already got it, sir."

"Of course you do. I keep forgetting—"

"It's okay, sir."

"Maybe it's good I keep forgetting, huh?"

I know what he means.

I'm a girl, just a girl, who never should've had to be in charge in the first place.

Jenessa tilts her head back. Her large eyes worry me with questions.

"Melissa said it's just some puzzles or something, remember? You don't have to talk if you don't want to."

Nessa's grip relaxes. I wouldn't tell her something that wasn't so. I lean in and gather her backpack from the seat, a gift from Melissa before we left the house. It contains two sandwiches, a clean pair of underpants, and a few children's magazines.

"That's Snow White on the back," Melissa says, *turning the backpack over.*

We look at her blankly.

"Don't you know Snow White? She's a princess. You know, the Disney princesses?"

"She knows Cinderella, ma'am. From her shirt."

"Right! Cinderella is one of the princesses. I'll have to dig out Delly's princess books for you, Jenessa."

Nessa claps her hands and does a silly dance.

We smile, Cinderella building a bridge between our woods and civilization. For a moment, we all stand on it equally, comfortably. For a moment, we belong.

Ness reaches for my father's hand, and we make an awkward train, zigging up the building's steps and zagging down the polished hallways. I picture him in my mind, pushing open the beige door with the MRS. HASKELL nameplate glued to the front, discussing the letter and our case while I cooked beans and washed clothes in the creek and smushed cockroaches scurrying across the tiny countertop, oblivious to the coming end of our world.

Mrs. Haskell looks awfully happy to see us.

"Awww," she says as Ness flies into her arms.

Familiar faces are priceless for my sister. In a sea of trees turned into a sea of total strangers, familiar means everything.

"Hi there, sweetie. Hi, Carey. Won't you come in?"

My father motions me in front of him with a sweep of his hand. We all settle into chairs opposite Mrs. Haskell.

"How's it working out so far, Mr. Benskin?"

Folders are piled high on every surface but her desk. Even an empty chair boasts a rising tower of paperwork stretching toward the ceiling, steadied by the wall the chair leans against.

"We're doing well, I think. Right, girls?"

Jenessa leaves Mrs. Haskell's arms and sidles over to my father, climbing into his lap. Mrs. Haskell turns to me, waiting.

"Yes, ma'am. We're doing right fine," I say, forcing a smile.

"That's good to hear. I dare say we may have a happy ending in the making. 'And they lived happily ever after.' Who doesn't love a happy ending?"

I think of Jenessa. *We have to stay together. That's our happy ending.*

"Let's get down to business. I'll be working with Jenessa today, and you'll be in a room on your own," she says, motioning toward a few loose pages on her desk. "These are written tests. Answer what you can."

She hesitates, and I wait, watching the struggle play across her face.

"Excuse me for asking, but you can read *and* write, can't you?"
My cheeks burn.

"Yes, ma'am. We both can. I taught Ness through books. I also taught her her sums. Mama found a chalkboard at a yard sale, and we used that. We had some old schoolbooks, lots of Winnie-the-Pooh books, and the poetry of Mr. Hopkins, Mr. Wordsworth, Lord Tennyson, Mr. Tagore, and Miss Dickinson, to name a few."

Mrs. Haskell exhales, looking relieved.

"That's really good, Carey. Jenessa's lucky to have a sister like you. It's much easier to teach reading, writing, and numbers to children when they're younger."

Nessa grins, like she's so smart and it's all her own doing.

"All I ask," I say, the mama bear rising, "is that you don't make her talk if she doesn't want to."

"Are you sure she can talk?"

"Yes, ma'am."

"How do you know?"

"Because she talks to me."

I shift in my seat, feeling like I'm betraying Nessa's trust. But the fact of the matter is, her choice to remain mute concerns me, too. As if it isn't bad enough we're poor, backward folk; Jenessa's lack of speech is enough to cast her as a freak. She's so trusting, so innocent. That's what worries me the most.

"She talks to you? When was the last time?"

I look over at Jenessa, who's thumbing through a *Highlights* magazine fished from her backpack. She stares at the page, transfixed by a dog that bears a clear resemblance to Shorty.

"Yesterday."

My father looks from me to Jenessa. Surprise and relief flood his face. He exhales loudly as he fiddles with the ball cap on his head.

He doesn't want her to be a freak, either.

"What did she say?"

I look over at Nessa again, who seems relaxed, paying no never-mind.

"She said Shorty was hers."

My father laughs until his eyes tear up and his face turns kidney-bean red. When he finally gets hold of himself, he sputters out the words.

"That's right, honey. That old hound dog was half-dead when we found him in the woods. I bet she'd understand the feeling more than most. He's hers all right."

And that's the thing about little kids. Even when they're not listening, they're listening.

Nessa flies to my father and weaves her arms around his neck. She looks like a twig that'd snap on the first bend, wrapped up in his tree-trunk arms.

I'm overcome by a feeling I don't know how to hold. It's the opposite of hardship and worry. *The opposite of cigarette burns, dwindling camp supplies, and creek-cold bones.*

Mrs. Haskell, her eyes bright, clears her throat. "Okay, folks. Carey, you can see yourself to the room next door. That's right, the one to the right. Mr. Benskin, you can sit in the waiting room. I'll be working with Jenessa at the table here. Carey, take these with you."

She holds out pages. I lean forward in my chair and take them from her hand.

"Please print your name and age on the top right, and answer as many questions as you can. There's no passing or failing—we just want to see where you are."

"Yes, ma'am." My palms sweat and my jeans stick to my legs. "I'll do my best."

"Good. Now, Jenessa, your tests are like games. Do you like games?"

Nessa's eyes grow wide and she nods.

"Good. You sit in the chair right there."

We drag ourselves out the door, both of us hesitant about leaving her.

"Jenessa will be fine with me. I promise. Now, shoo, you two."

My father makes his way toward the waiting room, but I linger.

"It's okay, Carey. Really." Mrs. Haskell looks me straight in the eye. "She'll have fun."

"If she needs me, you'll send her right next door, ma'am?"

"I will. And I almost forgot."

Her heels click over to me, and she holds out a long yellow stick with a sharp black tip on one end and a brownish orange cylinder on the other.

"This is a pencil. I know you know what a pen is, right? I saw some in the camper."

I nod. Black ink, called a Bic. Mama hoarded them in an empty tea can.

"Well, a pencil is the same sort of thing—a writing instrument. You write with the sharp end, and see this hard, spongy thing here? That's an eraser. If you make a mistake, you can erase the markings you made with the eraser."

I marvel at it. "We could've used one of those when Jenessa was learning to write." I take it from her outstretched hand.

"Well, you can keep it, if you want. See what it says on the side?"

I read it out loud. "'Children and Family Services of TN.'"

"TN is the abbreviation for Tennessee."

"Where we live," I say softly.

"Right. Now, off you go."

Me and my pencil enter the assigned room, and I lay out the pages on the long table. I can't see tables now without thinking of a plate of bacon. I wish there was bacon, too.

The first part is easy:

Carey Violet Blackburn

Age: 15

It could be worse, I tell myself as I struggle over the first few questions. *You could not know how to read or write. You could've had no books, no schoolbooks, or, even worse, no motivation to teach Ness or yourself.*

To my surprise, once I get started, I know most of the answers, and the math is even easier. I think of the algebra and trigonometry texts Mama brought home from the yard sale, and those endless hours we filled with history and science, poetry and Pooh.

I won't lie. There were times I daydreamed about what it'd be like to get out of the woods, go to college, and play in the symphony, when Jenessa was older and didn't need me so much. No way I'd turn into Mama. My moods are steady, dependable. I'm not bipolar; I'm sure of it. I won't do drugs. I took care of myself *and* a baby. I kept us safe, kept us fed, kept us smart.

I finish the pages in no time, in under two hours, according to the wristwatch Melissa gave me before we left.

"Carey, honey, wait."

I slide my shirt on quickly before she opens my bedroom door.

"Yes, ma'am? Do you need help with Nessa?"

"No, she's downstairs, ready to go. It's just that I have something for you. For luck."

I stiffen, not sure what to do. "For me, ma'am?"

"This was mine when I was in college. It was a high school graduation gift from my father."

Delaney, passing by, stops to listen.

"Hold out your arm."

I do. Melissa buckles on the thin straps of a wristwatch. It's the most beautiful thing I've ever seen. I can't believe she's giving it to me.

"Mom!" Delaney squeals.

"You have my watch from college graduation. You have plenty of watches, Delly," she calls out as Delaney stomps down the hallway.

"Don't worry about Delly. She can have one of my other ones, if she wants another that badly."

Now, I stare at the tiny hands, no thicker than a strand of Nessa's hair, as they tick tick tick around the face. The watch is delicate, with a golden rectangular frame and a creamy mother-of-pearl face, with blond leather straps and a tiny gold buckle to hold it in place.

It's fine—right fine. I've never owned anything so fine before.

I fill in the last question and put down my pencil. I decide I love pencils. Such a convenient invention, if ever there was one. Stretching my legs, I peer out the windows on the back wall. The glass is rectangle-shaped, and the consecutive panels stretch from waist height to high above my five feet, seven inches.

I survey a courtyard filled with children Nessa's age and younger, swinging on swings and hanging from bars and climbing a round-shaped cage with ladder rungs.

Women dressed like Mrs. Haskell cart folders in their arms and talk to grown folk who watch the children from benches. Some of the women remind me of Mama—worn-out clothes and hair askew, puffing on cigarettes like no one's business, and, even from my perch, quite obviously putting on the dog, plain as a slice of moldy muskrat meat.

A river of feelings courses through me when I think of Mama. Her memory snaps around me like a cheap bear trap that'll never let go.

Where is she? Why did she leave us? She could've at least said good-bye to Nessa.

I jump at the sound of the door opening. A shiny-headed man peeks through.

"I'm looking for an empty room."

"You can have this one, sir."

"Don't forget your papers," he says, pointing.

Tripping over my feet, I gather up the sheets and slide past him through the doorway, careful not to touch.

Feeling sneaky, I peer through the tiny glass window in Mrs. Haskell's office door. True to her word, she and Jenessa are bent over some sort of puzzle made out of yellow, blue, red, and green wood pieces.

I watch them for a moment. Nessa is smiling. That's all I need to know. I continue toward the waiting room.

My father sits in a chair in the corner, sunlight pouring in from a window above as he reads a newspaper. He folds it and drops it on his lap when he sees me.

"How did the test go?"

"Fine, sir."

I sit in the chair farthest from him, swinging my feet.

"Glad to hear it. Do you mind if I take a look?"

I walk over and reluctantly hand him the pages. The place where my hand held the paper is wrinkled and damp. It's impossible to miss the look on his face as he scrutinizes the top sheet, looking up at me and then back at the page.

I lean forward to see what he's stuck on, following his line of vision. It's just my name at the top, like Mrs. Haskell told me to write.

My father looks up again, his brow furrowed.

"What's wrong, sir?"

"You were supposed to put your age on here—"

"I did. See there—" I motion at the page, uncomprehending. "It's right under my name."

"But you put down *fifteen*."

"Yes, sir."

My stomach does a wobbly cartwheel, realizing something I haven't yet. It did the same when I saw him in the woods.

He lets out a long, slow breath, which smells like toothpaste and cigarettes.

"You were born fourteen years ago, Carey."

Blood beats in my brain like a drum.

"Fifteen, sir."

My father looks away, squinting into the afternoon light. He shakes his head no. The room shrinks around me, like I'm Alice and I ate the tiny cake. My eyes refocus, and my mind uses all its energy to wrap around his words.

"*Fifteen*," I say again, emphasizing the *fif*, as if I can make it true by repeating it.

"Fourteen. I'm sorry, Carey."

The hallway is a blur as I run down it, out the front door, and through the parking lot. *Can't breathe.* I squat behind his truck, panting, my T-shirt sticking to my back.

No! I can't be fourteen when I was fourteen already! Mama couldn't have been that screwed-up!

My mind fills with the whooshing and crashing of the Obed River. The whispering trees, calling for me, wondering why I've left them. I'm just like Mama.

I want to go home! My home!

The eaglets. I concentrate on the eaglets. Ness and I watched them every day after they'd hatched. She was still talking then.

"*Oh no!*" Nessa cries. "*The eaglet's nest is fallin' apart. Look, Carey. It's bwoken!*"

"*No, it's not.*"

"*Yes it is. Look at it!*"

I gather her onto my lap, her cheeks slick with tears.

"No, Ness. Over time, the mama eagle pulls away the straws one by one until the babies are left balancin' on the branches."

"You're lyin', Carey Blackburn! Why would she be that mean?"

"It's not mean. It's love. If the mama kept bringin' them food and they stayed in their comfy little nest, they'd never be brave enough to learn how to fly or to venture out into the world."

Jenessa takes in a ragged breath, thinkin' it over. I play with her hair, waitin'.

"The baby birds are just like us. Right, Carey?"

"How do you mean?"

"Brave, like us. Our mama isn't here. Does that mean we're flyin', too?"

I give her a squeeze. She doesn't know it, but she's my wings.

"You bet we are, baby. In our own way, we're flyin', too."

I wonder if the chipped water jug is still there, and the kettle. I think of the key in the hollow hickory. What if someone else finds it?

I hate Mama. HATE her. What kind of mother forgets the age of her child? What kind of mother can't even keep a birthday straight?

"Hey, you."

My father stands above me, blocking the sun. He nudges my cowboy boot with his work boot.

"I'm sorry, kiddo. I don't know why she would've lied to you, unless it was to keep you two disguised."

"Or she forgot." I don't look up. "Jenessa's still six, right?"

"Yes. She got that right."

I hug my knees to my chest, my arms aching, I hold on so tight. We share the silence for a bit—six minutes, according to my wristwatch—and then he fixes to go back into the building, stopping after a few paces to turn back to me.

"Don't you go anywhere, you hear? I don't know if you're think-ing about running, but your sister needs you here."

I look up at him, my face swollen and tear-stained.

"*I* need you here. And Melissa would skin me alive if I came home without you. She's pretty attached to you two, if you don't already know it. She's expecting me to bring both her girls home."

I swallow my emotions in an audible gulp. He walks back over, nudges my foot again.

"Are we clear?"

I nod, as mute as Jenessa. Then I watch his feet walk away, al-though it still feels like he's walking toward me in all the ways that count.

I wonder, in the darkest puzzle piece of my heart, if he'd say those words if he knew, really knew, about the white-star night.

Jenessa would never tell. It had sucked the words right out of her.

I carry the secret close as skin or breath or pee. It rode in the truck with me as surely as those three garbage bags. Even with hours and miles between us, the truth hunkers down fat as a tick tucked into the moistest, darkest place.

Quick as the rabbits I used to shoot for breakfast, I sprint across the asphalt to the bushes and let my breakfast fly.

"*You have a bird's stomach,*" *Mama says, none too pleased.* "*You have to get those nerves under control, girl. Why you so scared? No one here but your mama.*"

She was barely there, the last year, and still not there, even when she was. And that's not counting the times she was there and a per-son wished with all her might she wasn't.

7

It's been three weeks since we arrived at our father's farm, and yet it feels like a year in some ways.

Looking at Jenessa, you'd never know she was the same little girl. Her body, kindling thin and all angles upon arrival, is now pinker and rounder, with the start of little dents Melissa calls "dimples" in her cheeks and at the back of her knees. Her huge, haunted eyes are as sweet as they've always been, but the edges of worry have crumbled away, not all of it, but most. Those eyes sparkle brightest when she's with Shorty, and there's many a time we sit and watch them play, her company melting years off the old hound, "undoing the gray," as my father likes to joke.

Last week, Melissa took Ness into town for a haircut, and my sister came back with her blond curls brushing her shoulders, framing rosy apple cheeks. In her new shirts, jeans, chinos, dresses, shoes, slippers, and nightgowns, she looks like a girl, a normal little girl, not the forlorn soul huddling over a tin cup of never-ending beans.

I haven't fared as well, with so much on my mind. I haven't gained more than five pounds, if I'm lucky. It's the bird nerves, like Mama said.

At breakfast, I eat my bacon but pick at the eggs. I'm snug-warm in a pale blue terry-cloth bathrobe, a gift from Melissa. And yet, I'm keening fierce for the campfire, for the early-morning bird chatter launching the sun into orbit as I shiver and poke the sleeping coals awake, the morning not just a vision but a feeling, a scent, a taste that enters your pores and coasts through your veins until it fires up your very soul.

Melissa interrupts my daydreaming, her back to me as she pours herself a cup of coffee from the carafe on the kitchen counter.

"I think it's your turn, Carey. We need to get you some new clothes. Not just for school but to keep you warm and comfortable, too. Winter's coming. At the least, you need a new coat."

"Yes, ma'am."

It's impossible to say no to Melissa (especially when she's talking up a new winter coat!), but not because she's bossy. More because her intentions are always in the right places.

Melissa waits until my seat belt clicks before she turns the key and proceeds down the driveway. She waves to my father, who's chopping firewood, and to Nessa and Shorty, who are playing fetch out front.

She hums to the radio, to slower songs I've never heard before. I sneak a few glances at her, and she catches me, winking at me, and I can't help but smile back. At least until we reach the ginormous (Delaney's word) bustling place called "the mall," and I change my mind less than five feet from the entrance.

"What's wrong, sweetie?"

My feet remain glued to the blacktop. I can't look at her.

"Carey? Look at me, sweetie."

I look into her face, my own expressing the tangle of emotions churning my breakfast and flushing my cheeks.

Melissa looks pained, which surprises me. She takes a deep, steadying breath for both of us and then smiles her reassurance, with the kind of strength dredged up from a backbone of steel. Steel. *For me.*

"Here. Take these."

She drops the key chain to the SUV into my open palm.

"You can wait in the car, okay? I'll pick up a few things, and then we'll go home. How does that sound?"

"Good, ma'am." I summon up a tiny grin, all monkey arms—awkward. "Thank you, ma'am."

"Do you know how tall you are?"

Longing runs down my innards like Pooh's honey as I think of the Growing Trees, two hickorys side by side, where I'd carved ascending notches as I'd marked my height on one and Nessa's on the other.

"Five feet, seven inches."

"How about your feet? Do you know what size?"

"My sneakers are an eight? And they fit right good."

Same size as Mama's. But I don't say it out loud.

Slumping in the passenger seat, barely blinking, I people-watch my eyes out. There are lots of girls my age dancing around women like Melissa, as excited as Shorty when I hold up a bone and he weaves between my legs in rapidfire anticipation.

I smooth my hair, seeing the girls' perfect locks. Melissa made mine perfect just last week.

"Unless you want to change your style, I only need to take about an inch off the ends, straight across the bottom. I could do it for you, if you'd like."

The ends look chunky now, and I can't stop turning around to see them in the mirror.

I watch women navigate kids with wires hanging out of their

ears, their heads bouncing rhythmically. I follow the wires down to little square boxes clipped onto their belts or disappearing inside jacket pockets.

Some talk into rectangular devices pressed to their ears, called "cell phones," or hold them out in front of them, thumbs tapping wildly. If you did that in Obed, you could fall down a ravine or step on a venomous snake. Not paying attention, you'd miss the snippet of baby rabbit flashing by or the red shuffle-fox who could easily be persuaded to visit from time to time in exchange for bread crusts or wild blackberries, twinkly tinfoil or a busted shoestring.

Delaney has both devices, and she laughed at me when I first asked Melissa what they were. In the middle of the conversation, Nessa's head whipped toward me, her eyes wide as the harvest moon. I shook my head no.

"We can't call Mama."

Why not? Jenessa's eyes shout.

"Because Mama don't—doesn't—have one of those fancy phones."

Delaney turns to Melissa, incredulous.

"She's kidding, right? How can anyone in this century, let alone on this planet, not know what a cell phone is?"

Melissa's lips press into a hard line. Delaney throws up her hands, her signature gesture, I've learned by now. She glares at me before turning back to Melissa.

"What? What did I say this time?"

Melissa shakes her head slowly, a look passing between them.

"Fine. If you think I'm bad, Mother, wait until she goes to school. The kids'll eat her alive if she doesn't get with the program!"

School.

Each time I replay that conversation, my blood pounds in my ears and my stomach jumps like catfish in the Obed River.

It only takes Melissa one and a half shopping hours, the end of which I spend dozing. I quickly grow tired of scrutinizing my reflection in the mirror, studying the girl who lives in that glass. I hadn't known I was beautiful until Melissa confirmed it. Going by her voice, it's supposed to be a good thing—like winning the Mega Millions, which my father plays twice a week, or bringing down a fat buck.

Only, I don't see it. All I see is me. And I know me. And that word doesn't fit me. I still look exactly like the girl who lived in the woods. You can take the girl out of the woods, but not the woods out of the girl, I reckon. I still look owl-eyed, pointy-chinned, serious. I still look like I know more than I should, which I do. I still look like I'm hefting huge white-star secrets. I'm surprised every day that no one else can see.

Rap rap rap!

I open my eyes and see Melissa looking in, toting a bunch of large white bags that bump against her thighs.

"Could you pop the trunk for me?"

I watch her eyes remember. I like that she forgets.

"Here. Let me show you how."

She disappears from view, reappearing by her own door.

I know how to unlock the doors, so I do that. One flick of a switch. It's amazing.

"Thanks, Carey. See this button here?" I lean toward her, nodding.

She pushes it, and I spin in my seat to watch the trunk open automatically.

"Now you know."

She smiles softly and disappears around the back. I sit up straight and wipe the sleep from my eyes, smooth my hair again, and wait.

"Just a sec, and we'll be on our way home," she calls out.

Home.

That word. It creeps across my consciousness like a plump cat-

erpillar. You don't want to hurt it, but you don't know what to do
with it, either. To which I tell myself, home is wherever Jenessa is.
It's as simple as that, really. It doesn't have to mean more than
that unless I want it to. One *h* word can't wipe out my Obed life.
Nor can it wipe out Mama. Even if sometimes a huge part of me
wishes it could.

We carry the humongous bags to my room. I carry a heavy one
filled with rectangular white boxes. I have no idea what goes into
rectangular white boxes. But they look so clean, so fresh and new.
For a moment, everything that's good in the whole wide world must
fit into rectangular white boxes.

I vow to keep the boxes, too.

I'm so curious and excited, I don't even flinch when Melissa leans in
toward me and gives me a hug, her eyes dancing.

"Let's unpack the loot," she says, and I don't know what *loot*
means, but it sounds like it must be at least as good as rectangular
white boxes.

The first bag is full of so many colors, I can't even name them all.
I most definitely can't call the first items "undergarments," because
the plain word dishonors the silky beauty of the pretty colors and
patterns. There are matching bras to go along with them, some
with small cups and some that remind me of tank tops cut in half. I
glide my fingers over the material as Melissa pulls out packs of
socks, some colored, some white, some up to the calf, some stopping at the ankle. There are even two pairs of panty hose I could
swear are made of flesh-colored spiderwebs.

Another bag contains a pair of gloves fashioned from the softest
material I've ever touched—"cashmere," Melissa says, then explains
what cashmere is.

"Isn't it the most amazing thing you've ever felt?"

"Right soft." Gently, I lay my cheek on the glove, imagining a whole pillow made of the stuff.

"Do you know what cashmere is?"

I shake my head no.

"It's the silky, fine wool at the roots of the hair of the Kashmir goat."

"A goat?"

"I know. Isn't the world so interesting?"

I smile my yes, my attention turned back to the loot, to another pair of hand coverings with a thumb but no separate fingers, made of thick, scratchier material.

"That's wool, and it comes from sheep. It's not as soft, but it's thick and warm. They're called 'mittens.' It can get pretty cold most winters."

She says it like I don't know, like I don't know cold the way I do. I like when she forgets. I think of early mornings with my clumsy hands purple as I rubbed Nessa's little fingers, her skin denting yellow, then glazed-over white as we huddled together in the camper, frostbitten if we weren't careful, our winter coats buttoned up past our throats, and underneath, sweatshirts, the hoods tied snugly under our chins. We wore two pairs of jeans apiece, and a spare pair of socks on our hands once the feeling returned to our fingers.

It was warmer outside in the snow, where we sat on logs around the fire I coaxed to life from coals each morning, and if we had tea bags, we'd drink cups of orange pekoe. There, I could peel off the covering and warm my hands to the point that I could play for Ness, the ghosts of Bach, Vivaldi, and Beethoven crouched on the log, the notes sparkling like the icicles hanging from the branches above us.

Sometimes, Nessa skipped and danced to the music to keep warm, her feet scratching white circles around the fire as I heated

the leftover squirrel, hiding the bits of meat in thick beans sweet-
ened with brown sugar, lucky with a few squares of bobbing fat.

My new clothes don't smell like wood smoke, and neither does
my hair or Jenessa's anymore. I never thought I'd miss it, but I
do . . . in the same way I miss the crisp ceiling of stars and the wanwood leafmeal that made up our floor.

"Look in the next bag," Melissa urges, her voice gilded with ex-
citement.

I unpack two pairs of jeans, fancy as all get out. Jeans just like
Delaney's.

"Bedazzled jeans. They're bedazzled with gems and rhinestones,"
she explains as I run my fingers over the glinting swirls and patterns
along the bottom of the legs. "Delaney and her friends brought
them back into style."

Along with a few plain pairs, I count seven pairs of jeans in all.
Seven pairs of jeans. It's right unimaginable. My fingers wander over
to one pair, washed-out blue, with a small hole I trace around the
knee.

"Can you believe that's the in thing? Even in the woods, you
were sporting the style," Melissa says, winking.

I laugh, startling myself with the sound. But it *is* funny. All these
girls with hot water and warm houses and store-bought clothes wearing washed-out jeans with holes in them.

The next bag is filled with tops—a few sweater pullovers, a few
button-downs made of flannel, also soft in my hands, and some of
what Melissa calls "turtlenecks" to wear beneath them. There are
more T-shirts, some short-sleeved, some long. My bed is a rainbow
for the senses. Melissa leaves and then returns with six packs of
hangers in white, pale blue, and pale pink colors.

We turn to the next bag, the one with the white rectangular
boxes. My breath catches in my throat. Box after box is filled with

shoes. I pull out a pair of ankle-high boots that look like my dad's work boots, a pair of white Keds, another pair of sneakers in dark blue with the word *Converse* and a star on the sides, and a shiny pair of shoes with little heels that look as fancy and wobbly as Mrs. Haskell's. Another box contains a pair of snappy snow boots with faux fur tufting the tops. I gasp when, from the last box, I pull out a slinky pair of knee-high boots in rich brown leather, so beautiful that my eyes grow as wide as Jenessa's.

This can't be for real. It can't be all for me. *Luck is as rare as butter for Mama, Jenessa, and me.*

"These items should start you off right. Your closet's going to look the way it should—nice and full. Go in and try something on."

Needing no second invitation, I grab a bright purple bra with cups and a matching pair of underpants, a pair of bedazzled jeans, and a long-sleeve T-shirt splashed with flowers melting into different colors down the front. I close the door of the closet behind me.

My clean, warm toes sink into the plush rug, and I hold my breath as I put my arms through the bra straps, the A cups padded and the tricky clasp taking me a few tries to hook. I turn sideways in front of the mirror. I actually look like I have something up there now. I pull on the underpants, amazed that Melissa sized me so perfectly. I turn back to the mirror, holding my breath, afraid to open my eyes. When I do, I can't believe the girl staring back at me *is* me.

It's so wonderfully, truly frightening, but in a good way, like Delaney says.

I slip on the shirt and jeans, smile shyly at the stranger in the mirror.

Melissa knocks on the door. "Are you decent?"

I push the door open without turning, frozen in the looking glass. Melissa clasps her hands and gasps, her eyes on my eyes in the mirror. We stare at the strange girl, the poker-straight hair woven into a thick French braid by her gentle hands that morning, and the large blue eyes blinking in disbelief. The bedazzled jeans flash in the light as I turn left, then right.

"Look at you, Carey. You're absolutely gorgeous. You could be a model in a magazine."

I can't take my eyes off myself. Hair clean and styled, no smoke smudges on my nose or cheeks. Hands slender, lotioned, nails clean. My old life kicks within me, but on the surface, the woods are gone. I look like Delaney. Like the girls in the mall parking lot. A brand-new Carey. No one would guess what I did.

I tear my eyes from Melissa's as I tear up.

"Oh, honey," she says. "It's okay for things to go well for you. It's about time. Don't you think?"

"I reckon." I duck my head, noting her own white Keds. "Thank you kindly for the clothes. For shopping for me—". My voice cracks, and the sentence melts away. She smiles wide enough for both of us.

"It's my pleasure, honey. And hey—"

I find her eyes again.

"Thanks for not calling me 'ma'am.'"

I go back to the girl in the mirror, and I can see it plain as day, like a photo negative of the woods. The girl standing on the rug practices a smile. The mirror girl throbs on the inside. Melissa locks her arms around me, holding me against her. I feel womanly softness against my wing bones and her heartbeat tapping against my back. She rests her chin on my head, her eyes solemn. We both stare at the girl in the mirror, a creature that can't be fully captured, not even in mirror glass.

"You deserve all of it, Carey—all of it. You always have."

She pauses, seeing me, *really seeing me*. Like she knows.

"That girl in the woods is amazing. Don't you ever stop being that girl in the woods, you hear me? Braids and new clothes can't take away the best parts of you. You hold on tight to your heritage. That girl in the woods raised a baby, took care of her sister, kept her fed, warm, safe. That girl in the woods is special. Especially out here."

I nod, my voice a wavery whisper.

"Thank you."

I hope she knows it's the girl in the woods who's thanking her.

"You're braver than most girls your age will ever have to be. Don't let anyone tell you differently."

I feel the cool air move in where her warmth used to be, as she walks out of my bedroom to check on Jenessa. She doesn't have to say so; I know her well enough by now to know that's where she's going.

I walk over to the window, where I see Jenessa smiling and giggling and whispering to Shorty in the field below, bolder when no one's around. Shorty lies on his back with his legs in the air, grabbing Nessa's arm in his huge mouth and letting go as she laughs and laughs.

Melissa walks down the path toward her, and Nessa's smile grows large enough to swallow the sun. She flies into Melissa's arms, laughing as Melissa spins her in circles.

Please don't let me wake up. Please, Saint Joseph, don't let this be a dream. Let me have this. Help me to know how to have this. Don't let us wake up cold and hungry, Jenessa's eyes begging me to make it better. Please. Never again. I may not deserve it, but Jenessa does.

Melissa takes Nessa's hand and they walk across the grass toward the kitchen door, while Shorty tears around, doing what my father calls a "rabbit hop," streaking ahead and doubling back, like he knows, somehow, these times are special. I know, because I have that same feeling.

For a moment, I almost forget how the date of my classroom debut's rapidly approaching.

"You'll start on December first, and there'll only be a few weeks until Christmas break. It'll give you a chance to dip your feet in the water without being overwhelmed," Melissa had said, brave enough for both of us.

I don't know. I don't know how it's going to be. All I know is, if I want to be normal, I'm going to have to work at acting normal. Talking normal.

Fake it through until I make it true.

8

"You have to sit still if you want me to braid your hair like mine."

Jenessa is excited to be going into town, and she squirms under my hands. Shorty lies next to her on my bed, pushing her hand with a wet nose each time she stops scratching his back.

"You girls almost ready?"

My father peeks in through the open door and grins at the two of us.

"Yes, sir," I say, braiding a little faster. My fingers trip over a turn and I let that part out, rebraiding the strands so there are no bumps.

Downstairs, sitting on the couch, my heart beats fast, thinking of those test results. *What if we failed? What if we're stupid for real and they don't want us anymore?*

"Is she going to be in any of my classes?" Delaney stops to talk to my father on her way to the living room. "She won't, right, because she'll be, like, a freshman, and I'll be a sophomore. Better yet, if they keep her back a grade, we'll be in two separate schools," she adds, perking up at the thought.

"Mrs. Haskell will let us know. I haven't seen the test results yet myself."

My father is clean-shaven and chipper. *Chipper*: his word. I sneak a longer look at him. He winks back.

"Sometimes the fourteen-year-olds end up in sophomore English," Delaney says, fretting. "If she ends up in sophomore English, can she be put in a different period?"

I don't know him well enough yet, but I can sense Delaney is wearing on his last nerve.

"She's your sister, Delaney. You'd think a girl would want to help her sister," my father says.

Delaney glares at him.

"She's *not* my sister! She's not even my real *half* sister. If Mom had let me keep my bio father's name, no one at school would even know—"

"They're registered under their mother's maiden name. So your secret is safe. Go clean up your room, Del. Your mom said it's a disaster area."

It's a voice I hope he never has reason to use on me.

"Ashley is having everyone over for study group. I go every Thursday afternoon, and stay for dinner. You know that."

"You can do your homework here tonight, in your room."

"That's so unfair! Mom!"

I watch Melissa through the window glass, raking leaves.

"Life's unfair. Now, march!"

Nessa shrinks against me as Delaney stomps by, her nostrils flaring like the devil himself. I glare right back at her. I've seen scarier things in the woods. So has Ness.

I think of my father's words, saying we're sisters. I hadn't given it much thought, nor had I framed it that way in my mind.

But he's right. Only, we're stepsisters, like Melissa said. We share no blood.

"C'mon, Ness. I don't want to make us late."

Nessa follows me outside, with Shorty bringing up the rear. Melissa holds the hound by the collar, where he pulls and whines and complains in a chortling howl.

"Not today, old man. You can ride with me tomorrow," my father says, affection smoothing his words.

The drive to Mrs. Haskell's office is quick, now that we know the way. We sit in the waiting room, Nessa flipping through a picture book, *The Tiptoe Guide to Fairies*, from the rack on the wall. I wonder if she misses the wood fairies, the only friends she's ever had, besides me.

"Hello, folks. Come on in."

Jenessa runs up for her hug. Mrs. Haskell gulps the rest of her coffee and gets right to the point.

"You will be pleased to know that both girls scored out of their age groups, Mr. Benskin. Jenessa, going by your age, you should be in first grade. But you've tested as a second-month third grader."

I beam at Ness, who smiles sweetly, not grasping the terms but knowing it's something right proud. My father slaps his knee and grins.

"Well, I'll be damned."

"You did a great job, Carey, at keeping up both your educations. You, my dear, tested as a solid eleventh grader. Both of you scored two grades ahead of your peers."

My father smiles at me now, and I force a grin, my face feeling funny. Especially when I think of Delaney.

"What does it mean?" I ask, skeptical.

"Oh, it's nothing to worry about. I'll recommend placing each of you ahead one grade. That way, you won't be too far out of your age groups. If the material is too easy, we'll revisit the situation in the future. What's most important is your social adjustment."

She turns to my father.

"While I believe the girls could keep up academically if they were placed two years ahead, they also need to fit in socially. Taking their history into account, and Jenessa's speech impediment, I feel that placing them ahead one grade is a solid compromise. That would be my recommendation to the court."

My father nods at her words. We all watch him rub his chin as he continues to grin.

To my surprise, he turns to me.

"What do you think, Carey? Sound manageable?"

I'm not sure what I think. I'm still not finished thanking Saint Joseph that we're not stupid as a hill of beans after all those years in the woods.

"I don't know." Then I surprise us both. "What do you think we should do?"

All eyes trail to my leg, which is jiggling wildly.

"I think Jenessa will be fine starting off in second grade. She's sophisticated enough. And you'll do fine as a sophomore. I think the woods matured you, compared to girls with more contemporary upbringings," he says.

I jump when he leans over and curls his hand around mine. He gives my hand a squeeze, and then, just as suddenly, lets go.

"I have no doubts you can handle skipping straight to your sophomore year. There are AP classes if you need more stimulation, and we can always bump you up another grade next year," Mrs. Haskell says.

I nod, still unsure.

"High school is a social experience," Mrs. Haskell adds. "It'll give you time to adjust before you have to start thinking about college."

College? It'd always seemed as likely as going to the moon.

"Then it's settled," I say, woods-firm. Perhaps the woods *had* made us older. I'd just never looked upon it as a good thing. "I'll do my best, ma'am."

I smile at Nessa with all the confidence I can muster.

"You're absolutely sure?" Mrs. Haskell says, scrutinizing my face.

"Yes, ma'am. Ness and I didn't have much else to do *but* study. We both like learning, and Ness is right scrappy. Talking or no talking, she can hold her own."

"That brings us to the next item on our agenda. Jenessa's talking, or lack thereof. Carey, you'd mentioned she'd been diagnosed in the past?"

Nessa stares out the window, zoning out. I betray my sister, letting it look like what it seems—like Ness is bored by the grown folks' talk. My heart speeds up, then slows down. Ness would never give up my secret.

"Yes, ma'am. She's always been quiet, but she stopped talking a little over a year ago."

"Your mother must have been concerned."

Annoyed was more like it.

"When she didn't start talking again, Mama took her to a speech therapist in town."

"So, who are you?"

Mama waits, her eyes marble-hard.

"Ness is Robin, like Christopher Robin, and I'm Margaret, from Goldengrove unleavin'."

"You girls and your book nonsense. Okay. Robin and Margaret. Your father?"

"Dead."

"Your address?"

"You answer that. Ness and I talk little as possible."

"Good girl," Mama says, beamin'. "That's right. Let me do the talkin'."

Mrs. Haskell pigeon-scratches on her pad. "Do you remember the doctor's name?"

"No. But I remember the building—it was gray—and there was a child therapist next door. I remember because we went in that office first, by mistake."

Mrs. Haskell turns to my father. "We probably won't be able to get the records from that visit, but I'm not concerned. I think a speech therapist is a good idea, though. I'd like to recommend once-weekly visits. Since Jenessa has a stable home life with both a mother and a father, I think once a week would suffice."

My father turns to Jenessa, his voice luring her from the window view back to us with words soft as an embrace.

"What do you think, kiddo? Would you like to visit with a nice lady who could help you with your words?"

Nessa nods, avoiding my eyes, and I swallow hard. But I smile weakly in her direction, and she smiles an apology in mine, all without looking at me.

I can't blame her, wanting to be normal. Wanting to let go of the past.

Saint Joseph, please let Ness's words come slowly so I have time to figure out what to do before she spills the beans.

Mrs. Haskell eyes me in a way that lets me know she knows there's more, but the moment has passed. Ness has gone back to watching the warblers on the windowsill, and my eyes are empty of the secrets she seeks.

"Does she speak in full sentences when she does speak?"

I rip my eyes from my sister and turn to Mrs. Haskell, feeling two hundred years old, at least.

"Yes, ma'am. Sentences and paragraphs, like anyone else. She doesn't talk above a whisper, though. She doesn't want anyone to hear when she does."

Mrs. Haskell turns to my father. "I'd have to agree, in my professional opinion, that the diagnosis of selective mutism is an accurate one. Her mind is fine, obviously. Just, for some reason, she chooses not to use her voice."

They both look in my direction, waiting for me to add to the conversation, but I don't. I can't.

"So, these will be my recommendations to the court: that Carey enter tenth grade, Jenessa enter second, along with once-weekly sessions with a speech therapist. Any questions?"

I shake my head no and look to my father.

"Thank you, Mrs. Haskell. Do we need to go to the next hearing?"

"You're welcome to, if you'd like, but it's not necessary. I'll present the points we discussed, give a status report, and it'll all be over in a matter of minutes. Then I'll prepare and file the paperwork."

"We'll leave it in your capable hands." My father gets to his feet, motioning for us to follow. "Let's go, girls. Melissa's making a special dinner for you two. To celebrate."

Jenessa gets to her feet and hugs Mrs. Haskell good-bye without her usual pluck.

"She's just tired," I say.

But Mrs. Haskell's eyes bore into mine, digging deep as the hickory roots of the Hundred Acre Wood, if not deeper. My eyes trip over hers, and I'm the first to look away.

I take Jenessa's hand as we cross the parking lot and she leans into me in her usual way. It's hard to keep my mind from going back to that night, the night we swore we'd never talk about.

"What happens in the woods, stays in the woods. You hear?"

I shake her bony shoulders, forcing her to look me in the eye.

"You hear?"

Only, that night became the next day, the next night, and the next.

I know it's my fault Ness went silent. I kept telling myself there were worse things than silence. Worse than Jenessa losing her words would be for her to lose me, like we lost Mama. I'd give my own words to make things different, I would. In the truck, I curl my hands into fists, the nails pressing red half-moons into my palms. I want them to. I want to hurt.

You're just trying to save your own skin, you coward. That's what it's been about all along, and you know it.

Saint Joseph as my witness, I hope that's not true. I lean down and kiss Nessa's head, her fine hair sticking to my lips.

What else was I supposed to do?

Once again, I feel the white-hot hatred toward Mama. I let the feeling trickle in without the usual filters, and it feels good because it's the truth. She'd left us alone while she did who knows what. The books she brought back, the broken toys, the smelly old clothes— they were the consolation prizes.

Only, it's no consolation, alone in the woods, two young girls short on options. She never should've left us there, that time or any other.

What else could I have done?

Nothing. We weren't strong enough. One day, I'll be paying the consequences, not Mama, and I burn harder.

But not today, which is its own sort of consolation.

9

Jenessa is crazy in love with family dinners. She's gotten a handle on her eating at this point, no longer stuffing herself or wolfing down her food. She uses her utensils in a civilized manner, doesn't use her fingers except for stuff like fries or hamburgers or sandwiches, and looks forward to setting the table and helping Melissa in the kitchen before and after.

We've all found Nessa in the pantry on more than one occasion, silently mouthing the labels with her finger in the air, counting off cans, but now it's different. A person only has to look into her face to see she's dazzled by all the bounty.

Mrs. Haskell said we shouldn't worry, that Nessa's food fascination will pass with time. I'm relieved not to have to worry about feeding us anymore. I have a ton of extra time on my hands now that I'm not shooting and preparing our meals. Melissa says that's her job, minus the shooting part.

Her canned-food stash, lining shelf after shelf of a walk-in pantry that dwarfs even my large clothes closet, consists of more than just beans. There are cans of olives, mixed vegetables, beets, corn, string beans, asparagus, button mushrooms, tomato paste, noodles, and so on, although Melissa prefers fresh, then frozen, whenever possible. She says she likes to have the canned goods for the wintertime, when the farm is snowed under and she's down on supplies.

That's an apt description of now (minus the low supplies). Even Delaney has been home this last week of November, the high school closed due to snow days.

Back home, I help Ness out of her coat and boots, my stomach growling at the wafting scents of Melissa's celebratory dinner: spaghetti and meatballs, with golden crisp garlic bread hacked off in thickly buttered hunks.

At the table, I take Delaney's hand in mine, and Jenessa's in my other, bowing my head.

"For what we are about to receive, let us be thankful," my father says, glancing at me and Ness when he says it.

Delaney can't drop my hand fast enough.

"Enough of the suspense! Tell us how it went!"

My father grins at Melissa, an electricity flowing between them. *Love.* It's the same that flows between Ness and me, better than a million dollars, and more filling than a whole pantry of canned goods.

"We don't got nothin'."

Her arm winds back, and she lets it fly.

"Jenessa Blackburn! You pick that up this instant!"

She stomps her foot in protest, and I get up and pick up the Pooh book myself, wipin' the dark, rich soil off the inside pages.

"What do you mean you got nothin'? You have these books, for one. Books are like whole new worlds," I say, my voice reverent.

"So?"

"So, that means you have the world. And you better take care of it," I say, handin' the book back to her.

"I want a Barbie," Nessa says, snifflin'. She hugs the book to her chest in apology.

"*You have a Barbie.*"

"*Not that one. I want a* real *Barbie. From the store. With clothes and tiny shoes and nice hair and a clean face.*"

"*Tell Saint Joseph.*"

"*I did. And he won't give me none. All I get is nothin'.*"

"*That's not true. You have love. My love. That's better than a Barbie any ol' day because it never gets lost or old or dirty.*"

"No effin' way!"

A speck of food flies from Delaney's mouth and lands on the side of the bread tray.

Now, that's gross. I rouse myself, tuning in to the conversation.

"There's no way she's going to be in my class! She's *fourteen,* remember? I'm *fifteen.* That makes her a *freshman,* not a *sophomore.* Do the *math.*"

Delaney turns to Melissa, her eyes flashing. My father's hand holds a slice of bread lifted halfway to his mouth. I can tell by the set of his jaw that he's fuming. I half-expect to see smoke curling from his ears, like a character from one of Nessa's cartoons.

We watch him dip the bread in the sauce and chew methodically. Then: "You watch your language, Delaney. I won't tell you again."

"Mom!"

"He's right, honey. No need to speak to us that way. Not unless you want to be grounded."

"But *Mom.*"

"Delly honey, Carey's and Jenessa's homeschooling pushed them both up a grade. It's not the end of the world. Your dad and I discussed it, and we agree that advancing them at least one grade is best."

My cheeks burn when Delaney scoffs at Melissa's use of the word *homeschooling.* The veins twitch in my father's forehead, his eyes trained on Melissa. He keeps still, even when Delaney scrapes her chair across the floor, leaving scuff marks behind.

I wait. *Will he hit her?* I'm ready to grab Jenessa and run.

Delaney throws her napkin onto her plate, and to my surprise, her eyes pool with tears.

"I don't count around here anymore, do I? Not since his *real* daughter arrived."

"Delaney!"

Melissa looks aghast, and my father looks like he's been punched.

Jenessa's mouth hangs slack, full of half-chewed food. The kitchen is silent as we listen to Delaney stomp through the living room and up the stairs.

"Oh boy. Teenage girls." Melissa attempts a shaky smile, glancing at us and then away, tucking a strand of hair behind her ear. "Well, that went over well."

"Mel, I swear to God—"

Melissa's face turns fierce, like a mama bear protecting her young.

"It's a lot to get used to, Charlie. For *all* of our girls."

I'm taken by the effort Melissa makes to bite her tongue—her decision not to say more in front of Nessa and me. She was brought up right, unlike our mama. The rest of the words flow between their eyes, until my father visibily softens.

No switch. No black eyes or bruises.

Looking down, I follow the slight movement of legs as my father's foot finds Melissa's under the table.

"I'll go talk to her after dinner," he says.

I can see it in her eyes, how much she loves my father.

"Thank you, Charlie."

———

I guess it *would* be a big adjustment, to have sisters all of a sudden, but I'm not the best judge. I've always had Jenessa. I can't imagine life without her.

With her as a captive audience, I'd recite poetry or stories, and Jenessa, bundled up in her baby snowsuit during camper winters, would dance in her car seat after I'd moved it into the camper and propped it in the corner. I'd play my own souped-up version of "Pop Goes the Weasel," like Pa Ingalls played for Laura and Mary, Carrie and Grace in their own woods. Nessa would swat at the air with her chubby hands as she cooed to the music.

I still see echoes of that baby in her eyes, those eyes that could swallow a person whole and spit you out gooey with love.

As my father reads the paper after dinner and Melissa loads the dishwasher, I sneak to my room, shut the door tight, and pull out my violin. I learned to play by watching Mama, mimicking her notes and finger placements, sometimes right, sometimes corrected. She was more patient back then.

"*That's right, Carey. Hold the string there, and keep your bow level.*"

"*Like this?*" Even I'm surprised by the perfect notes I carve out of *wood and air.*

"*That's it! Right fine playin'. You're a natural, child. All you have to do is develop your calluses, and you'll be playing every song there is to play.*"

Sometimes we'd played together, her rendition perfect, mine full of clunkers. But eventually, I got better, and our music rose up smooth and seamless.

When she went into town one time with her violin and returned without it, she hadn't explained, but I figured she'd sold it for food, and she had, but that wasn't all.

"*These are for you.*"

"*For me?*"

Mama hands me a slew of books, thin, full of parallel lines and strange markin's.

"Them there are music books. Them things are notes. If you learn to play from sheets, you'll be able to play anythin' in the world."

"Just like you, Mama."

"Yeah, well. You just mind your g's and keep up your book learnin'. That way, you sound smart on the strings *and* in the world."

Over the years, I learned each piece from front page to last, playing for her and Ness on the evenings she stayed at the camper, which wasn't anymore after the white-star night. Eventually, I didn't need the books anymore. She called it "playin' by heart."

Even though playing reminds me of Mama, I feel worse when I don't play. It feels like my soul is lost outside my body, howling to get back in. These past weeks, with my violin lonely on the closet shelf, I'm sure it pined for me the way I pined for it. I just wish it weren't so tangled and complicated.

Tonight, my captive audience is Nessa, who's snuggled up against Shorty on the bed. I know I'm playing soulfully when Shorty points his nose toward the ceiling and howls in mournful accompaniment.

Right away, I notice the shadow beneath the door, which lingers while I play. And I think of what Melissa said about *the big adjustment,* and I wonder what it would be like to have an older sister, or even a friend close to my age.

I spied on Delaney through the kitchen window as I pretended to wash a dish or rinse a cup. The sleds and saucers looked fun, and so did the girls laughing and pushing one another into the snow.

Melissa appears in the doorway, her cheeks rosy with cold.

"Why don't you join Del and her friends? Doesn't it look like fun?"

"Thanks, ma'am," I say, but my feet don't budge.

One-two-three-four-five-six-seven-eight girls, I count, with Delaney the queen.

I smile shyly at Melissa, but my insides are an avalanche of slush. I'll never be like those girls.

"You'll make friends once you start school," she says knowingly. "You'll see."

But, I don't know. I think of the woods, and I still feel like that girl—filthy, lacking, backward. I don't know the hip music, the slang, the cultural references, what's "cool."

I don't know how to be like them, how to think like them.

I'm hoping it'll be easier for Nessa, since she's still so young. But can a person make friends when they don't talk? Will the other children tease her, make her cry, cause her to yearn for the woods like me?

I wonder where Mama is, what she's doing, if she has friends. I want to stay angry at her, but lately what I'm feeling is sorry for her. She remains in the old world, a cold, colorless world with all the energy a person can muster spent on sheer survival.

As soon as the *Mazurka-Oberek* is over, Jenessa bounces on the bed and claps her hands, giggling when Shorty burrows his head into her lap, watching us from upside down.

I bow like a real performer, imagining people throwing roses onto the stage like they did for Mama.

Glancing at the bottom of the door, the shadow flickers, then disappears.

"Music is a bridge," Mama says, blowin' meth smoke through the melancholy strains my violin leaves hangin' in the air, the notes decoratin' the woods like ornaments on a Christmas tree. "It connects folks on a higher level, sayin' what words can't say."

Maybe it says what Delaney can't say, also.

Part II

THE MIDDLE

It's always useful to know where a friend-and-relation is, whether you want him or whether you don't.

—RABBIT, FROM *POOH'S LITTLE INSTRUCTION BOOK*

10

Melissa calls it fate when school reopens on Wednesday, December 1, the exact day I'm supposed to start. The snow has been divided and conquered, plowed to each side of the roadway, and the buses are running again. However, Melissa takes her mom job seriously, driving Delaney to school on those slippery, snowy days—which means driving all three of us now.

"I'm going to drop you girls at the high school first, so I can get Jenessa settled into her new classroom."

"Don't you worry about Carey, Mom." Delaney turns to me from the front seat, her face sweet as pie. "I'll take her to homeroom and introduce her to everyone."

Melissa looks harried as she switches on her blinker and turns right, weaving her way through the high school parking lot and coming to a stop along the sidewalk by the front entrance.

"Well, I registered her last week, and took care of all the paper-work. You sure, Delly?"

"Sure I'm sure. No self-respecting sophomore shows up for homeroom with a parent in tow."

I'm paying little attention to either of them at this point, as I take in the building, so large that I have to blink to be sure I'm really seeing what I'm seeing. I could get lost in there and no one would find me for weeks.

"You're absolutely sure?" Melissa darts a look at her watch.

"Yes, we're *sure.*" Delaney throws her arms around Melissa, and my teeth ache. "We can look out for each other. Didn't you say that's what sisters do? It's more important you take care of Jenessa. Right, Carey?"

I swallow the lump in my throat and nod. Melissa surveys me in the rearview mirror. I force my own pie smile.

"If they ask, Mrs. Haskell sent her records along two weeks ago, so there's no need for her to go to the office that I know of."

"Then we'll go straight to homeroom. C'mon, Carey."

Melissa looks as dubious as I feel, but another glance at her watch seals the deal.

"Okay. I'm counting on you, Delly, to get her to homeroom and her classes today."

Melissa turns to me. "By the end of the day, you'll be an old pro."

Delaney snickers as I step out of the SUV and slide on an icy patch of asphalt. I fumble with my violin case, wondering why I even brought the dang thing. I must look like a doofus (Mama's word for me). I wonder what word Delaney would use—something different, perhaps, but meaning the same. I barely have time to give Ness a hug and kiss, what with Delaney tugging on my arm and bossing me around.

"You'll be right fine, Ness. Remember what I told you. Be a good girl. Have fun."

"Yeah, yeah, yeah, whatever," Delaney says, waving at Melissa as she pulls out. "If you don't get moving, we'll both be late."

I watch the SUV until it disappears, almost jumping out of my skin when a car horn blares behind me. I scurry up onto the sidewalk. Delaney pokes me in the chest.

"And don't forget—you're Carey *Blackburn*, not *Benskin*. Got it?"

Easy enough. Ever since the woods, I've been Carey Blackburn.

Saint Joseph, look out for my little sister today. Let the other girls be nice to her and let her make some friends. Please let it be a day of smiles. Her life's been hard enough.

On beans I pray.

I take a deep breath and shift the knapsack strap so it's no longer biting into my shoulder. My violin has a strap, too, superglued onto its case by Mama. I turn to Delaney, all prepared for her mocking words and breathy look of annoyance.

But she's already gone.

I tug off the wool hat with the tassel on top (the tassel reminds me of saplings sprouting early) and stuff it into my coat pocket. I can only imagine what my hair looks like. I think of Delaney, hatless this morning, her hair perfectly swooped and curled.

Surreptitiously, I wipe the moisture from my upper lip. Flat hair (but clean), face glistening, lugging a scuffed violin case that screams *secondhand* . . . Delaney's right. It's hopeless.

Get a grip. All you have to do is ask someone where to go. What's wrong with you? The woods at night were worse than this.

I follow a group of boys who are laughing and elbowing one another through the front doors, swept up like muskie in a strong current. Against the wall stands a formidable glass case filled with statues—trophies—and plaques. The glass is as clean as a mirror, and I catch myself, cheeks pinked, mouth frozen in an O like the choral mouths of Renaissance angels—or fish face. I press my lips together, swallow hard.

The hallway stretches infinitely to the left and right, with a staircase on either side of the glass case, the polished banisters curving up to the second floor.

"Move it. You're blocking the way."

A guy who must be a senior, going by his size and voice, pushes through the throng. I step backward as the river of faces whitewater by. I could kill Delaney on the spot, for two reasons: First, because she's "ditched" me (her word) on my first *ever* day of school, and, second, because I'm actually scanning faces for a glimpse of her Barbie-doll face and peacock strut, since, whether I like it or not, she's all I've got.

Pathetic. (My word.) But I'm sure she'd agree.

So many strange faces.

We gawk at one another like wild animals and humans, only I'm not sure who's who.

Too many faces.

I swallow down the breakfast threatening to rise, pleading with myself, only in Mama's voice.

That's all you need, child, to be known forevermore as Puke Girl. Buck up! Life ain't no picnic!

"Are you lost?"

I concentrate on his face as it slips from two back into one. I will myself to breathe.

A boy! I'm talking to a boy.

"Do-dooo I look lost?"

He cracks a smile.

"Actually, yeah. You have that befuddled, new-girl look on your face."

I think of the girl in the glass case, her eyes wider than a cornered pheasant's. His voice is steady as a handle, so I hold on to it, and he grins at me, holding my arm at the elbow to steady me.

"Where are you headed?"

"I'm a sophomore," I manage to say, "and I have no idea where to go."

"Do you know your homeroom number?"

I shake my head no.

"The teacher's name?"

That I do know.

"Mrs. Hadley," I say. "Do you know where she is?"

"I had her for homeroom last year. C'mon. I'll take you."

"Won't I make you late?"

"You," he says, eyes shining like Nessa's when she's up to no good, "will be my excuse. A decent one, for a change."

Without asking, he untangles me from my knapsack and hefts it over his shoulder. "Don't forget your violin."

I grab the handle tighter and he leads the way, parting the sea of students, some of whom smile or wave at him.

"Watch where you're going!" a girl with glasses says as the neck of the violin case pokes her in the side.

"Sorry," I mumble. *Why did I bring this clunky thing with me?*

The hallway trickles down to a few stragglers, and I jump higher than a rabbit when a bell explodes above us.

"That's the warning bell. No worries. We're almost there."

I follow him like Shorty follows Nessa, and realizing this, I feel the heat creeping into my cheeks. *Get a grip!* I almost walk past the door, but he grabs my upper arm.

"This is your door. Second one from the end, that's how you remember. Mrs. Hadley will assign you a student buddy to get you to your classes. That's how she rolls."

He sticks out his hand. "Ryan Shipley, vice prez of the junior class and all-around shepherd of the lost and befuddled."

I shake his hand, and he looks at me like he's waiting for something.

"Hey, Ry!"

"Hey, Travis."

I stand there like a bump on a log.

"Carey," he says for me, "Blackburn. Right?"

It's as if a gust of Hundred Acre wind set the trees rattling in their skins of ice, only it's my bones rattling. Gran called the feeling "someone walking over your grave."

And then it's gone. He drops my hand. I want to ask him how he knew. But the words won't come.

"Good luck, Carey," he says, turning to grin at the woman who appears in the doorway, her lips pursed like Nessa's after her first-ever sip of grapefruit juice. (Pink, of course. But still.)

"Aren't you late for class, Mr. Shipley?"

"I sure am, but for good reason: I took it upon myself to deliver this new girl into your capable hands." He winks at me.

I listen to the exchange, note the begrudging affection in her voice, and, his attention diverted, I stare at him openly. He's the first boy I've ever touched, let alone talked to. I want to reach out and touch his hair. *Does boy hair feel different from girl hair?* I like his face. I see both clouds and suns.

"Well, that's a valid excuse, although I do believe you find too many of them, Mr. Shipley," she says, giving me a sidelong glance and then looking longer, like people have ever since I got here, like they can't stop looking. She pulls her eyes from mine and tilts her head at Ryan. Her chalky finger stabs the air.

"I'm sure there's more than chivalry going on here. You'd better skedaddle."

She strides to her desk and returns with a yellow slip of paper. "Now, shoo."

"You're a hard woman, Mrs. Hadley," he says, winking at her this time.

"Oh, shoo!"

He sprints down the hallway, slides to a stop at the staircase, then takes the stairs two at a time.

"And you are?" Mrs. Hadley peers down at me, her face all business.

"Carey Blackburn."

"Ah, Carey. We've been expecting you."

I peer through the doorway, where a gaggle of girls giggle and whisper. Delaney scowls from their midst.

"Nice boy, Ryan Shipley," Mrs. Hadley says, watching my face.

The heat creeps up my neck as I nod in agreement.

"Delaney Benskin would agree."

I glance back at Delaney, who shoots me the evil eye.

"Come on in and find a seat." Mrs. Hadley guides me through the door with her hand on my back. My elbow still feels warm where Ryan held it. "When you're seated, I'll make the introductions."

I keep my head low as I walk the aisle farthest from Delaney. I feel like I'm walking the gauntlet. More giggles when my violin case bumps between my thighs and I trip, catching myself on the end of the desk of a skinny girl with metal things on her teeth.

I choose the desk in the back corner, safe as a key in a hollow tree. I stash the violin case behind my chair and drop my knapsack on the floor next to me, not even remembering that Ryan gave it back to me.

"Delaney liked Ryan all last year. And he doesn't even hang out with the pops."

She's small, like the girls who dance on beams and do backflips on weekend television.

"The pops?"

"The popular kids. Ryan does his own thing. I know he's into astronomy. Last year, he built his very own telescope! Just in time to see the Geminid meteor shower. He said it was *ah-mazing*."

I note her rosy cheeks, the caramel freckles, the screaming red hair, and the whitest skin I've ever seen on a living person. She can't be much older than Jenessa, and yet there she sits in the desk next to mine.

"You're Carey, obviously," she says. "Mrs. Hadley told us you'd be joining the class. I'm Courtney Macleod, your student buddy. But they call me 'Pixie'"—she makes a sweeping gesture that encompasses her elfin stature—"because of my particular situation. I also have the misfortune of being the smartest twelve-year-old in the state of Tennessee—or maybe it's the shortest. I can never remember, exactly."

I giggle, liking her instantly.

"Carey Blackburn," I whisper, offering my hand like Ryan offered his. "I'm fourteen and I tested as a seventeen-year-old. They skipped me a year."

I don't tell her that I'm feeling right better about it, after meeting her.

Courtney grins. "Us geeks need to stick together. Of course, I mean *geeks* in the nicest way. Another plus is that Delaney despises me," she says wickedly.

"An added bonus."

"For sure . . ."

Pixie's voice trails off as she all-out stares at me.

Is there something on my face? Am I doing something uncool without realizing it?

"What?" I whisper.

"Sorry. I don't mean to be rude. But you have to be the most beautiful girl I've seen outside of a magazine. It's hard not to stare. Look. Everyone's doing it."

I look up and into so many pairs of eyes, I want to shrink myself into a river mink and hide at the bottom of my knapsack. Delaney's friends quickly look away. She fumes.

"You must be used to it. I bet people have been doing it your entire life."

I smile weakly.

"Not that I'm gay or anything," Pixie adds quickly. "It's just impossible not to notice."

Gay? Does she mean happy? I make a mental note to ask Melissa later.

Mrs. Hadley clears her throat loudly in our direction and then addresses the students.

"People, please welcome Carey Blackburn to the sophomore class."

All eyes stare at me openly now. Delaney and her friends feign disinterest, busying themselves with textbooks, notebooks, and pens.

"Class will come to order. Carey, this is both your homeroom and first-period English. Do you have your book with you?"

I ignore the whispers as I dig through my knapsack for *The Winter's Tale*, my nervous hands sending other texts skating across the floor. The girls titter. Pixie uses her foot to herd the wayward books, pushing them next to my chair. I hold up my copy, the front cover pressed with the dusty tread of Pixie's combat boot.

"Good," Mrs. Hadley says. "Delaney, please read aloud from where we left off."

"'Now, my fairest friend, I would I had some flowers of the spring that might become your time of day . . .'"

Her voice betrays none of the drama and angst she subjects us to at home. As she reads, I pick up the spilled books and shove them back into my knapsack, squishing my bag lunch, but I don't care. Pixie juts her head toward the knapsack.

"Didn't anyone point out your locker?"

I shake my head no. I don't tell her that I don't know what a locker is. I bet Delaney and her ladies-in-waiting would get a good laugh out of that.

"I'll show you after class," she says.

I pick up my book and hide behind it, pretending to follow along, but the words just blur across the page. I try to adjust to the yellowish light humming from the long overhead bulbs. I feel the walls pressing in, the manufactured quiet stifling. I can smell the human animal: breath, hair, perfume, gum, and even cigarette smoke. *I can't breathe.* I feel like one of Nessa's chipmunks pressed to the back of the rusty birdcage while healing from puncture wounds or a snapped leg.

I peek at Pixie. She mouths the words of *The Winter's Tale* by heart, eyes closed, her love for someone named Shakespeare more than obvious. Shakespeare's words sound like a foreign language to me, a language everyone seems to know *except* me.

"Don't you just love Perdita," she says, opening one eye. "Have you ever seen the painting by Anthony Frederick Augustus Sandys? She has flaming red hair, just like mine."

I shake my head no.

"In a dream, Hermione appears to Antigonus and says, 'Name your child Perdita.' It means 'loss,' or 'the lost she.' They leave the infant on a seacoast, but a shepherd takes her in and raises her. Later in life, it turns out she's the princess of Sicily. Can you believe it? She grew up thinking she was one person, only to find out she's another."

The princess of Beans. Just like me.

"The painting's in my art book at home. I'll bring it in so you can see."

"Thanks. I'd like that."

No one told me it could happen when you least expect it, without a plan, a map, or a prayer to Saint Joseph.

A friend. I've actually made a friend.

This time, it's Melissa's voice I hear.

Good things come to those who let them in. All you have to do is take a chance.

After class, I follow Pixie to the office, where she stands on her tiptoes in an attempt to see over the counter, banging her palm three times on a round metal bell. She turns to me, sighing.

"You can see why I nag my mother to let me wear heels. She thinks I'm trying to grow up too fast. I just want to see over counters."

She's a piece of work, as Mama would say.

"Courtney Macleod. What can I do for you?"

A sleek woman approaches, looking like what Delaney would call "super-hip." I immediately covet her coal black boots, formfitting and zipped to her thighs.

I'd love to have me a pair of them boots.

Pixie gestures toward me. "This is Carey Blackburn. She needs a lock and a locker assignment."

The woman stares at me for a moment, before she catches herself and clears her throat.

"Ah, the new girl. Mr. Alpert told me to be on the lookout for you, Carey. Nice to meet you."

She extends her hand, and now I'm the one staring. Her nails look like jewelry, they're so fine: long, perfectly square, pale pink nails, with a thick white line drawn across the tip of each.

"Nice to meet you, ma'am," I say, carefully taking her hand and shaking it.

"Mr. Alpert is the principal, and he's not too scary, as long as you're not in trouble," Pixie explains matter-of-factly, and the woman behind the counter smiles. It's obvious she knows Courtney and likes her, too.

"That would be correct," the woman agrees. "But neither of you girls strikes me as the troublemaking sort."

"No, ma'am."

"Girl, I stand out enough," Pixie says with a wave of her hand.

"I'm Ms. Phillips, by the way. Mr. Alpert's secretary. If you have any questions, or if you need *anything*, I'm your go-to person."

"Thank you, ma'am."

"Isn't she so polite? Not like some of the girls in our class. Not like Del—"

Ms. Phillips's face folds into a frown, but Pixie stands defiant.

"I'm just sayin'—" She catches sight of the wall clock. "Dang. I'm going to be late for AP physics, *again*. Later, ladies!"

She rushes out the door in a blur of striped leggings and a knapsack almost as big as she is.

"Here's your locker number, your lock, and your combination." Ms. Phillips places a slip of paper and a cold metal lock in my hand. "No contraband, or we'll have the authority to search your locker. That means no meds without a prescription, no weapons, no illegal drugs, paraphernalia, or objectionable materials."

"Yes, ma'am."

She looks me over, satisfied. I still don't know what a locker is.

"You're going to do fine here, Carey. Just get to your classes on time and mind your teachers."

She hands me one of those half slips of yellow paper.

"It's your late pass. You're late for second period."

She gestures for my schedule, which I give to her.

"Economics. First door on the right, second floor. Go up the big staircase and make a right."

"Yes, ma'am."

"And don't worry," she says as she ushers me into the hallway. "Most of us don't bite."

Even a backwoods girl like me knows better than to be the new girl in a large gathering of teen folk. Food smells waft out from under the glass doors as I peer down at the round tables, the people milling about, hear the clatter of dishes tangled up in words, music, laughter. It reminds me of a pack of wolves celebrating a kill.

I reckon the talk with Delaney this morning didn't help matters, none.

"You're brown-bagging it?"

"Why?" I say.

"You're such a goober."

I listen through the window as Melissa warms up the SUV. A goober is slang for peanut, according to a book I'd read on Georgia, USA, exports. But I'd probably sound like a goober, telling her so.

Delaney waves a twenty-dollar bill in my face.

"This is how you do lunch in the civilized world."

I stare at the riches. I've never even held a twenty-dollar bill, although I touched a five once, rolled into a tube Mama used to snort with. I couldn't see the pictures too good.

Twenty dollars. Twenty dollars bought a half hour with me, with Mama taking the money first, before shoving the men with the fat fingers into the camper and shutting the door behind us. I hated getting undressed. It was so cold, you could see your breath.

"You're clueless. Positively clueless, Blackburn. Take your bag lunch. Be a goober on your first day. Just don't sit anywhere near me. Got it?"

I glower at her. She's about to say more, and then her eyes train on my feet.

"I know my mom bought you brand-new boots. Why are you wearing those old things?"

"I just am."

I think of Jenessa and her thumb. Me and the violin. Me and these boots. Even better if they piss off Delaney.

I decide to bypass the cafeteria altogether. My skull throbs with the buildup of noise, people, sights, scents. I discover the door to a barren courtyard hosting a huddle of maple trees, and stone benches, cold but dry. I sit, my violin next to me. I stare at it. It stares back.

Occasionally, a student walks by, eyeing me through a glass hallway that makes up one of the courtyard walls, but, other than that, the space is mine.

I sit on my hat for added warmth and replay the morning. When I hadn't seen Pixie again, I'd finally broken down and asked a tall, gangly girl if she could lead me to my locker. The lockers are ingenious; so much easier to carry around books for a class or two, instead of the knapsack, which weighs a ton.

Delaney and her friends wouldn't be caught dead lugging around a knapsack.

Delaney shares two classes with me so far, English lit and American history, and she gives me a wide berth in each, as do her friends.

"Birds of a feather stick together," Mama said.

It's even more true here.

I exhale, long and straight, no wiggles for the first time today. The woods were a luxury of sorts, I reckon, cut off from the rest of the world. The peopled world is so fast, so loud and busy. Always things to do, with none seeming all that important. I've taken to popping aspirin most afternoons, my head punching back at all the hustle, bustle, and noise.

I watch a phoebe land on the cornice and characteristically pump

its tail. Nessa healed a phoebe of a broken wing in the Hundred
Acre Wood. The fledgling's feathers were a silky grayish brown,
with its stomach a happy yellow surprise. I pretend the phoebe followed us here, seeing how it's such a sturdy, resourceful critter.

Fee-bee. Feeeeee-bee.

The bird sounds like it's calling itself.

I take my violin from its case and, positioning my bow, imitate
the sound.

Fee-bee. Feeeeee-bee.

When Ness was younger, she loved to trace the dark, discolored
mark under my chin where the violin continually pressed, a mark
she called my "purple flower," blooming from years of playing.

I close my eyes and slide into Vivaldi's "Spring," and even the
phoebe stills to listen. I ride the notes back to the Hundred Acre
Wood, to the sway and dazzle of sun-drizzled branches, the wanwood leafmeal a spicy carpet, the air crisp as a bite from a rare apple,
as the Obed River rushed off to bigger things.

Some days, the longing for the woods breaks the ache in two
until I can't breathe. I slip into Brahms' sonata no. 1 in G Major, my
lunch completely forgotten, along with the constant motion, the
tittering girls, the awkward fit of this outsider's world. My bow glides
across the strings and I play by heart, from the heart, as Mama
taught me, my lashes wet and then my cheeks, the strings vibrating
the stars behind the daylight, the notes deliberate as switch strokes
at times, a caress from Saint Joseph at others.

"Woo hoo! Bravo!"

I hit a clunker, almost dropping my violin. He leans in the doorway, his gloves smacking together, his eyes sparkling like Obed sun
off freshly fallen snow.

"Wow. And to think they were calling you 'Clumsy Carey' just
this morning."

"Is that what they're calling me?" I say, drying my face and hoping he doesn't see. "Could be worse, I reckon."

I put down my bow, rest the violin on my lap.

"You looked like you were in another world. In orbit."

I blush, but I don't look away. *Ryan Shipley*. My heart leaps, but I don't understand why.

Say something.

"You look cold," I say, my own teeth chattering.

"Hold that thought."

He returns less than a minute later, a thick coat in his arms. I wait for him to pull it on. Instead, he walks over and drapes it across my shoulders.

My heart beats upside down when he plunks down next to me. *So close.* I think of what Pixie said about him, my cheeks burning. *With cold*, I tell myself. But even I don't believe it.

"You can really play. I mean, *wow*."

An icicle crashes to the ground behind us.

"What are you doing out here anyway?" he asks, as if he's been looking for me.

Has he been looking for me?

"Playing the violin," I say.

Our laughter echoes off the walls.

"Where did you learn to play?"

I feel myself smiling the way Jenessa does when Melissa praises her. I always knew I was good; I've practiced enough. But the fuss everyone makes continues to surprise me.

"My mother was a concert violinist. She taught me from the time I was four or so, and I loved it. She said it's in our blood."

"It must be, if you can play like that."

The phoebe pokes its head out over the cornice.

Fee-bee. Feeeee-beeeee.

We look up at the bird, and I answer back with my violin.
Fee-bee. Feeeee-beeeee.

"You must play somewhere, right, where people can listen and there's heat and stuff?"

We're both grinning. I can't stop. I think of what Mrs. Hadley said about Delaney, then push the thought aside.

"I've never played for anyone but my mother and my little sister. Not on purpose anyway."

"You can't be serious."

I nod, my chest puffed up like the phoebe itself. And then I think of Mama. Mama, playing her meth'd-up clunkers, or nodding off over the violin, me darting forward to catch it as it fell from her hands. *The music couldn't save her.* I think of Delaney's twenty-dollar bill, and what fifty would get you, and I see Mama's toothless face, laughing at me when I asked her why I couldn't play for the men instead.

"That's not the kind of playing they want," she'd said, shaking her head at me.

He'd never understand, and I could never explain.

"Please don't tell anyone," I say, the words tumbling over each other. I'm shivering, and I can't stop. "This here is private. Okay?"

His eyes fill with disappointment. "That may be one of the saddest things I've ever heard," he says, shaking his head. "You're a prodigy. Gifts like that are for sharing. Otherwise, what's the point?"

I think of a deer I cornered once, terror rising from its coat in steamy puffs. I'd lowered my shotgun, ashamed. Its face had been swallowed up by the same eyes Nessa wore the night she stopped talking.

If I hadn't been lost in the violin, I might've heard sooner. Heard in time.

"Please don't say anything. Please?" My eyes well. "Please?"

He looks like he's been struck as the tears slip down my cheeks. *Dang tears.* I almost never cried in the woods.

"I'm so sorry, Carey. I didn't mean to push. I was just saying—ah, hell."

"No worries," I say quickly, like he'd said to me this morning. I pull myself together, surprised by my reaction. "It's just that I have so much to juggle right now, and everything's so different—"

"You don't have to explain. Your playing, you're just so—I got carried away." He leans in, giving my shoulder a bump. "Sorry."

"It's okay. I just—" I look at him, my cheeks burning. "I reckon for now, I just want to blend in."

His eyes warm me like our crackliest fires, the ones inside the house.

"You, Carey Blackburn, could never blend in. Believe me," he says, his words soft as cashmere, "that's the truth. But, if you want to keep them thinking you're Clumsy Carey—"

I give a wobbly laugh. "Yeah, I reckon."

"Then who am I to stand in your way?"

His eyes flicker to the building, where two guys yell his name and press goofy faces against the glass. He tucks his hands into the armpits of his sweater, the way Jenessa and I did in the woods. His eyes hold mine, causing my stomach to flip.

"But we know better," he adds, winking. "Right?

I hand him back his coat. "We know better."

I watch his back, his feet crunching through the snow. At the door, he turns, his eyes centered on me, the *real* me.

Fee-bee. Feeeeee-bee.

"Catch ya later, then, CC."

The door clicks shut behind him, and a moment later, the bell rings. I fit the violin and bow back in their bed of crushed velvet, my hands clumsy with cold. I take three big bites of my tuna sandwich and swig the apple juice in the container down to its last drop before dropping the rest of my lunch into the trash can and crunching my way to the door.

I've survived my first lunch period as the new girl.

I feel as proud of myself as I did catching my first fish or starting my first fire.

Prod-i-gy: *person with extraordinary gifts; extraordinary thing.*

I'd looked it up as soon as I got home.

"Could you please pass Jenessa the butter?" I ask politely.

Jenessa wants to melt a pat of butter on top of her peach cobbler.

"Ewwww." Delaney wrinkles her nose.

Even after weeks of good food, Nessa remains slim like Mama, destined to be long and lithe and beautiful. Everywhere we go, grown-ups and kids alike stop to stare at her. At us. Before Pixie, I would've thought it was because we were backwoods losers stickin' out like sore thumbs.

Good old Pixie.

Delaney ignores my request, although the butter dish sits right in front of her.

"I got it." Melissa, smiling an apology in my direction, waves me to sit back down. She passes the butter to Nessa as Delaney feigns ignorance, concentrating on her plate, where she pushes around a few stalks of asparagus.

"Not a big pat. A pat-pat," I tell Jenessa.

When she reaches for another, I shake my head no.

I still can't get used to the taste of beef. It's so different from pigeon, quail, squirrel, deer, and rabbit. Going back in my mind, I catch the glint of my hunting knife as I deftly gut a rabbit with a few skillful strokes. We've yet to have rabbit at my father's house.

"How old do we have to be before we're allowed to have a boy-friend?" Delaney asks with a sidelong glance in my direction.

I cut into my baked potato, fuming.

"Sixteen," my father booms in his no-nonsense voice.

"How old to wear makeup?"

"Fifteen," Melissa says. "Tastefully."

Delaney smiles triumphantly.

"Why?" ask Melissa and my father together.

"Oh, no reason," Delaney purrs, careful not to look at me. "Just checking."

They exchange a glance. Melissa shrugs.

"Hey, Mom," Delaney says, her mouth full of cobbler. "You work too hard. How about Carey and me clearing the table and loading the dishwasher?"

Melissa puts down her spoon, her plate empty except for a few sugary smears on the dessert dish and a few crumbs pressed against the sides.

"That would be lovely, helpful daughter of mine."

She looks over at me for confirmation. I flash a smile of consent. I might be too shy to show it, but I'd do anything for Melissa. Just for all she's done for Jenessa, I could never pay her back.

I turn to Ness. "Teeth brushed and homework before TV, okay?"

Ness nods enthusiastically.

It's obvious from her good mood and voracious appetite that her first day of school went well.

Melissa confirms it.

"I spoke with Jenessa's teacher today, Mrs. Tompkins. She said the children were very welcoming, especially after she explained your sister's speech issue. She asked the children, 'Who wants to be Jenessa's classroom buddy?' Every single child raised a hand."

Ness beams from her chair.

"The class project is sign language, so they can bond with Jenessa, and she with them. Isn't that so thoughtful of Mrs. Tompkins?"

Melissa pushes back her chair, dabbing at her mouth with her napkin before placing it on the table. She squeezes my shoulder reassuringly as she passes, and I think of how Ryan bumped my shoulder earlier.

Ness copies Melissa, dabbing her mouth with her napkin before pushing back her chair and taking Melissa's hand. They reunite with a tail-thumping Shorty, who's anxiously been awaiting Nessa's arrival before the popping fireplace.

Nessa collapses onto the rug and pulls Shorty onto her lap, practically disappearing beneath the old hound. I think of Mama's sticker on the bottom of my violin case, a swirl of black and white completing a whole circle, called "yin and yang." That's Nessa and Shorty.

Melissa gathers up her crochet bag, choosing colored balls of yarn for the night's knitting.

"Five minutes with Shorty, okay, then bath, teeth, and homework," she says.

Jenessa's giggles are muffled by Shorty's fur, but her hand waves in the air, giving a thumbs-up.

"Ouch. That's unnecessary," I say as Delaney elbows me hard.

"You didn't think I was going to do this all by myself?"

"It was your idea," I grumble.

With Melissa and Nessa in the other room and my father out feeding the livestock and chickens, it's just the two of us in the too-bright kitchen.

"You bring in the dishes," she orders. "I'll rinse and stack."

I glare at her, unmoving.

"Truce, okay? Just get the dishes. Or we'll be here all night."

I hand her plate after plate, and she rinses them under the steaming water. I watch, mesmerized, as I've been since the first day, by the convenience of inside faucets. She has no idea how good she has it.

"Marie said she saw you in the courtyard with Ryan today."

I scrutinize her face, but it's unreadable. I think of how Ryan sat next to me and the way my heart flipped over, and I almost drop a dinner plate.

"Careful with those. That's part of a set that belonged to my great-grandmother. They'll be mine, when I marry."

Delaney grabs the plate from me roughly, almost dropping it herself. As always, I can feel her measuring me. Measuring me against herself.

"If I were you," she continues, "I'd watch out for Ryan. He's a player. And a junior. I wonder what your father would say about that."

I think of the creek in the dead of winter—silent, rock-hard, impenetrable.

Be the creek.

I center on Melissa, who's speaking to my sister, her words soft as a lullaby.

"We'll have to ask Santa for crochet needles for you. Would you like to learn?"

Ness nods happily, playing with Shorty's front toes.

"That's your defense? You're going to pull a Jenessa on me?" Delaney demands.

I shrug, hand her another dish. I'm not going to discuss Ryan with her. I can barely discuss him with myself. I peer out the window over the sink, the glass frosted by the cold outside and fogged by the warmth within.

Delaney reaches her finger toward the glass. I watch as she draws a large R, then a circle around it, then a slanted line through the circle.

"Just stay away from him, you hear?"

I don't take well to people telling me what to do.

Never have, never will.

"Or what?" I demand.

What can she really do to me?

Delaney reaches into her pocket and pulls out a sheet of paper folded into squares. The blood drains from my face. I could kill her right there on the spot.

"Or this," she says, "is going to end up taped to the walls at school."

"That's mine." My voice cracks. "Give it back."

Her eyes flash, and she begins reading to herself.

"To Whom It May Concern,

I'm writing in regards to my daughters, Carey and Jenessa Blackburn.

I removed Carey from her father's home without his permission while she was in his legal custody.

His name is Charles Benskin, and you can find him through the National Center for Missing and Exploited Children.

I have issues with methamphetamine and bipolar disorder, and can no longer care for the girls. You can find them at a camper in the woods of the Obed Wild and Scenic River National Park.

If you enter from the first scenic overlook and follow the river, you'll find the camper in a clearing about seven miles out.

Please know I'm sorry for what I did.

Sincerely,

Joelle Blackburn

"Wow. Your mom is pretty effed up."

I dart forward and rip the paper from her hands. She grins, the victor either way.

"That's just a copy. I have more where that came from. You think Ryan Shipley could really like a backwoods freak like you? We only took you in out of pity."

I stand next to myself—that's how it feels—and watch helplessly as my arm pulls back and my fist balls, ready to hit her harder than I've ever hit anything.

"Go ahead—I dare you, *freak*," Delaney hisses, not even trying to defend herself. "Show them who you really are—white-trash garbage whose mother didn't bring her up right, let alone want her."

To my horror, a dam breaks.

"You're pathetic, you know that? I wish they'd never found you. I wish your crack-ass mother had taken you with her—"

"She was smoking *meth*," I hiss. "And I didn't ask to come here."

We're both breathing heavily.

"What's your problem with me anyway?" I say, the white heat filling my body. "I reckon you have everything a person could ask for. You even had my father. Why do you hate us so much?"

Delaney laughs, a hollow, bitter sound. "Are you kidding me? I never had either one of them. Not even my own mother! It was all about *you*. It's *always* been about you! Were you alive? Were you dead? Oh, there's another sighting. No, it's not her. Were you hungry? Safe? Warm? Carey this, Carey that. It was always All *about you*."

I watch the tears slip down her cheeks, the perfect facade melting into one of misery.

"You girls okay in there?" Melissa's voice is light, calm.

"We're fine, ma'am. Just finishing up."

Delaney slaps the dish towel over my shoulder.

"I'm through here," she says, her eyes hard. I watch her back, straight and proud, as she walks away.

Once she's gone, I ball up the paper and shove it to the bottom

of the garbage. Then I hold on to the edge of the counter for support and cry until I'm all cried out. I reckon a good cry has been
a long time in the making, and I cry until I'm empty, but a good
empty, like the speckled shells left behind by flapping quail babies.

My mind wanders back to the Hundred Acre Wood and I close
my eyes, remembering the frosty breeze painting roses on our cheeks
and setting the branches chattering; the stars blinking thoughtfully
from their perilous heights; the crackling fire accompanying my
violin; and Nessa clapping at the end, propped up against me for
warmth.

I even yearn for Mama, just for a second, before I snuff out her
memory like the candle stubs we read by when the kerosene lamp
ran low.

I close the dishwasher after filling the tiny compartment with
dishwasher soap like my father taught me. I wipe down the counters and then the stainless-steel double sinks.

Fee-bee. Feeeeee-bee.

The little bird lands on the windowsill, tilting its head curiously,
regarding me with sympathetic eyes.

I think of Ryan, of how I played for him, how he made the violin
happy again, instead of melancholy and achy. He watched my soul
ride the notes to all the private places: happy, sad, unsure, scared.
In his eyes, I was CC, not the backwoods freak.

Would that change if he knew? If my life in the woods got
around school? If Delaney showed him Mama's letter?

My breath comes fast, and I work on slowing it down. In, out. In,
out. I reckon I'd die if Ryan found out about me—if he looked at me
and saw the old Carey with the dirty nails and smoke-smudged face,
the ripped jeans and the cat-pee coat.

"I'm taking Jenessa up for her bath," Melissa says, peeking in
through the doorway.

"Yes, ma'am."

After she's gone, I splash water on my face and dry it with a sheet of paper towel. I still can't believe they come from trees. It makes me right sad. I use the sheet to wipe off the R circle, too, clearing the glass in time to see the phoebe ride the current and alight on the barn roof. A streak of light rims the bottom of the door, where my father finishes up the evening feed.

Does he think the same as Delaney? That his daughters are backwoods freaks? White trash? Whatever that is, it even sounds nasty. Delaney had to be lying, saying that he'd looked for me. Mama said she sent him letters but that he never wrote back. Why did he let Mama take me, knowing himself what she was like?

I slip up the stairs and close the door behind me, crawling into bed fully clothed, like in the woods.

I listen to Melissa singing to Nessa in the tub. *Three blind mice. See how they run.* I let the sounds wash over me, clutching at the peace that comes from knowing Nessa's not a burden to Melissa. She loves my little sister. Anyone can see it.

I pretend she's our mother, our real mother, and the woods are just a bad dream erased with a bubble bath and a nonsensical children's song.

The last thing I see before I drift off is Melissa's crescent-moon smile.

She opens my door quietly, reaches in, and flicks off the light.

"Sleep tight. Don't let the bedbugs bite."

I sure hope they bite Mama.

11

Marie reads out loud while I stare out the classroom window.

"You okay?"

Pixie whispers from the side of her mouth, pretending to take notes as Mrs. Hadley regards us sternly.

"I'm fine. Shhhh."

Pixie is amused by this, by my shushing her. With her hair on fire and her peculiar fashion sense—a canned-corn yellow sundress tied across the shoulders of a tie-dyed long-sleeved T-shirt, with multicolored striped tights underneath, laced into combat boots (Delaney owns a few well-worn pairs herself), Pixie couldn't stick out more if she tried.

"Well, you don't look okay. You look nervous. Like something's bugging you," Pixie says, pressing.

Now I'm the one talking out of the side of my mouth.

"I'm *fine*. You're going to get us in *trouble*."

Pixie pretends she's concentrating on the book in front of her, fooling Mrs. Hadley, who turns back to the notes on the blackboard.

"Delaney giving you shit about Ryan?"

I stare at her.

"What? Because I said *shit*? It's just a word," she says matter-of-factly, turning back to *The Great Gatsby*, yawning and flipping a page. "Can you believe they make us read this *shit?*"

She giggles, and I can't help but grin.

Bored myself, I watch Pixie use her pen to connect the freckles on her arm into the shape of the stainless-steel dipper we'd used to scoop our rabbit stew.

She stares proudly at her handiwork. "That's the Little Dipper, like I see over our house at night."

I think of the violin constellation, twinkling down over the camper, and nod appreciatively, my eyes back on my book as Mrs. Hadley turns around.

"Courtney, I'd like you to read the next page, please."

"Busted," Pixie whispers out of the side of her mouth.

I follow the words as Pixie drones on, her dislike of the story comically apparent. But, something else catches my eye—a familiar grin filling up the rectangle of glass in the classroom door.

It's Ryan, pointing at his watch and making exaggerated chewing motions.

Mrs. Hadley marches to the door and throws it open, catching him mid-chew. Pixie uses the moment to ball up a sheet of notebook paper and hit me in the head with it.

"Score," she proclaims under her breath.

"Look, everyone. It's Ryan Shipley," Mrs. Hadley says, and even I have to laugh.

"This isn't trigonometry! I'll have to report you, Mrs. Hadley, if you don't produce my trigonometry class at once," he says.

"Get to class, Ryan, before I report *you*."

"Yes, ma'am," he says, winking at me.

"As you were," he says to the class, saluting and clicking his heels. Mrs. Hadley closes the door, shaking her head, like we're all impossible.

I settle back in my seat, smiling, until I remember. I turn slowly toward the left. Delaney looks away and proceeds to make a big production out of folding a sheet of notebook paper into squares.

"Psssst."

I turn to Pixie, whose eyes are shining.

"You're soooo lucky," she whispers. "Ryan *definitely* likes you. Damn, girl, I wish I were older—believe me, you'd have some stiff competition."

I force a smile, but my insides jump like I've eaten the tumors we found in some of the catfish a few summers back. I can feel Delaney staring at me, but I refuse to look. My mind's a jumble.

The important question is, Where can I meet Ryan for lunch this time? I reckon the courtyard's out. It needs to be a place where Delaney and her friends won't find us.

I scribble like I'm scribbling *Gatsby* notes, then tear the sheet from my notebook and pass it to Pixie.

Can you pass a message to Ryan for me? Don't let on, okay? I don't want Delaney to see. Ask him to meet me in the library at lunch.

Pixie nods, making it appear as if she's nodding at something Mrs. Hadley is saying.

And that's that.

"Mrs. Hadley?" Pixie stabs her hand in the air, waving her arm frantically.

"What is it, Courtney?"

"May I have a pass to the ladies' room?"

Mrs. Hadley checks the wall clock. "The period's almost over. Can't you wait five minutes?"

Pixie shakes her head violently, scrunching her face in agony.

As soon as Mrs. Hadley turns to retrieve the girl's room key, a key that dangles from a block of wood with the room number wormed into it, Pixie winks at me and collects her things.

"Here you go." Mrs. Hadley motions for her to come to the front of the room.

"Catch you tomorrow," Pixie says into my ear, "when you can tell me all about it. *Bon appétit!*" she adds in a strange, high-pitched voice.

I regard her blankly.

"Like Julia Child. You don't know Julia Child?"

"Is she a sophomore?"

Pixie giggles. "Gawd, girl. You have so much to learn."

I see him before he sees me. Fawn brown hair, fine like my own, but his is slightly wavy. Eyes that light up an open face, with a smile that tunnels under my skin as if I've bitten off a piece of the sun and the warmth now lives inside me.

I reckon I sound like a goober, but there aren't enough words to describe the pull. It's like Nessa's magnets. Indigenous. I think of the men in the woods. But somehow, Ryan stays Ryan. I remember what Delaney said in the kitchen, before things got so emotional.

"Girls like you have to be careful, you know."

I rinse Jenessa's plate, licked clean by Shorty when Melissa wasn't paying attention.

"Girls like me?"

Does she mean the woods?

"You know you're gorgeous. There'll be lots of guys liking you for how you look."

My face heats up, thinking of guys liking me at all.

"Believe me. Been there, done that. Don't let it go to your head. High school boys are all about one thing: getting into your pants. You'll see."

I stare at her, horrified. The men in the woods were bad enough. Not boys, too.

Not Ryan.

I smile as he catches sight of me.

Why *does* he like me? Because it's obvious he likes me. Is it because I'm new? Is it the violin? Could it be like Delaney said?

All of a sudden, I'm unsure. *What am I doing?* I think of Delaney and Mama's note. I think of the circles burned into my shoulder and the white-star night, which makes my stomach jump. It's strange how those times feel realer than here, no matter how many days lengthen the distance between then and now.

I keep my eyes on Ryan's, touching my violin case reflexively. I see relief flood his face, as if he wasn't sure I'd show. He meanders in my direction while smiling hello at students along the way. I slide down into the study carrel. What *am* I doing?

I know nothing about boys and whether they like me, let alone how to handle girls like Delaney, *especially* if she tells people about the woods. I'm playing with fire, and I know what happens when people play with fire. I mean, I wouldn't even know what study carrels were if the sign—NO FOOD OR DRINK ALLOWED IN THE STUDY CARRELS—wasn't posted on the wall above me.

"Hey. Pixie told me to meet you here. Why all the cloak-and-dagger?"

I don't know what he means, but I get the gist.

"It's a long story," I say, stalling as I search the library for Delaney and her court—namely, Ashley, Lauren, Kara, and Marie—but, just as I suspected, the library isn't their hangout of choice.

"Let's get out of here, CC. It's lunchtime, after all."

I smile when I hear his stomach grumble and mine answer in kind.

Ryan slings my knapsack over his shoulder. I grab my violin case, still not sure why I constantly drag it around. I don't want to

be "Fiddle Girl," as Delaney called me, either at school or at home.
I don't want anyone to make me play . . . to make me remember
Mama, or being in the woods.

The best place for the instrument remains shoved at the back
of the closet shelf. But each morning, I can't bear to leave the thing
behind. I think of Ness's old blankie, a "security blanket," Mama
called it, worn to a rag. I just wish my version wasn't so clumsy to
carry around.

"I know where we can go," Ryan says, leading me through the library and its maze of books and out the back door, through a grotto
of trees. We cross a sizable snow-encrusted field, the kind people
chase balls around, and before I can react, he takes my free hand
and leads me into the woods.

The trees grow thick, like in the Hundred Acre Wood, and I
smell the familiar old twang of earth and shade. Ryan doesn't know
it, but I'm more Carey among the trees than anywhere else. I breathe
in the musky aroma of old leaves and freeze-dried earth. We find a
large flat rock.

"You have a strap on your violin case. Like a guitar case."

"Yeah. Mama—my mother—glued it on. So she could carry it
over her shoulder."

"Just stand there for a second, okay? Don't move."

I freeze while he pulls out a camera from his pocket. The click is
loud in the stillness.

"Done. Come sit."

I do.

"May I?" he asks, and I nod. I watch him open my knapsack and
pull out a crumpled brown paper bag, which he sets in the space
between us. "I brought a bag lunch, too."

With a flourish, he pulls a banana from a side pocket, a foil-
wrapped sandwich from another, and a Baggie of black disks

with white between them from a zipped compartment inside his coat.

"Do you like Oreos?"

I nod, acting like I know what he's talking about.

I empty my sandwich, a green apple, a Baggie of Pringles, and two small containers of apple juice onto the rock. Ryan grins. With a flourish, he pulls a dented package of something named Twinkies from the depths of the same pocket that housed the banana.

We survey the spread before us.

"It's a feast," I say, forgetting myself. And it's true. Where I come from, this is a bona fide feast.

"It's a winter picnic," he says, "and this will be our tablecloth."

He removes his scarf and spreads it on the rock. I help him move the food onto it.

"It's beautiful," I say, waiting for him to laugh at me, but he doesn't.

"I only have one regret." He hands me half of his meat loaf and ketchup sandwich. I hand him an apple juice and half of my PB&J.

"Which is?" I take a swig of my juice.

"That you can't play violin with food in your hands," he says.

I laugh. "I reckon it'd be worse if I were a singer."

"I'd love to hear you play again."

I chew my sandwich slowly, and when the familiar heat flushes my neck and face, I let it. Deep down, I like the way it feels. *What's wrong with that?*

"I don't mind playing for you," I say, giving him a quick look.

I stay still as he reaches out with his fingertips and lightly traces the purple callus under my chin.

"I still think you should play for people—in the Memphis Symphony, maybe, or in the school band."

I take the Twinkie he hands me, closing my eyes in delight as the cream filling twinkles on my tongue.

"My mother played in public, and she found it so stressful. She lost the joy, she said. I don't know what I'd do if I lost the joy."

I search for phoebes in the branches above us. Looking up that way, I see the branches spiral out in overlapping circles, trunk to trunk to trunk, forever and ever.

"You're not your mom, though," he says.

I feel it again, the rattling. Someone walking over my grave. I look into his face and see so much, I have to look away. It's like if I look too long, he'll know all about me.

The only person I've ever been close to is Jenessa. It's amazing to see the same potential for closeness in his eyes.

"I know. But I already stick out so much, coming here in the middle of the semester, not knowing anyone. Being younger."

"Pixie can help you there. She's in the same boat, and she sure doesn't mind sticking out."

We laugh, thinking of Courtney. *If only I could borrow a cup of her gumption . . .*

"Where did you live, before you came to Tupelo?"

I can't tell him we lived in the Obed Wild and Scenic River National Park, tucked away like termites inside rotting, lightning-split trunks. But I can tell him the surrounding town.

"Wartburg. With my mom and my little sister."

"Where did you go to school?"

I use the word Melissa so generously attributed to my and Nessa's prior education.

"We were homeschooled."

I see an understanding enter his eyes.

"That explains soooo much. So the high school experience is totally new to you. I get it now."

I drain my juice, nodding. "It's like a whole different world."

We fall into a comfortable silence, broken only by the snow cover sliding from the oak and hickory trees surrounding us.

"So, Delaney's your sister."

I stare at him, mouth open, food on my tongue.

"No worries. I can keep a secret."

I chew, absorbing the gravity of this breach of my secret life. *Does anyone else know?* I swallow the food in a lump.

"Delaney is my stepsister. My father married her mother. We don't share blood or anything."

"And you're not the best of friends, obviously."

"Not yet."

We both smile at that. Then I surprise myself.

"I reckon it's tough, Jenessa and me popping up out of the blue like we did."

Ryan nods, but he's gone to school with Delaney for years and knows her better than I do. Perhaps because of Mama or my bond with Ness, it means more to me than it does to Delaney.

"What's your stepmom like?"

That's easy. "She's wonderful. She really is. And she's amazing with my sister."

"What about your mom?"

"Mama?"

He takes a bite of banana, offering me a bite. I shake my head no.

"Was your mom good with your sister?"

I take another bite of Twinkie. Again, I don't know how to answer. I'm not used to sharing, especially information about ourselves. After all those years sworn to secrecy, I'm not sure I'll ever get used to it.

"She tried to be. She did her best by us, I reckon. But she had her own stuff to deal with." The lie tastes bitter, tainting the moment. I wish I'd never said the words.

Ryan stares off into the distance, avoiding my eyes, like he knows I'm lying. All of a sudden, I'm feeling naked as the trees without their snow cover.

"I reckon you know something you're not saying," I venture. "I'm not stupid."

He scrutinizes my face, then looks away. My leg begins to jiggle. I rest my arm on my thigh to make it stop.

"I don't know if I should say anything."

"Please," I say quietly, swallowing the lump in my throat. "Just say it."

I watch him reach inside his coat pocket and pull out a piece of white paper folded in squares. My heart pounds as I think of Delaney and the *R* circle on the window glass.

He already knows. He's trying to find a way to "let me down easy," as they say on TV.

I take the paper from him, my hands shaking, and unfold it on my lap, smoothing out the creases. But it isn't Mama's letter. It's worse.

I see a picture of a little girl with a Po doll in her arms, below the words MISSING AND ENDANGERED. The words disappear as I stare at the little girl, who still looks like me. Five years old, barely. Top middle teeth missing. Wearing a stripey maroon pullover, hair still pumpkin-seed blond. Easy smile. So easy, I ache at the sight of it.

My voice comes from far, far away.

"Where did you get this?"

I'm breathing fast. I can't stop; soon, I'm panting like Shorty after chasing tennis balls, and the trees seem to run in circles around me.

"Here, take this. Put it over your mouth and breathe in and out as deeply as you can."

I take the lunch bag and follow his instructions. In. Out. In. Out. Until the trees slow to a stop and the ground sinks back into place. Ryan reaches out to steady me, but before I can stop myself, I push him away.

"Where did you get this?" I wave the flyer at him, my voice on the verge of hysteria.

"My mom. I was talking about you, and she remembered some old newspaper clippings. She saves newspaper clippings in a scrapbook. The flyer was in there, too."

"How many people have seen this?"

I flinch as his eyes register surprise, then hurt.

"No one! I wouldn't do that. Why would I do that? I just thought—"

"What? That it'd be fun to humiliate me?"

"It's not like that." Ryan pleads with me. "CC, I didn't mean—"

"My mother is not a kidnapper! This is *bullshit*."

I don't know why I'm lying to him. I don't know why I'm protecting her.

"Forget it. Let's just—"

Ryan watches helplessly as I scramble to my feet. I'm glad to see him off balance—just like me. I shove the flyer into my knapsack before slinging it over my shoulder. I snatch up my violin case, smacking his knee with it. Reaching out, he places his hand over mine as I clutch the handle tight.

"I'm sorry, CC. I didn't mean— I wasn't trying to—"

"I don't want anyone to know about Mama!"

How many other people have seen this flyer? How many people remember? Is that why they stare at us? Because they know? Do they know about the woods, too?

I wrench my hand from his and make my way back to the building, marching through the footprints we'd made on our way out, my heart as cold as my toes, but my anger colder.

This was a mistake, coming here. I'll never be the same as these girls, no matter how many pairs of bedazzled jeans I own.

Back in the library, I hide in a different carrel, unseen by Ryan as he sags through the library, his face stormy, his eyes devoid of their usual light.

You did that. You hurt one of the only people who bothered to be kind to you.

My chest aches. I don't know the right words for it, but it aches so hard, I can't breathe. My innards feel tangled as a net of bluegills. I reckon I'm just so sick of the tangles.

Even though Mrs. Haskell used the word, too, I still don't want to believe Mama stole me. Mama took me away to protect me—she wasn't the bad guy; my father was! *But then, why do none of the stories add up? Why isn't he the man Mama made him out to be?*

Without realizing I'm doing it, I reach across my left shoulder and rub the burns on my back. *Like Mama's worry beads,* I think, and stop.

Can you even hear me out here, Saint Joseph? Is it too loud for you to hear me?

I think of our lives in the Hundred Acre Wood, the days painted yellow (phoebies), rusty crimson (Christopher robins; to Jenessa, all robins are "Christopher robins"), blue (with blue jays, or possibly tears), and the woods themselves, a living thing, unfurling in shades of beauty, pain, misery, awe, joy, all swirled together, never running out of new and different combinations.

Mama did what she had to do. She *saved* us.

Then why the burns? Why the switch?

I ignore the bell when it rings, and I do know the term for what I'm doing—*cutting.* Cutting class. I blend into the other students in the library, pretending I have independent study hall like everyone else.

Over in the reference section, I find a book on national parks. I leaf through the pages until I find Obed Wild and Scenic River National Park. I study the pictures. The familiar tide of homesickness washes over me.

This is never going to work. Maybe for Jenessa, but not for me. I'm like Ness's broken-legged chipmunk, which had to be shaken and poked out of the birdcage once it healed, preferring the familiar, even if the familiar was a jail. Home is home.

A tree for every word of Pooh ever spoken. The Lady of Shalott curtseying before a minuet. Lancelot bowing, his hair a ripple of sunbleached wheat. My "puffed-up library," as Mama called it, a scooped-out nook carved by ancient tree roots in the high bank, close enough to be by Ness, yet far enough away to be alone. Boards wedged between rocks becoming shelves that housed whatever books I was reading at the time.

In Obed, I was queen of the world. In the zone, violin wailing, all the animals stopped to listen to a bow coax music from wood.

Here, there's always noise. Pointless sounds. Electric lights humming, keyboards clicking, phones chirping, music playing, people chattering. My head is Thanksgiving Day–full, and I hate it.

But it doesn't matter, because I need to be where Nessa is, and Nessa needs to be with me. She sacrificed her words because of the white-star night. I'll sacrifice my sanity, if it means keeping her here.

Back at my father's house, with all the pomp and circumstance of an Obed red-shouldered hawk funeral, I shove my violin to the back of the highest shelf of my closet, pull some white rectangular boxes in front of it, fuss a little more, then stand back, satisfied.

I'm not that girl anymore. The fiddler in the woods is dead. I'm like a wild bear balancing on a ball in the circus: I'm no longer one or the other. I'm The New One. The One I Don't Know Yet. And, as Delaney likes to say, it kinda sucks.

After dinner, a quiet one with Delaney at school for a late cheer practice, I sit cross-legged on my bed, my geometry book open on my lap. It doesn't take long to work out the answers to the problems in the notebook next to me, even though my mind keeps returning to Ryan and the look on his face.

I can't let Mama ruin one more thing.

I have to apologize. I know it. And yet I hesitate even as I imagine it, walking up to him and saying the words. No one warned me that being close to people meant hurting sometimes, both them and you. And then I think of Mama. If I'd learned anything, it should've been that.

A small knock and a short bark, and I can't help but smile.

"Come in."

Shorty climbs onto the bed in stages, eventually stretching out next to me, using my thigh as a pillow. I pat the bed.

"Come sit for a minute, Ness."

Jenessa climbs up and snuggles against me. Her skin smells like cake. Like Melissa's famous butterscotch cake, and, on further inspection, I see flour on her shirt. Dried batter above her lip. I push the books and papers to the end of the bed with my feet.

"You look good, Ness. You look healthy and happy."

What she does next surprises me.

"I am," she says softly. Me and Shorty sway toward the sound of her voice, like flowers to the sunlight. "I love it here. Don't you?"

Her eyes are pleading, hoping. Sometimes it's easy to forget how perceptive she is, especially where I'm concerned. Her silence makes a person forget her quick memory, the braille way she reads people, her mind sharper than the waddle-badger and the shuffle-fox combined.

I remember what the speech therapist told Mama.

"If she talks, don't make a big deal out of it. We don't want to give her mutism any more power than it already has. The same goes for her silence."

"It's nice here, yes," I tell her, forcing a smile. And it's not a lie. It *is* nice here, with a warm bed, new clothes, a quiet belly, toasty toes. We can even go barefoot in winter.

"I like Melissa. Isn't she nice?"

I have to lean in close to hear her, but even so, it's progress— whole sentences of it.

"She's wonderful. It's obvious she thinks you're wonderful, too, Ness."

I pull her closer, breathing her in. Strawberry shampoo. Baby powder. She rests her head on my chest and my heart swells. Regardless of how I feel about myself, I'm so happy for her, I could bust.

"You're not ever gonna leave me, are you, Carey?"

I watch her hands play with Shorty's ears, arranging them on his head as if they were a hairstyle. I'm sad that she doesn't know I wouldn't.

"Wherever you are, I'll be there. Remember?"

"Like in the Hundred Acre Wood," she says, lifting her head to check my eyes. "You said we'd always be together."

"And I meant it."

But, for the first time that I can remember, she's not sure she can believe me. It makes my chest ache all over again.

I recite one of her favorite Poohisms. "'If ever there is tomorrow when we're not together. . . . there is something you must always remember. You are braver than you believe, stronger than you seem, and smarter than you think. But, the most important thing is, even if we're apart . . . I'll always be with you.'"

She looks up at me, and for a split second, I see her campfire eyes shining back, the ones from before the white-star night.

"But I want you here for real, " she says, pouting. "Not in my heart, but for real."

"I'm here, baby." I take her hand. "See?"

"I'm never leaving, Carey. Even when I'm older than old."

"I bet I know one of your favorite parts about being here," I say, teasing her. "No more beans."

"Uh-uh," she says, correcting me with a grin. "Human beans."

I could eat her up.

"Did you finish your homework?"

The campfire goes out, and she shakes her head no, scrambling from the bed and motioning to Shorty. The dog lowers himself slowly to the ground and proceeds to stretch, rump poking the air, front paws splayed, back leg centered beneath him. It looks like one of Melissa's yoga positions.

"Could you close the door, please?"

They disappear with a click and it's just me again. Backwoods, clumsy, square-peg me. Circus Bear Carey, and I reckon that's not the worst folks could call me.

Jenessa would be fine. If they didn't want me anymore, she'd be fine. That's the main thing.

Ness would always be okay, if she had Melissa. Melissa would raise her as if she were her own—she already is. Even Delaney loves Nessa. We all know it, no matter how hard she tries to hide it.

Another knock, and I wonder what Jenessa forgot.

"Come in."

Only it's Melissa, bearing a tray of butterscotch cake and a glass of chocolate milk. She sets it down on the night table, smiling at me.

"It's strange to have daughters who do their homework without being scolded into it," she says.

We stare at each other, the word *daughters* hanging in the air, dainty and unexpected, like the first snowflake of winter.

I look her in the eye, woods-brave. "Thank you, ma'am."

"For the cake? It's no bother."

"Not just the cake." Monkey arms sprout from my shoulders, but it's important. "She's happy here."

Her eyes smile at me, warming me, like the eyes of a mother from a book. Just when I think she's about to cry, she blinks back the tears and gives a little laugh.

"I really care about your sister. About both of you, for that matter."

She looks away, taking a moment, then finds my eyes again.

"I don't want to make you uncomfortable." She pauses, straightening the edge of my quilt so it hangs straight. "Can I assume your back looks something like Nessa's?"

I look away, in answer. I know she hears it.

"You must've been pretty brave, fending for yourselves in the woods."

I wish something fierce it were true. Wish I felt it.

"Your dad asked if you'd help him outside," she says softly. "You can have your cake afterward."

"Yes, ma'am."

I slip from the bed, feeling self-conscious as I search for my socks. She pauses in the doorway, watching me.

"Are *you*, Carey?" she asks.

"Am I what, ma'am?" I find my snow boots half under the bed, hidden behind the dust ruffle.

"Happy here. Perhaps just a little?"

I busy myself by pulling on boots. Ryan makes my heart soar like a kite. This here makes my heart feel gnawed on, like one of Shorty's bones. But it's not her fault.

"You've been very kind to us. I could never repay you."

"But . . ." she says sadly, waiting.

"It's not—it's just—it's just that I—"

She crosses the room in two strides and enfolds me in her arms. I hear sobs, muffled by her thick sweater, before I realize that it's me crying. That's *me*. When she kisses my hair, I close my eyes, making a memory, one I can take with me wherever I go.

"We knew it would be harder for you, sweetie. Especially for you. And that's okay."

But it's not.

She sinks to the bed, pulling me with her. We sit together, not talking. I want to be the girl in the mirror glass, the lucky girl who has it easy, the girl who forgets all about the woods and the horrible things she's done. I want to be like Delaney and go to sleepovers and listen to the cool music and dance around my room in my new jeans. But I don't know how to be that girl.

"The day before your dad went to get you two, we spent three hours with Mrs. Haskell, asking all sorts of questions. How could we make you girls feel at home. How could we help you fit in. Things like that."

She smoothes my hair from my face and caresses my cheek with the back of her hand.

"Mrs. Haskell gave us ideas as to what to do, what not to do, how it might go, what problems to expect. But in the end, even if we did everything right, she said it all came down to time."

"Time?" I sniffle.

"Time. Time to get used to things, time to forge new bonds, new associations. There's no rushing time. She said it wouldn't always be easy, and that you girls might be homesick or angry or confused. She said that no matter what happened, the best we could do was just love you as you are."

"She said that?"

"Yes. Your dad couldn't understand how you girls could ever be homesick, especially after the way you were living. But I could. We make attachments to what's familiar. We find the beauty, even in the lack. That's human. We make the best of what we're given."

I think over her words. It's true.

"And all of this"—she makes a sweeping gesture—"isn't what you're used to. We even thought it might be best if we homeschooled you, but Mrs. Haskell was right. Better to face your fears and make a new normal, instead of sitting around worrying about it."

She stands up and smoothes down her apron. "It'll be okay, sweetie. If you let it."

Like she knows for sure. Could she?

"Your dad's waiting for you."

I let her tug me to my feet.

"This is yours, too, Carey. I know it's different. But it's yours."

I take back my hand, like a leaf letting go. It hurts too much to hang on. So why does it hurt so much to let go?

"Thank you, ma'am." I look at her, then look away. "I reckon Delaney's not too happy, though."

If they make me leave, I'm taking this new coat with me, I think as I zip up my puffer coat—that's what Melissa called it, a "puffer coat"—and pull on my mittens. The quilted waist-long white coat sprouts a hood lined in faux ermine. Or at least in my mind it is.

Melissa stops in the doorway and turns, her face thoughtful.

"Delly was used to things being a certain way, too. Although she'd never met you, you were already a part of her life. Not an easy part, either. So, Delly needs time. We all need time. Thank goodness we have plenty of it."

She leaves me alone. I pull on the strange cap with its interwoven threads of blue-, pink-, and yellow-speckled wool, the braided ties hanging from the earflaps. I turn and catch myself in the mirror.

I'm always unleaving.

The woods girl stares back with her grim face, eyes the color of stormy skies. I blink, and the One I Don't Know Yet blinks back.

Outside, I follow the light. I can hear my father moving around in the barn as I crunch my way through the snow and slide open the door. He's flipping down straw bedding for the four goats to sleep on, while the donkeys, one cocoa brown and the other softest gray, munch hay in their stalls with half-closed lids.

My father ducks his head in greeting.

"I'll be with you in a minute."

"Yes, sir."

I watch him use the muck rake to pick up the last of the manure, tossing it into a huge wheelbarrow.

"You can sit there," he says, motioning toward a bale of straw. "Let me just latch the stalls."

He locks the animals in for the night, the goats watching me with their strange keyhole irises. They're kind of cute, actually, with their nubby horns, which instantly remind me of Pan, god of the wild, keeper of shepherds and their flocks, nature and mountain wilds, hunting and rustic music. *Wooded glens. Violins around campfires. Margaret's Spring.* The goats are a huge hit with Nessa, if not with Shorty, who constantly tries to herd them from one place to another. My father slides the barn door open a smitch and leans in the opening.

"I know it's difficult to talk about . . ." He pauses to light a cigarette, the smoke curling out the door and disappearing. "But I wanted to ask about your mama."

I fidget on the bale, plucking a piece of straw just to have something to do with my hands.

"Your mama hit you girls?"

I think of Melissa, and nod. I can't meet his eyes, either.

"She left you on your own in the woods? More than just that time we found you?"

Again, I nod.

"I know you said your sister stopped talking last year. What I want to know is why."

I command myself to breathe. In, out. In, out. I've rehearsed the words in my head so many times, it should be easy.

"She never talked a lot to begin with, sir. It wasn't like there were lots of folks to talk to anyhow."

I see it in his eyes, the struggle not to push.

"Ness was five," I continue. "After a few months, when she stayed like that, Mama took her to the speech therapist in town."

"Was there a precipitating event?"

"'Precipitating'?"

I know so many words. It's perplexing to come across so many I don't.

"Something that upset her. There must've been a reason."

I look at the animals, so warm and safe. The cocoa brown donkey peers at me, waiting for an answer, too. I don't know what to say. All the prerehearsed words aren't as easy with my father's eyes upon me and his forehead creased with concern.

"I don't know," I say, trying not to look away, because *liars look away*. That's what the man in the woods had said. I tremble, trying *not* to remember. My father pulls a blanket from a shelf and drapes it over my shoulders.

My teeth chatter the words. "Thhank yyyou, ssssir."

His work boots are water-stained at the toes after dumping and filling buckets for the animals. Neither of us talks for a long spell, but I can feel his need to know. I think of Perdita, as lost as me:

One of these two must be necessities
Which then will speak, that you must change this purpose,
Or I my life.

"Well, if you think of anything, let me know. We want to help Nessa get past this."

I nod as I hand the blanket back. "Yes, sir."

Outside, I let out my breath in a large white cloud. I'm shivering even while my T-shirt sticks to my ribs. I follow along the wall to the back of the barn, sliding down into a squat. I wish I had that paper bag. The lady on the late-night "infomercial" called them "anxiety attacks." They're becoming all too common lately.

My father has no idea what he's asking of me. None of them do. Only Jenessa, who loves me too much to tell—literally. Jenessa, who's willing to give up her words altogether to keep me close . . . a sacrifice I let her make because I'm too cowardly to say the words myself.

What kind of monster am I, to let a six-year-old bear my sins?

I hate myself, hate what I've done. I've thought it through backward and forward, and I still can't find an answer that spares us both.

I wipe away the tears angrily, the wool chapping my cheeks. I cry too easily since coming here. I hate that, too.

As long as Ness is safe, the rest doesn't matter.

I think of Mama, the tears giving way to numbness. She was only being herself, leaving us in the woods. *"Just cuz a person don't like the truth don't make it less the truth."* Mama's brain doesn't work right. She called it "manic episodes." Diagnosed bipolar when she was my age. She didn't have a say in it, either.

Saint Joseph, can you hear me? I don't know what to do! It seems no matter what I do, a little girl gets hurt. You tell me—what's worse? Jenessa losing her words, or losing me?

What if I tell them and they don't want me anymore?

I roll up the leg of my jeans, my skin moon white in the darkness. I run my mitten over the scar, flat and gray, like a rut in the back of my calf where the flesh rubbed away. The metal edge of the folding table had done that. I hadn't felt it happen until afterward.

"Charles! Carey? It's freezing out here! Jenessa is hoping Carey will give her her bubble bath. Are you two coming in?"

I'm surprised when my father covers for me.

"Carey went for a walk—I told her not to go too far. Tell Ness that Carey'll have to give her a rain check."

"Well, don't you be too long, then. I have water on for tea."

"I'm just finishing up, and then I'll be in."

Their voices ring out clear as crow caws carried on the back of the frigid air.

A few minutes later, I hear my father's footsteps crunch through the snow and the sound of boots knocking against the back stairs before the door clicks shut behind him.

It's only a matter of time. I know it for sure now. And then I won't be able to stay here—either because the law won't let me or because it won't be good for Jenessa and her new family.

I reckon Miss Charlotte Brontë summed it up best.

Speak words of kindled wrath to me
When dead as dust in funeral urn
Sank every note of melody
And I was forced to wake again
The silent song, the slumbering strain.

I don't care about myself. Not really. I might be a coward now, but I wasn't when it really counted. If there are consequences, so be it. It's why I'm not like Mama. It's why we made it, Jenessa and me, and why we always will.

12

If you ask me, it's a strange teenage ritual on a Saturday night to gather together at someone else's house to eat snacks and drink pop. I mean, didn't we all just eat dinner, pop included?

"That's not the point," Melissa says, amused. "It's a chance to get to know your classmates and make friends outside school. You'll have fun," she says with a grin. "I wouldn't imagine the Carey I know to be scared by a little party."

"Who's scared?" I fire back, taking the bait, but still. "Anyway, I promised Pixie I'd go. Her mother won't let her go otherwise."

Delaney, eavesdropping in the doorway, rolls her eyes. I put away the last of the silverware, the cleanup helping burn off nervous energy.

Nessa likes to listen to our conversations from the kitchen table after it's cleared, where she swings her legs and draws pictures of Shorty and my father scrunched beneath rainbows that take up half pages, or of Delaney and Melissa smiling beneath bulbous yellow suns. The drawings aren't half-bad, actually. They crowd the refrigerator doors, held in place by tiny black magnets. I count another three drawings taped to the pantry door, and one sketch of our woods through Jenessa's eyes, framed and hung on the dining room wall—the first Nessa ever drew for Melissa.

That one's my favorite, drawn in old, familiar Bic, the trees scratching the page with a straight-lined elegance, the camper in the clearing, the creek running off the bottom of the paper. Nessa could be an artist, one day.

"It's nice of Carey to take Courtney to the party," Melissa says, giving Delaney an impromptu hug as she passes.

"Mom, really. You're messing up my hair."

"I'd imagine she has one tough row to hoe," Melissa continues, "being young and accelerated. It doesn't surprise me you two would hit it off."

I bristle. "Why? Because we're freaks?"

I watch Melissa climb barefoot onto the counter to put away the crystal bowls on the cabinet's top shelf. My father doesn't like it when she does that. He wants her to use the step stool, even if it's a pain to unfold and heavy to drag in from the hallway closet.

Melissa climbs down and turns to me.

"Freak? Where did you hear that?"

We both look at Delaney through the archway, where she languishes on the sofa, reading *Star* and *People*. *Freak*'s a word she'd use forever if I admitted that, one, I don't know who any of the people in *People* are, or why some of the older women look like cats—cats with huge lips—and two, to me, the teens look bizarre with their blinding white smiles, impossibly perfect hair, and expensive purses and bags. Ness and I could've lived in the woods for a year, maybe two, with the money it costs to buy one of those "Louis Vuitton" bags.

A horn bleeps outside. Delaney rushes to find her coat, then pops her head through the doorway.

"I'm going now. Bye!"

Melissa stops her.

"Are you sure you don't have room for Carey and Pixie, Delly?"

I cringe. Adults can be so optimistic. Delaney's face could wither one of Nessa's smiling paper flowers into a petalless, slumped brown shoot.

"Sorry, Mom. We're going to Kara's house first, and then the party. I can't make the girls wait."

Melissa looks at me, and I'm the slumped brown shoot. Not that I'd go to the party with Delaney anyway. I'd rather eat skunk, which (thanks, Saint Joseph!) Nessa and I never had to do.

"We understand. Have fun, honey. No drinking, and wear your seat belt! And no texting while driving, you hear? Anything untoward, and you have them stop the car and I'll come pick you up."

Delaney groans. "And I'd be the laughingstock of high school."

"I don't care. At least you'd be a live laughingstock!"

The front door slams behind her just as my father comes in from the back.

"Who's slamming doors around here?"

Jenessa raises her hand and giggles.

"Oh, you think so, huh?"

He descends on Ness with tickling fingers, her bubbly laughter loud and infectious, so close to real words, I almost expect her to talk out loud. Smart as the shuffle fox, she slides under the table, but it's obvious she doesn't really want to escape.

"That's enough now," Melissa warns. "She just ate dinner."

Still laughing, my father helps Jenessa back into her chair, her hand so tiny in his large one. I know it's considered impolite, but I can't help staring at him. It's like finding something you didn't know was yours, and the only way to get to know it is to look and look. With his tousled hair and wide smile, he looks younger and happier than he did that first day in the woods. He doesn't look like a guy who doesn't care about his daughters.

Everyone loves Nessa. Melissa, Delaney, Mrs. Haskell, Mrs.

Tompkins, the entire second-grade class, and obviously, my father. It should be hard for Ness, like it is for me, but for her, it's
not. It's like when we went food shopping with Melissa last weekend and on the way home, the SUV caught one green light after
another.

Lucky. Easy. That's how it is for Jenessa.

I smile at her, a pink smile, seeing the candy necklace she's
gnawing on. She must've gotten it at school. Or from Melissa. She's
eaten most of the candy beads, except for the pink ones.

A strong rap on the front door, and we all turn our heads.

"I'll get it," my father says.

I watch from my chair as he greets Courtney and her mom. I'm
surprised by how young Pixie's mom is.

"Would you like to come in?"

Pixie's mom shyly holds out her hand. "I'm Amy Macleod. Carey
is all Courtney talks about."

Pixie turns almost as red as her hair. "Mom!"

"Let me take your coat," Melissa says warmly.

I've been ready for ages. My puffer coat hangs on a peg by the
door, with thick wool mittens the color of dusty rose shoved in a
pocket apiece. I'm wearing the new boots, which cling like a second
skin all the way to my knees, and which, Melissa says, fashion trends
aside, are really equestrian boots.

I reckon they look good with my black leggings and the chunky
jay-colored cable-knit sweater that almost skims the tops. Even
Delaney had looked me over appreciatively, for the split-second before she caught herself.

"I have an idea," my father says. "How about I drop them off at
the party, and you two ladies can visit, perhaps have a cup of tea?"

"That's a wonderful idea, Charles. What do you say, Amy?"

Pixie grins, looking from me to her mom and back again.

"I think that sounds lovely."

My father takes Amy's coat and hangs it on the peg where mine used to be.

"After you, ladies," he says to us, with Pixie hanging on his every word.

It's obvious she's never had a father, either. I puff up like a Christopher robin. I don't mind sharing at all.

Pixie giggles as my father gives us the lowdown before letting us out of the SUV. We're parked in Marie's driveway, the birthday girl, one of Delaney's closest friends. The whole sophomore class has been invited. From the looks of things, almost all have come.

"No drinking. No smoking. No drugs. Got it, girls?"

"Yes, sir."

Pixie pulls a serious face, but she can't keep it up.

"Don't worry, Mr. Blackburn. I'll keep Carey out of trouble."

My father and I exchange glances, but neither of us corrects her. That's when I realize she doesn't know about Delaney and me.

The winter air is exhilarating, when you're snug in a puffer coat. I pause in the driveway, squinting into the headlights as my father honks once and then backs out onto the road.

Marie's house is at least the size of one million of our campers put together.

"Scared?" Pixie says, reading my face.

Two freaks out past their bedtime, I think, like Delaney had cracked earlier, cackling like a Halloween witch.

"No," I say, drawing myself up taller. "Contemplative."

"'Contemplative'? What is this, a funeral? You'd better file away those SAT words for tonight, Blackburn. It's time to par-TAY."

Pixie dances crazy, and I grab her arm before she slips on the sleekness coating practically everything. Even though Melissa says everyone uses salt. *Salt, to melt ice from steps and walkways.* And no, not the kind we use on our chicken or steak.

"That woulda sucked. Thanks, Carey."

I think of Mrs. Macleod, who looks just like Pixie, red hair and all.

"You look just like your mom, you know."

"Everyone says that. Probably because she looks so young. She got pregnant with me in high school. She was *fifteen*. I'm not supposed to say or anything."

I think of Ness. "It's hard to raise a baby when you're that young."

"I know. I told my mom how you used to take care of your sister all the time, before you moved here, and she said I could go tonight, if I went with you. I still can't believe she said yes!"

"Yup, that's me." I smile wryly. "Old reliable."

"You kinda are, though. I guess we both are," she adds, sighing.

"But not tonight. I reckon we're going to guzzle pop and eat unnecessary snacks with the best of them!"

"You don't get out much, do you, Blackburn?"

"Like you should talk."

We stand side by side, admiring the house. It's breathtaking, draped in Christmas lights, both clear, twinkling bulbs and long strings that mimic icicles. I've never seen anything like it in my whole life. Lights on houses and spiraled up the trunks of trees, even. The lights sketch the dark into a fairy world, like straight out of one of Nessa's picture books.

"By the second week of December, whole neighborhoods will be decked out. We'll take some drives so you girls can see the lights," Melissa had promised, and it was a promise she'd kept.

I knew a little about Christmas from before the woods, although

I was so young, I don't remember much. Jenessa, on the other hand, has spent her life Christmas-free. We'd been too busy surviving to celebrate.

Pixie pulls on my coat sleeve. "Let's go in. I don't want to spend my whole first party shivering in the driveway!"

I hold her up all the way to the front door.

"You've got some heels on those shoes, huh?"

She blushes with delight that I've noticed.

"No tiptoes. See?" She rings the doorbell.

"I think we're supposed to just go in," I say nervously.

But then the door opens and Marie peeks out, regarding us with lofty amusement.

"If it isn't Pixie Macleod and Fiddle Girl," she purrs.

Pixie gives a little hop in place and Marie smiles.

"Oh hell, if you're that excited, come on in."

"Thanks," Pixie gushes, pulling me in behind her.

The noise is like an assault—the house vibrating with laughter and music and chatter. My heart thumps sideways, out of rhythm with the driving beat.

"Look!"

Pixie drags me into a room off the hall. There's actually a whole separate room for coats.

"Feel that in your chest? Isn't it cool? It's dance music, like at the clubs."

I keep my coat on. I'm wishing I had my violin case, just to have something to hold on to. Even worse, I'm wondering if there's a way to get a spare case and take the handle off. I could hold it in my pocket, where no one could see.

Pixie tugs my sleeve.

"Aren't you going to hang up your coat?"

"I think I'll keep it on."

What if someone swiped it? It's the nicest coat I've ever owned. When I wear it, I feel like civilized Carey. Carey with a hope.

"Suit yourself. If you get too hot, you can always hang it up later."

Back in the great room (Pixie knows these things), the noise squashes me like a bug against the wall.

"You're the literal definition of a wallflower, you know that, Blackburn? Don't you want to dance?"

I shake my head no, my smile glued in place. I can't breathe. Can't think.

"You, um, go ahead. I'll—I'll be fine."

Pixie sashays off across the polished marble, the room's furniture huddled against the back and side walls to make way for dancers. She stops at the glass fireplace in the center, rubbing her hands together. She smiles and waves at a group of girls from English lit, who wave her over. They dance together in a circle, laughing and shouting over the din.

She makes it look so easy. I feel a twinge, watching her. Jealous. Jealous of Pixie.

I imagine dancing, something I've never done in my life, and Delaney and her ladies-in-waiting laughing and pointing.

I jump when a skinny guy leans in toward me, his head wagging to the beat.

"Want some?"

He holds out what looks like a homemade cigarette, the smoke sweet, like when Ness and me threw moss into the campfire.

"What is it?"

"Fun."

I stare at him blankly.

"You're joking, right? You really don't know what this is?"

I shake my head no, and he laughs like a hyena, so loud that the group next to us turns to stare. He leans in toward me, and I recoil at his breath. *Like Mama on the moonshine.* I inch away.

"Stuck-up bitch. All girls like you are stuck-up bitches."

I think of my shotgun. Just the sight of it, steadily pointed, could set the knees of grown men quaking.

Pixie catches my eye and gives two dancing thumbs-up. I smile a shaky smile. *I can do this.* I inch along the wall. I have no idea where I'm going. *I'm a scientist in the wild,* I tell myself, *observing the social behavior of caribou.* But I'd be lying if I didn't admit that a part of me keens to be a caribou, too.

"Sorry," I mumble as I bump into a couple. I catch my foot on a root, only here, it's someone else's foot. My arms flail.

He catches me, his body shielding me from the gyrating crowd, and I hang in his arms. It's as if I'm one of Nessa's Disney princesses; we've been dancing, and he dipped me.

"You," he says.

> *But Lancelot mused a little space;*
> *He said, "She has a lovely face;*
> *God in his mercy lend her grace,*
> *The Lady of Shalott."*

I fall into those eyes that feel like swinging real high with your head thrown back.

"Lucky I was here to catch you. You could've been trampled."

By caribou. Just the thought alone hurts.

I think of the way it felt, screaming at him in the woods. My face screwed up. The words ugly. I'd come undone. I'd never come undone before.

"Ryan," I say, my voice barely a whisper. I search his face, but it's like the open book has closed.

He sets me back on my feet.

I stand next to him, our arms touching, watching the crowd. I want to say something, anything, but the words won't come. He leans in toward me and forces a smile, a smile that doesn't reach his eyes.

"I haven't seen you around all week." His breath is minty fresh, like Delaney's Tic Tacs. "I'd say you've been avoiding me. Have you been avoiding me?"

I look away, my chest expanding with that all-too-familiar ache that seems to await me around every corner.

"No. I don't know."

"Well, is it yes, or no?"

"It's just . . . I just—"

"Just what? I no longer deserve any common courtesy? People make one mistake with you and they're out in the cold?"

"No! I didn't think you'd want to see *me*. I thought—I mean, I thought that—"

He turns my face to his, but unlike Mama's, his grip is phoebe-belly soft.

"I thought we were friends," he says.

My eyes fill, but he doesn't let go.

"I was hoping we were more than that, but at least friends." His hand drops to his side. "Either way, that's not how you treat people who care about you. At least not where I come from. Was I wrong about you? I thought . . ."

I wait, until I can't wait any longer. "What? Thought what?"

"That you were different. That's all."

Right then, my heart breaks. It's like it's been waiting to break forever, and Ryan's words crack it wide open.

"I am different," I squeak as the tears slide down my cheeks. "That's the problem."

My life's a tangle of past and present, like two separate puzzles with their pieces tumbled together. Nothing fits.

"No kissin', ya hear? Touchin's fine, but no kissin'. This ain't romance; it's b'ness," Mama says, her words spit out like buckshot.

The man's eyes glint. His face is already flushed. But they always listen to Mama.

He expects me to be afraid. His eyes register his disappointment when he sees I'm not. But it's been this way as long as I can remember.

"Time rubs the shine off things," Mama says later, when she finds me crying on the cot. *"You'll get used to it."*

"I don't want to get used to it. I don't like it."

"We need ya' pullin' your weight around here, girl. No one wants to be the garbageman or the undertaker, but someone has ta do it."

It's a vicious circle, what a girl can get used to. And compartmentalize. That's what the psychology textbook called it—"compartmentalization." "Sexual desensitization."

> *Out flew the web and floated wide;*
> *The mirror crack'd from side to side;*
> *"The curse has come upon me," cried*
> *The Lady of Shalott.*

Ryan reaches out a tentative hand and catches a tear as it glides off my chin.

I'll always be different. I tried to tell him, that day in the courtyard. That picnic in the woods.

"I'm sorry for upsetting you or scaring you or whatever I did that day, CC. But don't you know I'd know what a big deal it is? I can't begin to imagine what you and your sister must've gone through. You could've trusted me, you know. I'd look out for you."

For me? Or the girl in the woods? I can't tell where one ends and the other begins.

"I get it, Ceec. I mean, literally, I get it."

I wait, listening. I reckon it's the biggest gift a human being can give to another. It's what I should've done all along.

"I live with my mom. She's a single mom . . ." He pauses, taking a deep breath. "My father went to prison on domestic-abuse charges. He knocked out my mom's front teeth and broke my arm one night when I was seven. My mom was in the hospital for a week. All because we were out of beer."

I listen with all I have.

"No one knows. Well, except for you, now."

The color green. Bright green. Then it's gone.

"I can't believe you're telling me this."

I didn't mean to say it out loud, but it's too late. I said it.

He reddens. "Why? You don't want to hear about it?"

"No, of course I do."

"What, then?"

"I'm just surprised, I guess. I thought—I mean, Delaney said—"

"What?"

I blush. "Delaney said you only liked me"—I fumble for the words—"because of my face."

We look at each other, but I look harder. I need to know the truth.

"It'll do, I guess," he says, smiling—a real smile—for the first time tonight. "But I wouldn't listen to everything Delaney says. Don't you feel it, too?"

"Feel what?"

"The affinity."

"'Affinity'?"

"*Kinship.* Like parallel roads. A history. You and me."

More pieces fall into place, thudding down soft as snow on snow, the memories resurrecting familiar bruises barely visible but still there.

"Ryan? Tell me."

"You sure you want to know?"

I'm not. I nod anyway.

"I don't know if I should."

"Why?"

"I don't know if it's my place. My mother said—"

"Your mother? Ryan, please."

"Okay, then. My mom and your mom were friends. You and I used to play together in my backyard. You really don't remember? Not even the swings?"

Not until now. The cogs and wheels turn, and I swing into the past. I see a golden-haired boy, older than me, hanging on to the swing next to me. Looking back is like looking into the sun.

"I remember," I croak. "It's in flashes, but I remember."

"Your mom went off her meds. She said it made the music sound furry. That's what she told me, out in our backyard."

"She meant her violin," I offer.

"My mom said she'd gone off her meds before, but this time, she wouldn't go back on them. My mom tried to help, but she couldn't."

"*You come here this instant, Carey Violet Benskin!*"

I jump from the swing, landing sideways on my ankle.

"*What, Mama?*"

I limp toward her. She meets me halfway, holding up a gold tube of lipstick, rolling up the tube until, broken in half, the color spills to the grass.

"*Makeup is expensive. It's not a toy. What did I tell you?*"

Her hand wraps around my upper arm, yanking me through the air.

She spanks me, open-handed, so hard that my skin burns right through my shorts.

"Joelle! She's only four!"

My eyes catch the eyes of the golden boy. Tears slide down his cheeks.

"Old enough to know right from wrong, Clarey."

"Your mom is Clarey," I say, dumbfounded.

"Clare. She saw the bruises on you. She said it was all the time, toward the end."

"I remember you." I squint at him in amazement. "I remember her."

"I remember the day she took you. I'll never forget that day. My mom had no idea. She said it was like any other day. Your mom picked you up from our house, but then you both disappeared. My mom followed your story through the newspaper, and your dad even went on the news a few times."

"Ryan! Joelle and Carey are here!"

Climbing trees, becoming the leaves.

Offering me half of a perfectly split cherry Popsicle.

Wrapped in the sun like a giant blanket, my golden friendship.

Swinging to the moon. Gone too soon.

"And you thought I was some random nice guy who liked your face," he says with a shoulder bump.

I just stare at him.

He rode between the barley-sheaves
The sun came dazzling thro' the leaves
And flamed upon the brazen greaves
Of bold Sir Lancelot.

"I remember. I can't believe I remember."

"Your mom used to read that crazy poem to us. About that lady in the boat floating down the lake."

"'The Lady of Shalott.' It's by Tennyson," I say. Only, I'd thought it was mine.

He smiles, and it's the boy smiling, the boy from before the woods.

"Right. It used to scare the bejeezus out of me."

"Because she dies."

"Right." He stares at me, relief softening his features. "I thought you'd died. When no one could find you."

"And then you found me. That first day at school."

"Guilty as charged," he says. "I saw your transfer records in the office one morning. At first, I couldn't figure out why you had your mom's last name, and not your dad's. But then I figured out you didn't want anyone to know."

"Why didn't you say anything?"

"I wanted to, but when you didn't remember me . . . I don't know. I thought for sure you'd remember me."

I want to give him a gift, too. So he knows I understand.

"You are nothing like your father, Ryan. I remember him, too."

I think of Mama. I know how much that matters.

"Thankfully. But the point is, everyone has a past, CC. Everyone has skeletons in the closet."

"'Skeletons in the closet'?"

"Things they want to forget. Things they'd rather keep hidden."

He pulls me close and I let him, his body as sheltering as the hundred-year hickory that shaded our picnic table.

"Does Delaney know what happened to you? That it was a kidnapping?"

"Melissa says she grew up dealing with the fallout."

"It doesn't seem like she's ever told anyone."

"She has her reasons, I reckon."

I follow his gaze to the ceiling, the middle carved out and replaced with a large glass dome. *Stars in the house.*

If I try real hard, I can imagine the sky is the Obed sky, virgin-pure and safe as a baby's suck. The stars chirp in Morse code dots and dashes, just enough to keep me lookin', and Jenessa sleepin'.

"So, you're supposed to forgive me now, and peck me one right here," he says, pointing at his cheek.

He leans down as I stretch toward him, but before he turns his head, I kiss his lips. I, The Carey I Already Am. When I don't reconsider, he kisses me back, his lips soft as gosling fuzz. I press my body closer in the places that count, and he puts his other arm around me. I lean into him as the music crashes and roils. I find his tongue, and set us both on fire.

And then he pulls back. Like he knows about the men in the woods, and doesn't want me anymore.

Looking through the throng, I see Pixie eyeing me, her mouth round and her eyes dancing.

"No breakin' and enterin'," Mama says, cockin' her head toward my crotch and winkin'.

This man is thinner. Twitchy. I don't like his hands. His nails are dirty. I watch as he crosses Mama's palm with gold: a fifty-dollar bill.

As if it's already pourin' down my throat, I retch, then swallow it back down.

"Mama, please. I don't want to do this."

"Do you want me to wake up Jenessa, then?"

I tremble, my legs wobbly. "No, Mama."

"Then get goin', girl."

"Carey, I'm sorry. I shouldn't have done that."

Ryan steps back, only a few steps, but it feels like miles. My eyes fill with tears despite my best efforts.

"Why? Because of my past? Because I'm fourteen? I'm not a little girl, Ryan."

He pants, working on slowing down his breathing.

"You're definitely not a little girl. But you have a lot going on. It might not be the best time for us to be—"

I reach out, take his hand, and put it between my legs.

"Carey!" He pulls away, fast, like he's touched a hot coal. I stare him down. *That's what men like.* But what I see is shock. Disgust.

I make my way down the wall, heading in the direction I'd been going before he found me.

"Carey!"

I keep going, ignoring him.

Caribou, of the Rangifer *genus, related to the old-world reindeers. Both males and females grow large, branched antlers. Name derived from the Algonquian* maka-lipi—*snow shoveler—due to their habit of using their front hooves to push aside snow in their search for winter food.*

"Carey, wait!"

He grabs my upper arm, and I tear it away.

"Carey. Please."

I shake my head, my cheeks burning, and take a step away. But he takes a step closer.

"Look at me."

This time, I do.

"Right now, I'm more interested in touching *this.*"

He places his hand on my heart. Barely an inch to the left or right, and he'd be just like the men in the woods. But his hand doesn't move. I put my hand over his, and he pulls me to him, enfolding me in his arms. He holds me, my body racked with sobs.

"Hey. It's okay, Ceec. It's okay. Just slow down. Okay?"

I nod, the material of his coat crinkling in my ear.

He kisses the top of my head. "I'm sorry about our picnic, about tonight, all of it."

He gives me a squeeze. I study his feet. He wears boots like my father's, but fancier.

"I've wanted to tell you ever since that afternoon." I fight for the words, fight for the sake of this new life. "I reckon I'm so used to being private and all, it's hard to get the feelings into words. But I'm sorry, too."

"Prove it," he whispers.

This time, I kiss his cheek like he wanted me to, smiling through the middle of it.

"Good girl. Let's get out of here." He takes my hand and weaves us through the crowd. I catch Pixie's eye again, and she motions at the girls she's with, waving for me to go with him.

"She'll be okay," Ryan says, following my gaze. "That's Sarah and Ainsley. I've known them since kindergarten."

He snakes us through the dancers, knuckle-bumping people I don't know and shouting above the music. I crane my neck for one last look at Pixie, but the icy blue eyes that grab mine aren't Courtney's.

Delaney looks like she could strangle me right here, right now. Our eyes stay locked until Ryan pulls me through the doorway into another room, shutting the door behind us.

A redbrick fireplace pops and crackles, the flames dancing in crazy shadows against the walls, and smack in the middle of an Oriental rug sits a grand piano, the mahogany polished to a mirrored shine. Outside, nosy snowflakes press against the sliding glass doors before flitting off into the night.

"Don't tell anyone," he whispers, sinking onto a crushed-velvet bench and lifting the lid to display the piano keys. "A secret for a secret."

My jaw drops as he plays the same piece I played for him in the courtyard, Vivaldi's "Spring." His fingers fly over the keys and the emotion builds, the notes delicate as a necklace of raindrops, ferocious as a wild boar protecting her young.

Ryan ends it with two notes. His rendition.

Fee-bee. Feeeeee-bee.

I laugh through my tears. It's perfect.

"My mom started me on lessons when I was four. She thought she'd have to superglue me to the bench to get me to practice. Instead, I loved it. There were times she had to drag me away for meals, or out into the sunshine because she said I'd become pale as a ghost."

"Your music is beautiful," I gush.

I smile at him, the softer, civilized version of myself. The girl from his backyard. The girl from before the woods. All it takes is one thought.

I'm not alone.

Ryan starts to play a piece I've never heard before. I close my eyes and ride the notes to their breathless end, my heart free-falling, like during my first elevator ride, then rising up, soaring like the eaglets with all the supporting branches gone, the only thing left being that leap of faith into the vast unknown.

I keep my eyes shut until the room goes silent. When I open my eyes, he's watching me.

Ryan lowers the lid and pops to his feet.

"I have an idea," he says.

He reaches into my coat pocket and pulls out my hat.

"I do appreciate a girl who chooses warmth over hairstyle."

He plays with the tassel for a moment before handing it back to me.

"Put your mittens on, too."

I regard him quizzically.

He reaches out and zips my coat to my chin, then does the same with his. We walk through the sliding glass doors and into the night. I'm glad for the horse boots, woods-glad. The snowflakes coat us in powdered sugar, and my breath rises like the smoke from my father's cigarettes, clouding, then disappearing.

"Can I show you something?"

I nod.

"Like this," Ryan says, falling backward into the snow. I copy him, falling into a spot next to him, my arms and legs outstretched, my head lifted so I can see his movements. He makes long, sweeping arcs with his arms and legs, open and closed, over and over, his boots thudding against each other.

I do as he does, grinning like a fool. Maybe he's crazy, but this kind of crazy is fun.

"Now, stand up like this."

I watch him extricate himself by first sitting up, careful not to mar the form. He gets to his feet and leaps to the side. I do the same.

He meets me where I stand, reaching for my mitten with his puffy glove.

"See?"

I stare at the markings.

"Snow angels," he says.

And they are. "Ooooo. They're *beautiful*."

He squeezes my hand, and I look at my mitten cradled in his glove. Before tonight, the only hand I'd ever held was Nessa's. I wish he'd never let go.

All in the blue unclouded weather
Thick-jewell'd shone the saddle-leather,

The helmet and the helmet-feather
Burn'd like one burning flame together,
As he rode down to Camelot.

I turn back to the angels, marveling. Just like the china angel on the mantel at home. The sweeping robes. The arc of wings.

"My sister would *love* this. I'll have to show her how to do it."

And I have something to show him, too.

"See up there, in the east? Those three stars in a row?"

I point, and he nods.

"That's the bridge. See those two stars above, and two below? That's the body. Those weaker stars beneath? They make up the neck. It's my constellation. The violin constellation."

Ryan laughs. "I'll be damned. It does look like a violin!"

"I used to tell my sister when she was younger, 'If we ever get separated, meet me beneath the big violin.'"

Hand in hand, we walk around the house, where he deposits me on the porch. I want to go back to our angels, to the soothing pressure of my hand in his.

"Do you want to know what us less visionary folk call it?"

I nod.

"Orion. Orion the hunter."

"Orion," I repeat. I can't wait to look it up on Melissa's laptop.

"They do have one thing in common, though."

"What?"

"They both use bows."

We grin at each other.

"Will you be okay?"

He motions with his head toward the door and the sound of laughter, music, and nonlethal screams. I'll never understand why teenage girls like to scream, minus strange men or bears approaching.

"Yeah. I'll be fine. I'll find Pixie," I tell him, my voice ringing out with a confidence I wish I felt. I glance at my watch. "It's almost time for Mrs. Macleod to pick us up anyway."

"Then I'll see you in school Monday. No hiding, you hear?"

He leans down and kisses my forehead, cocooning me for a moment in his puffer arms before stepping back.

"I almost forgot. I have something for you. Close your eyes." He unzips my coat partway, then stuffs something flimsy into the inside pocket before zipping me back up. "Don't look until you get home."

I watch him walk backward, holding me in his eyes, until he trips on something—a rock, a slick of ice—and his arms flail. I chuckle.

Once he's in his car, we stare at each other through the window as the car warms up. I smile when he traces CC into the condensation on the window, and when he pulls out, I wave until the taillights disappear, like stars plunging over the horizon.

> She knows not what the curse may be,
> And so she weaveth steadily,
> And little other care has she,
> The Lady of Shalott.

And then I'm back where I started, my teeth chattering, staring at Marie's front door.

I'm about the only teenager alive without a cell phone, as Delaney pointed out a few days ago, and I reckon at the time I didn't care. Now I'm wishing I had one something fierce. I'd call Pixie on hers and have her meet me out front.

Back inside, I scan the crowd. I don't see Delaney or her court. I wave back when Ainsley and Sarah wave, dancing with two guys who look vaguely familiar. Pixie isn't among them.

Newly brave, I find the wall and follow the smooth cream paint through another doorway into a spacious living room with leather chairs and couches and an entire back wall lined with books. People laugh and talk, and there's a group of girls sitting on guys' laps in front of a black woodstove, roasting marshmallows and hot dogs speared by long metal forks.

A folding table set up against the side wall holds a huge crystal bowl, from which a pretty girl with glasses and a sorrel ponytail ladles a red liquid into blue plastic cups. She motions for me to come over.

"Punch," she says, holding out a cup, "to get you into the spirit."

I take the cup gratefully, my throat scratchy from the cold, dry air.

"How much?" I ask nervously.

"Free. Or as much as you want." She giggles.

I take a big swig and instantly choke, white lightning spraying through my mouth and nose. The girl jumps back in disgust.

"Jesus!"

"Sorry!" My eyes water. I wipe my face with the napkins she shoves at me.

"You practically barfed all over me. You better have nothing contagious."

I don't tell her how me and Nessa got our shots two weeks before starting school, like we were Shorty or something. I also don't tell her about the itchy, pearly pinworms wriggling in the toilet bowl. We'd taken medicine for that, too.

The girl stares me down as she picks up her punch cup and throws back the contents in one gulp. She slams the cup down on the table.

"Ahhhh."

"What *is* it?"

"It's grain alcohol. What'd you expect?"

"*Moonshine?*"

"*Yep. I almost saved up enough for the 'quipment and the ingredi-*ents."

"*Moonshine.*"

"*I could sell it and make a profit. You, of all people, should be glad of that, girl.*"

My body will buy the still and the ingredients:

7 pounds baker's yeast

42 pounds brown sugar

4 pounds treacle (a thick, dark syrup produced durin' raw sugar-
     cane refinin')

1 pound hops

"*Where'll we get treacle, Mama?*"

"*You let me worry about that, girl.*"

The dormouse talked treacle at the Mad Tea Party.

Why not. The woods are their own sort of Wonderland.

"What if I had to drive a vehicle home?"

"Then you'd better hope it's a beater, and you'd chew this."

The girl flips a few foil-wrapped sticks at me.

I unwrap one and fold the gum into my mouth. "Thanks."

"Hey—aren't you Fiddle Girl?"

Before I know what I'm doing, I shake my head no.

"Sure you are. FYI, the kiddie drinks are in the cooler in the kitchen. Pop and juice, the G-rated kind."

I pick my way through a jungle of bodies, slowing down to lis-ten to a shaggy-haired guy in the corner play guitar for two girls. Not bad.

Back in the great room, I notice the massive staircase winding to the second floor. The bodies thin out as I ascend. On the landing, I hesitate before a dark hallway of closed doors.

I rap on the first one.

"Pixie?"

No answer.

"Pixie, are you in there? It's *time*."

"Go away!" a male voice growls, startling me, and I almost trample a cat with a pushed-in face. It hunches its back and hisses at me before skittering off.

What if something happened to Pixie? I'm in charge.

I never should have left her alone.

I knock on the next few doors, but there's no answer. I feel along the wall for a light switch, but I can't find one.

Would any of the guys hurt a little girl? What if they were drunk?

"Pixie!" I yell above the music. "Pixie!"

I have no choice but to go back to the first room, where I hear rustling, then silence.

Gently, I try the knob, surprised when it turns. Ever so slightly, I push the door open, my eyes adjusting to the light. There must be thirty candles burning, at least.

"What the hell are you doing in here, freak?"

I see much more than I want to—a guy's bare buttocks rising and falling over a girl, also naked, her breasts exposed as she twists out from under him.

The guy looks over his shoulder, eyes narrowed. "Didn't you hear her? GET OUT."

"Get the fuck OUT!" Delaney yells, half-hysterical.

I slam the door behind me, falling to my knees in my haste. Her shrill voice penetrates the wood.

"Shit, Derek! She knows!" Her voice quivers, on the brink of tears. "Shit! Shit! Shit!"

I fly down the stairs, knocking into Marie at the bottom. She glares at me like Delaney does as she works to steady a silver platter of small sandwiches.

"Watch where you're going. And for your information, the second floor is off-limits."

I'm so not in the mood. "I reckon someone should've told Delaney that," I snap.

She looks nervously from me to the upstairs landing.

I take one of the sandwiches. "Thanks."

She rushes up the stairs.

"There you are! Where'd you get the food?"

I whip around. Pixie stands with her hands on her hips, cheeks flushed, the hairs framing her face curly with perspiration.

"Marie has a platter. Wait a minute—there *I* am? Where've *you* been? I've been looking all over for you."

"You have any more gum?" she asks, watching me chew.

I'm still new to gum. I tend to chew it like cud.

I hand Pixie the sandwich, instead, which she inhales, her words garbled.

"I wish it were bigger. They call these finger sandwiches. I'm thinking of home and a honking big PB&J on pumpernickel—you know, the thick slices?"

I'm so relieved to have found her, I almost forget what I saw upstairs. Almost. I imagine my father's face on fire as he shouts at Delaney. I imagine Melissa's eyes, black as marbles, her arms locked across her chest, and I get it: It's the same out here as it is in the woods—the silent shame of young girls having babies. Even Mama didn't want that for me.

I see Delaney moving rhythmically in the bed, a smile on her face . . . a smile . . . until she saw me.

Pixie yawns so wide, I see her uvula.

"I was in the study, playing Scrabble with some of the freshman girls. *You* were the one who disappeared. With *Ryan*," she says, teasing me.

I grin, the happier events of the night playing on a loop. *Lips. Vivaldi. Snow angels. Lancelot.*

She grabs my arm and turns it, checking my watch. I trail her to the coat closet, where she finds her coat easily, slipping it from the hanger, and I help her put it on, like I do for Nessa. She turns to me as she wraps her scarf around her neck.

"This had to be the most amazing night of my entire life. I wish it weren't over already."

"Mine, too." I giggle. I feel like I could hug the world, like a big snow globe wrapped up in my puffer arms.

"I knew he'd kiss you," she says, leaning in to me.

"I didn't even know he'd be here."

"I did. He asked me on Friday if you were going"—her eyes glint conspiratorially—"and I told him, 'Hell yeah.'"

I laugh, realizing how much people underestimate Pixie. She comes in such an adorable package, but she's really light-years ahead of all of us.

She takes my bare hand in her gloved one. Each finger of her gloves is a different color.

"C'mon. I don't want my mom waiting too long."

We wrangle our way to the front door, but I stop and turn when I hear a familiar voice.

"Hey!"

Delaney leans over the second-floor balcony, her perfect hair a perfect mess. One collar blade of her white button-down blouse stands on end, but it's not that. Something's different.

And then I see it. Her eyes aren't defiant, superior, or icy. They're terrified.

Pixie pulls at me to go. I stare at Delaney for a long moment, waiting for the sisterly braille to kick in. It doesn't.

I turn and follow Pixie out the door.

"You girls have fun?"

Heat escapes in pockets out of Mrs. Macleod's open window. Pixie climbs into the front seat. I slide into the back.

"It was *awesome*, Amy!" Pixie sighs.

"*Mom*, please."

"It was AWESOME, Mom! I had the best night of my entire life. We ate birthday cake and danced all night, and the house was *huge*. There was this glass fireplace in the great room, and everyone was so nice to me."

"Cake?" I poke Pixie in the back.

"Um-hmm."

"Seat belts, please."

Pixie sighs, her face dreamy as she turns to me.

"Thanks, Carey, for the best night of my life."

"How about you, Carey? Did you have fun?"

Pixie giggles. I nod at Mrs. Macleod, and blush.

"It was quite a night," I agree, making a face at Pixie, then smiling at her mom, who smiles back in the rearview mirror.

We drive home through the slippery darkness, Pixie oohing and aahing over the Christmas lights strung across the houses, each display different, each amazing in its own right.

I remember Jenessa's face when we drove through town and she saw the lights for the first time. She thought it was her fairy world come to life.

There have been so many moments when we've smacked up against reality, struggling to gain our bearings and find our way clear. But not the lights. The lights are magical. Ness is young enough to make this world her real one, a place where sober people string lights on houses and trees, whole rooms exist for canned goods, and a fat old guy in a red suit leaves presents for children on December 25.

"Wait until we get the tree," Melissa says, her eyes shining. "A fresh-cut tree, with pine scent wafting through the house!"

"Imagine that," I tell Jenessa, her eyes wide, unblinking. "A tree in-side the house—hung with ornaments and even more lights!"

At our farm, it's dark and silent as the snow stops falling for the first time in days. Our own Christmas lights, ginormous bulbs of red, green, yellow, and blue, have been switched off for the night.

"Would you like us to walk you in?" Mrs. Macleod offers as I undo my seat belt and zip my coat.

"Thank you, ma'am, but I have my keys," I say, pulling the ring from my pocket and jangling it, "and it looks like everyone's asleep. I'll be okay. Thanks for the ride."

"You're welcome, Carey. Thanks for taking Courtney to the party. I know it meant a lot to her."

"You're welcome, ma'am. She had a good time. We both did."

"Hello! I'm right here!"

I chuckle as I close the door. Pixie scrambles over the seat and stretches out across the back, waving good-bye with her eyes closed.

I let myself into the house, shushing Shorty as he bays once, sniffs the party on me, then licks some off my hand. I struggle with my boots, leaving them standing in the mudroom, and pad down the hall in my stocking feet.

The fire in the living room is a pile of dying embers—sad, somehow. I perch on the rug before it, my knobby knees hugged to my chest. Good old Shorty, waiting until he heard the dead bolt click before disappearing up the stairs, back to Nessa.

I pat my pocket, remembering, my fingers closing around two shiny rectangles of paper. When I turn the key of the Tiffany lamp, there's just enough light to see.

There I am in black and white, in profile. From that angle, my violin case, slung over my shoulder, assumes the shape of an angel's wing.

The picnic in the woods.

It's the second photograph, though, that causes my breath to catch and sends me tumbling down Alice's rabbit hole.

A towhead girl and a gangly boy sit side by side in backyard swings. Her flaxen hair falls over one eye. His skinny arm is dwarfed by a neon green cast. Both wear grins for miles.

"Why didn't you say anything?"

"I wanted to, but when you didn't remember me . . . I don't know. I thought for sure you'd remember me."

I touch my cheek where he touched it, smooth my hair like he smoothed it, to feel what he felt. My cheek is winter cold, but soft, and so is my hand. His grip had been gentle and warm; hesitant, at first, and then bolder once we'd fixed things.

A starburst of headlights penetrates the front window, and it can only be one person. I search the face of the chiming clock as the beams wash over it. Five minutes to one, with our curfew extended an hour from the usual midnight. She'll just make it.

I hang my coat and take the stairs two at a time, closing the door to my room and forgoing the light. I hide the photographs under a sheaf of papers on the desk. I'm not ready to share them yet.

It was an awesome night, Saint Joseph. Did you hear Ryan play?

I barely breathe as Delaney climbs the stairs. Hallway light spills under my door. The shadow stands there, walks away, then returns.

"Good night," I call out to her sarcastically, waiting. But there's no fun in it.

The shadow hesitates.

Before I can rethink it, I throw open the door, grab her by the arm, and pull her in.

13

"Hey!"

She tugs her arm from my grasp and flips on the light.

"Like that hurts," I say, bolder after tonight. "Why do you have to be such a *bitch?*"

"'Bitch'? The high-and-mighty Carey, cussing? Where'd you learn *that?*"

"From the high-and-mighty Delaney. Get over it."

"What's your main problem, Blackburn?"

"You! You calling me 'backwoods freak' in front of people. Enough, already!"

Delaney rolls her eyes. But I refuse to let it go. I say the next softly, like a sucker punch to the gut.

"You know, if you call me a freak, you're calling Jenessa a freak, too."

My words pain her. Her eyes shift from angry and flashing to ashamed.

"Anything else?"

"I reckon there is. I want the letter from Mama—all the copies."

"Oh, you do? And what do I get?"

Like she doesn't know.

"My silence. I won't say anything to my father or your mom about tonight."

We size each other up like the waddle-badger and the shuffle-fox, those few times they'd crossed paths. Claws and teeth ready, but not necessary unless absolutely necessary, and everyone knows absolutes are rarely absolute. Especially after feasting on fermented blackberries.

"Fine. And for your information, I wasn't planning on showing the letter to anyone anyway."

"Oh, so you reckoned you'd blackmail me with it instead. It's obvious how much you hate me."

And it's like I flipped a switch—one waiting, all this time, to be flipped.

"I don't *hate* you. For someone so smart, you can be so dense. I'm just—" She stops and begins again, the clouds speeding up across her face. "It's not all about you, okay? I mean, I get it. You lived in the woods, cold and hungry with a drugged-up mother doing who knows what to survive. You have dibs on the monster bites of attention. I get that. But it doesn't make it any easier for me. It doesn't mean it doesn't suck, to be constantly shoved into the background."

The shame washes over me in waves. She's right. She's absolutely right.

"I didn't mean to make it all about me. I wasn't trying to—"

"I know. And that's exactly what I'm saying—it's complicated. The whole effin' thing is complicated. You . . . me—we're complicated."

She crosses her arms and turns away. I take the leap.

"I reckon it'll take time, Delaney. That's all. That's what Mel—your mom said."

She collapses onto my bed, her head on my pillow. She looks like someone different. Just a girl, like me.

"It was tough in the woods, huh?"

I swallow hard, nodding.

"I saw your sister's back." Her eyes are sorry, sharing the weight. "I die, thinking of Nessa out there," she whispers.

"I protected Nessa right fine."

"I'm sure you did. I didn't mean— Dad said—your father said you had a shotgun."

"Yup."

"Did you ever have to use it?"

I curl up in my mind like the accidental-hedgehog into a prickly ball of leave-me-alone. And then, whether a shift of light or shadow, the walls crash back into place. I'm the old Carey again. She's the old Delaney.

I lie. "How do you think we ate?"

"Meat well done, I hope. Or you'd both have worms."

I blush.

"So, Blackburn. A secret for a secret. That's the deal, right?"

She holds out her hand, and I pull her to her feet.

I think of her and Derek and their kind of sex. Smiling. Not for money. Enjoying themselves.

A whole different world.

"A secret for a secret."

She makes a fist and holds out her pinkie like a hook. I stare at it. "Just do it."

I do the same, and she hooks her pinkie through mine.

"Pinkie promise. Say it."

"Pinkie promise."

She lets go and wanders my room, her finger trailing the bindings of the poetry books lining the shelf above my desk.

"Hey, what's this?"

A corner of one of the photographs catches the light. Delaney moves toward it, sliding it out from under the papers. She studies it for a long, long time.

"Oh. My. God. I get it now." She holds out the photograph. "I can't believe it. Is that—"

"Me and Ryan. We knew each other as children."

"Oh. My. God." She stares at me, then back at the photograph. "Wow. Just wow. No words."

She puts the photo down and picks up the other. A tiny smile plays across her lips.

"This is a beautiful picture of you, Carey."

"Thank you."

I check her face. She really means it.

"Make sure you keep them somewhere safe. If it were me, I'd want to keep them forever."

I nod, not sure how to respond to this new, softer Delly. I think of the woods, the winter chill melting off into spring, how it's natural. Maybe this is natural. Maybe Melissa was right, and Delaney just needed time. Like all of us.

"On *that* note, I need to catch some z's. Night, Carey."

"Night."

She smiles at me from the doorway, and the chink, the tiny crack that let us in, remains.

I am the night bird, perched in the window seat. I reckon I love the concept of window seats. The world outside hums in black and white. It's 2:00 A.M. The snow wears the moonlight like perfume.

My conversation with Delaney plays on a loop, powered by surprise, I reckon. Because I picture Delaney throwing up her hands at the kitchen table. Screaming at the party. Glowering at me in the halls at school. And I realize it's all bluster.

Snow begins to fall, this boneless water turned mighty.
It's all bluster out there, too.
A world is a world is a world.
Or, as Jenessa says, human beans.
Not so different.

14

It seems like a dream at first, but by the second scream, I'm wide-awake and sitting up in bed.

"HERE, BOY! WHERE ARE YOUUUUUUUUUUU-UUUUU!"

Some kid is outside yelling, and I wish whoever it is would shut up. Sunday is my day to sleep in, and after last night, and with an English lit and a physics test coming up this week, I need all the sleep I can get.

"SHORTYYYYYYYYYYYYYYYYYYYYYYYYY!"

I open my eyes wide.

No way.

The voice is thick with tears. My bedroom door flings open and Melissa rushes in, her expression a mixture of pain and awe.

"You do know who that is, don't you?"

The whole world stops as I listen, and I shake my head in disbelief, making it look as if I'm saying no, when I mean yes.

"SHORTYYYY! COME ON, BOY! WHERE ARE YOU!"

In what feels like slow motion, I rise from the bed and hurtle toward the window. The scent of scrambled eggs wafts through the open door, and the wood is cold beneath my feet.

"SHORTY!!!! You come here this instant!"

I stare out the window, then turn to Melissa.

"Your sister's been out there like that the last hour or so."

Melissa sounds half-hysterical herself.

"I told you she could talk," I say, adrenaline strumming my veins. It feels like that moment before a lightning bolt hit in the Hundred Acre Wood, with the hair on our arms standing on end and the air humming with electricity.

I watch Jenessa stomp through the snow, her curls whipping left and right. She disappears into the barn, but I can still hear her screaming at the top of her lungs.

"SHORTYYYYYYYYYYYYYYYYYYYYYYYY!"

It's been so long.

"What's going on?"

"Shorty's missing. We've been out searching for him since seven. When Jenessa woke up without him, she came running downstairs, *talking*. It was the damnedest thing. She suited up, and she's been searching ever since."

"That's a lot of land to search."

I fly past Melissa and down the stairs, stuffing my feet into the boots I abandoned just hours earlier.

Hesitantly, not in her usual spear-head-dripping-with-toad-poison voice, Delaney calls to me from the kitchen table.

"The snowdrifts will ruin those boots, you know."

I jab my hands into my mittens and coil the scarf around my neck, pulling the hat over my head and whipping on my coat.

"Use my snow boots," Delaney offers. "They're right there in the closet."

"Thanks!" Quickly, I switch boots. "How about your sunglasses?"

"Go ahead."

I take them from the table and flip them on. I trudge out the door, and Melissa is right behind me, zipping her coat as she picks her way carefully down the frozen steps.

"Shorty!"

My voice echoes off the snow, the whiteness dizzying. I cut around the house in time to see Nessa back out of the barn, her cheeks sparkling with tears.

I run to her and hold her. "Don't worry. We'll find him."

We split up, Melissa going in one direction and Ness and me in another, checking under bushes and even in the scoop of the back-hoe, scanning the horizon where the gray squints through a smat-tering of trees farther out. I sniff. *Weather.* It'll snow again tonight, I reckon, if not this afternoon.

"It'll be okay, Jenessa," I say, squeezing her hand.

But she's no longer the meek, dependent little girl, believing in my every word.

"We'll keep looking until we find him," I say, my voice firm.

"Alive," Ness demands, her eyes darting around the hillside.

"Definitely alive," I say.

He has to be.

Please, Saint Joseph? Ness can't bear to lose this dog. It's her one good thing in a long, long time. Please help us find him. Please!

"Here, boy!" Ness continues to yell, her voice crackling with the effort.

Saint Joseph, please! Ness and Shorty go together like beans and brown sugar. It's like they were always waiting to find each other. They need each other! Please help us find him!

Jenessa plops down in the snow, her face hidden in her mittens, her shoulders heaving.

"Don't you dare give up! That dog would never give up on you, Jenessa Joelle Blackburn!"

She startles at the reminder of Mama, scowling at me.

I know exactly how she feels.

If you lead us to him and help us bring him back alive, I promise I'll come clean. I'll own up to what I did in the woods. I'll tell our father and I'll face the consequences. Please, Saint Joseph. Please!

I pull her to her feet.

"Melissa! Girls!"

We spin toward our father's voice.

I squint around the glare of snow, past the shiver of red maple to the clearing beyond. My father's arms cradle a still form, and my heart leaps sideways with fear and hope.

Oh please, Saint Joseph, let him be alive! My promise stands! Please!

Ness breaks out in a run, clouds of breath trailing behind her. From here, I wait, wait to read her sisterly braille, sagging in relief when a smile breaks out and she shakes her fists in the air.

I love you, Saint Joseph.

So many different kinds of tears in the world. I continue my clumsy trek, plucking my boots from the snow and crashing back down, my calf and thigh muscles screaming. Behind me, I hear Melissa doing the same.

My father stops to open and rezip his coat around Shorty's body, warming the hound with his body heat. Ness walks next to them, tearing her eyes from Shorty to share a kaleidoscope of emotions: worry, fear, exhilaration, shock, bewilderment, and, finally, joy.

I reach their side in four strides.

"What happened? Do you know?" My heart plummets when I glimpse a wide smear of blood on my father's coat sleeve. "Is he going to be okay?"

Please . . .

"I found him out past the clearing. He was probably chasing rabbits. Seems his collar snagged on a section of the old fence I'd

been meaning to tear down. Damn fence. I had to scare off two
coyotes. Looks like Shorty's been mauled. If Jenessa hadn't gone
looking for him like she did . . ."

We both turn to Ness, who coos to Shorty and strokes his head,
quite a feat as she keeps stride with us at a half run.

"I had a dream," she tells us breathlessly. I bite back tears at the
sound of her voice, her clear, sweet voice. "Shorty needed me to come
get 'im. I thought it was just a dream, but I woke up and he wasn't
there."

My father meets my eyes over her head.

"Will he be okay?" Ness chatters. Her entire body vibrates
with cold.

"I think we got to him in time. We need to get him to the vet,
though. But I dare say you saved his life, sweetheart."

Jenessa breaks out in a dance of joy. I myself feel light as snow.

"If you give me your keys, I'll warm up the truck," I offer.

He twists his body toward me, his coat pocket displaying a small
bulge. I reach in, grab for the keys, and take off at a run, my breath
melting into mist against my frozen cheeks. I tear into the driveway
and scramble into the truck, starting the engine and blasting the
heat.

"Mel, can you get Jenessa into the house? She's frozen stiff!"

They rush over the hill, and I notice how Nessa and my father
walk the same—Mama's long legs, his long legs, with the similar
placement of feet. She's imitating him, without even realizing she's
doing it. Belonging to him, regardless of blood. I throw open the
driver's side door.

Jenessa shakes her head vehemently, curls snaking every which
way, like Medusa.

"I'm going with you! Shorty wants me to go!"

I take Shorty from my father's arms and slide across to the

passenger side. I hold him on my lap, cradled like a baby, as my father drapes his coat over us. Ness runs around the truck and stands on tiptoe, framed by the window glass. I lean down and kiss Shorty's head for her. He licks my cheek weakly, trembling down to his tail.

"Mel—get her warmed up, and then meet us at Doc Samuels's."

Melissa nods and turns to my sister, who stomps her boot and bursts into tears.

"If you don't warm up, we'll be taking you to the hospital, too, honey. Shorty will be fine—we'll meet them there. You trust your sister, don't you?"

Nessa nods, crying in loud, gulping sobs. My father peels out as Melissa holds my sister firmly by the shoulders. I turn to look out the back window, watching her guide Nessa up the porch steps and into the house.

I remember Ness as a baby, how I had to use my body heat to warm her during those endless nights in the camper when she cried and cried for Mama, not realizing the mama she cried for was me.

It makes me shiver inside, just thinking how lucky we were.

Now, if only Shorty can be that lucky.

We sit side by side in Doc Samuels's waiting room, my cheeks and toes burning as they thaw. We handed Shorty over on arrival, unloading him into the doctor's arms. Now, in a back room, Shorty rests comfortably beneath warming blankets, his wounds debrided and sewn.

Turns out that coyotes hadn't mauled the old hound after all. It was the barbed wire that had ripped his flesh when he fought to free himself. The coyotes must've smelled the blood.

I shudder at the thought of what could've happened if my father hadn't gotten to Shorty in time.

"He's doing fine," Doc Samuels says, coming out to talk to us half an hour later. "You're lucky you found him when you did."

Doc Samuels looks me over with interest. "You the one who saved ol' Shorty?"

I shake my head. "My sister knew he was in trouble. It's like they have a psychic connection or something."

"Love is like that," he says, his eyes flitting to my father and then back to me. "The cold kept him from losing too much blood. Most dogs with body temperatures that low wouldn't have survived. That's one tough dog."

The doctor leaves us in the waiting room after pointing my father toward the full coffeepot. My father pours a cup and passes it to me, and I drink it black like he does, only caring about the way it warms my hands and my insides simultaneously.

He looks over at me every once in a while but says nothing. I can feel it in the room, though, beside the *National Geographic* magazines on the table, the laboring heater in the corner, the threadbare couch we sit upon. It surrounds us both, like an aura: our amazement over Jenessa's talking.

And now it's my turn. A promise is a promise. I turn to him, my eyes on his boots. I take a deep, shuddering breath.

"Remember you asked about Jenessa and what might've caused her to stop talkin'?"

It's like I've reverted. Like I've never left the woods.

He takes a sip of coffee without breaking eye contact.

"I know why," I whisper.

I don't know what's going to happen to me an hour, a day, a week from now, once I tell him. But it doesn't matter anymore. Folks don't do the right thing because it's easy. They do it because it's right.

"I figured as much," he says, his tone even. "I was hoping you'd tell me when you were ready."

He tilts his head and studies me, and in that gesture, I feel his genuine respect for our time in the Hundred Acre Wood. I let the strange feeling wash over me, enjoying it while I can.

I'm too old to act like a child. I know it now. Too old to play hide-and-seek with what's important. It's like the girl I'm going to be finally catches up with the girl I am, right there in Doc Samuels's waiting room.

I owe it to that girl.

The door bursts open, followed by a wave of cold air. Melissa and Jenessa stomp snow from their boots as Nessa turns to me, her eyes red and swollen.

"Where's Shorty? Is he going to be okay?"

I go to her and hold her close, her body shaking in my arms.

Then, I untangle myself and drop to my knees.

"Look at me," I say, taking her tear-stained face in my hands. "Shorty's going to be good as new. They're keeping him warm and letting him rest after cleaning and sewing his wounds. They have him sedated."

She looks at me blankly.

"Sedated means 'calmed down with medicine.' Like he's slow and sleepy."

Nessa laughs, squeezing me so hard, the breath escapes me. Then she runs to our father, who lifts her in his arms and spins her in a circle before sitting back down with her on his lap.

I get up and turn to Melissa, smiling shyly.

"We were thinking you two could take Shorty home. Doc Samuels said he's ready," I tell her.

She looks at my father curiously, then back to me. "We could do that."

I watch her search the office, knowing her well enough by now to know what she needs.

"Coffee is fresh, over there on the table," I say. I walk over, fill a cup, and take it to her.

"Thank you, Carey."

I can see Melissa's SUV out the window, a ribbon of exhaust weaving like a kite tail behind it.

"You left your car on," I tell her.

"I know. Delaney's in there. She was worried about Jenessa and wanted to come with us."

We both look outside. I see Delaney's foot propped up against the passenger-side window.

"She's not an early bird." Melissa laughs, shaking her head. "She's probably asleep."

Melissa remembers the coat folded over her arm.

"Here," she says to my father. "I thought you'd need this."

It's his heavy work coat, the one he wears in the barn when he's tending to the animals at night. It's perfect, actually, for where we're going.

Melissa pulls my father's scarf and hat from inside her coat and hands them to me. They're both warm and smell like her, like Beautiful, the perfume she wears and had bought for me, too, that day at the mall.

Once my father's coat is on, I hand him the scarf and hat. Melissa takes the bloodstained coat, the smears dried into rust.

"Where are you two off to?"

I can't believe the words leave my lips so easily.

"Back to the woods. I left something important behind. We're going back to get it."

She looks at my father and he smiles at her, a special smile she sails back to him. It's a language that reminds me of sisterly braille, or the unspoken bond between Jenessa and Shorty.

"We'll be back after supper," he assures her.

Jenessa slides from my father's lap and shuffles over, her eyes full of question marks.

"Are you sure, Carey? I'd never tell."

She whispers her words, dry as the rattle of winter leaves, and I ache at the sound of her retreat.

"I'm sure. It's time," I reassure her, managing to keep my voice steady. "You stay with Melissa and wait for Shorty. Make sure he stays warm on the drive home."

Nessa takes my hand in both of hers.

"Are you coming back?"

My heart breaks into new pieces, and her clasp tightens.

"I hope so. I mean, I plan to."

"Will you play me Brahms's Lullaby tonight? Instead of Pooh?"

I think of the violin shoved to the back of the closet shelf, how the parting scooped out a piece of my heart, like Melissa's melon-ball scooper. I'd shunned the violin because music is its own truth; there's no lying in the playing. Mama is woven into the notes, as are the woods. But I'd overlooked the bigger picture: It's the *best* part of Mama. The *best* part of the woods. The music transcended the dreariness, the hunger, the cold. Just like the truth transcends.

I look into those eyes I know as well as my own—better, even—and once again, I'm tearing up.

"I swear to Saint Joseph—"

"On a hill of beans," Jenessa says, finishing for me.

"Will you sing if I play?"

My voice breaks, and I "smile through diamonds," as Jenessa calls it. I think of how, in one day, because of one dog, our whole world has changed. It's been years since she's sung for me. I'm not even sure she remembers.

"I remember," she assures me, her eyes solemn. "I will."

I walk her over to Melissa, and they stand side by side, watching us leave. My father holds the door open, and with one last look at Jenessa, I walk through it. The leather strip of sleigh bells rings from the door handle, quite merry for the moment at hand.

Ness leans against Melissa's body, encircled by her arms.

I wave at them through the glass and Ness waves back tentatively, but like I told her, and more sure than I've ever been about anything, it's time.

We walk past the SUV. My father sees Delaney and pantomimes writing, mouthing the words *lit test* to her. She scowls at him. I catch and hold her gaze through the window glass. Her eyes are still worried, and not just for Shorty.

But I gave my word. Pinkie promise. Anyway, I don't want to be the kind of person associated with fear. I know fear too well, and I know its power. I don't want that kind of power. Not over Delaney or anyone else.

As I pass, I make a motion of locking my lips and throwing away the key—throwing *her* the key. *We're sisters, whether she likes it or not.*

I climb into the truck, with her eyes still on me. She flicks me a smile—the same smile from last night as she admired the photograph Ryan took of me.

I can only imagine those same eyes tonight, once she, like everyone else, knows the truth.

Part III

THE BEGINNING

You can't stay in your corner of the Forest waiting for others to come to you. You have to go to them, sometimes.

—PIGLET, FROM *POOH'S LITTLE INSTRUCTION BOOK*

15

It's been close to three months, and yet it seems like only yesterday that my father showed up in the Hundred Acre Wood. I never thought about going back to the woods together. I mean, during the tougher days at school I'd think of going back myself—*running away* is the term for it, I know now—and although I might not have known what to call it, that's exactly what it felt like: running away from everything in the civilized world that's oh-so-unbearably emotional.

I sneak a glance at my father, at the dead-ringer profile that looks like mine, and marvel how I used to worry that I was all Mama, in the ways that do and don't count. We couldn't be more different, it seems, and yet I belong to him. All those years in the woods and I belonged to him, too.

My stomach slips sideways like skeeters across the creek, and it's more than the truth coming out. The woods may as well be Mars now, despite my longing for them. I'm afraid to see what it used to be like—the way we used to live, what we'd accepted and settled for—from this civilized perspective. Just thinking of the cat-pee coat causes my ears to burn.

As we get closer, I start to remember the oddest snippets, like patchwork quilt squares tellin' me their stories.

*Mama blows meth clouds at Nessa and me, laughin' so hard, she
pees her pants. I scoop up my sister and tote her outside, proppin' her
on a log by the campfire, the flames jump-started with a few handfuls of
kindlin'.*

*Ness keeps almost fallin' over, catchin' herself with a jerk. It's two in
the mornin', after all. I'm flat-out annoyed, cold and tired myself. Only,
annoyed at Mama. Never at Nessa.*

I rest my face against the window glass, cool and smooth, and
watch the signs go by, the trees growing thicker, the road older,
other cars fewer. I think of that night, the one haunting me every
day since, no matter how hard I've tried to exterminate the memory. When we left the woods, that night came with us as sure as our
breath, our shadows, our eyelashes.

"It's gettin' dark, Ness. No more fairy huntin' for tonight, okay?
Nessa?"

"Okay," she says with a long sigh. "I'm comin'."

*I've spent the last half hour buildin' up the fire, not just to keep us
warm, but to cook over. My mind is elsewhere, itchin' to get back to the
violin. Mama's been gone for five weeks; I started markin' the days with
notches carved into the dyin' walnut tree at the edge of the clearin'.*

"What we havin' for dinner?"

"Food," I tell her. The point isn't lost on my smarty-pants sister.

*Jenessa wrinkles her nose, her eyes accusin'. "Beans again? Ain't there
other things in those cans?"*

"You ate rabbit for breakfast and the last can of ravioli for lunch. If
we don't eat the beans, there'll be nothin' left but beans, and then you'll
be eatin' 'em three times a day."

*Ness huffs and puffs her way over to the two-by-four swing. It took
scalin' a hickory like a flyin' squirrel and loopin' and tyin' thick rope
around the crotch of the fattest branches to make it work . . . to give her
a piece of childhood.*

Ness had watched the process from the leafmeal below, her eyes shinin'. By the time I was through, I had her believin' Saint Joseph had left the rope and plank in the forest just for her.

Little kids need somethin' to believe in. For them, it's as important as breathin'. And when Mama never fit the bill, Saint Joseph made a right good substitute.

"Here." I hand her a bowl with water and give her the rag from the table. "Clean your hands and wipe your face."

"Why do I have to? No one sees."

"I see. Just because we live in the Hundred Acre Wood don't mean we have to live like savages."

"Rowr!" Jenessa growls.

I watch her wipe herself down, face, neck, and hands, while I clear the foldin' table for dinner. I pile up my poetry books, our schoolbooks, and her Pooh books into a jagged tower, a tower I carry into the camper and spill onto the flimsy table that folds out from the wall, all the size of a doll's ironin' board, as Mama said. I yell to Ness through the open door.

"Get those other two rags and fold them on the table. You know how to set the table. You're no baby, right?"

I scold her gently. She's just turned five, after all. But that's no excuse to be useless.

Back at the fire, I load up our bowls with baked beans, the kind floatin' in a sweet brown sugar sauce. Into Ness's bowl, I ladle the three chubby squares of pork fat I find in the mixture.

I know Jenessa's too skinny. We're both too skinny, and although our mama is also skinny, and perhaps it's partly genetic, I know it has to do with our nutrition, with the careful rationin' of canned goods and the slim pickin's of bird, rabbit, and squirrel I'm lucky to shoot. I constantly salivate over the thought of wild turkey, but trackin' those noisy birds leads me too far from the camper and Nessa.

We sit at the table and eat quietly. The truth is, we're both ravenous, no matter the complainin' we do or what food we're sick of. We're luckier than some, Mama says. I reckon she's right. We have a bed, roof, clothes, food. I reckon we're crazy lucky. It's hard to imagine not havin' the essentials.

Finishin' quickly, I pick up my violin, gettin' bean sauce on the neck, but that won't hurt it none. I play in spurts, the notes clunky, determined to git it right.

Crack!

There's a feelin' that comes before danger falls. You can see it in the eyes of the deer or pheasant moments before the shot. Synapses firin' the instincts on, I reckon. Knowin' your life is about to snuff out, moments before the inevitable bang. I don't even remember settin' my violin and bow on the empty chair next to me.

Jenessa jumps up and freezes, her eyes widenin' until the whites show, her forgotten spoon drippin' beans onto the front of her patched pink dress. I place my index finger to my lips. Immediately, two fat tears pop from her eyes. We both watch the urine run down her legs, fillin' her sneaks and coatin' the leaves. We don't have time to hide before he stumbles into the clearin', his heavy boots makin' suckin' sounds as he tramps through the mud to our table.

I wrinkle my nose. From a few feet away, I can smell the moonshine, and lookin' into his eyes, bloodshot and unfocused, I feel goose bumps colonize up and down my arms.

"Where's Joelle?"

The tears flow fast and furious down Ness's face. I watch her spoon in free fall, bouncin' against the leaves.

"She went into town for supplies," I stammer at his feet, my stomach gathered up in one huge cramp.

"Don't you look away, girl. Only liars look away!"

I look into his eyes, and it's all I can do to hold his gaze.

"*Do you know our mama, sir?*"

I'm buyin' time, time to think of somethin'. I'm in charge. My steady voice fools even myself. My mind whirs a mile a minute.

"*I'm Carey. This is my sister, Jenessa.*"

"*Pretty little things, aren't ya?*"

My heart drops when he laughs, a soulless sound if ever there was one, capped off by a cobwebbed meth cough, a sound we know all too well. Jenessa leans over and empties her stomach on the ground.

In four lightnin' steps, he covers the leafmeal between us, his hand dartin' out to wrap around my throat.

"*You don't know what you're doin',*" *I say.* "*You're makin' a big mistake.*"

"*I asked you, where's your mama, girl? She owes me money and I'm not leavin' without it.*"

My fingers encircle his fingers, desperate to loosen the hold, my flesh burnin', his grip a vise. I cry out in pain.

"*Mama should be back any minute, sir. If you want to wait, you can have some food and—*"

"*Where does she keep the money?*"

I listen to my voice, small and placatin', like I'm talkin' to someone rational. Tears flow down my cheeks, but he don't let go.

"*I . . . I—we don't have no money, sir. But if you wait for Mama—*"

"*When's the last time she's been here? And don't lie to me, bitch.*"

"*Five weeks ago.*"

I tell him the truth. Maybe he'll let me go and go lookin' somewhere else. But he leans in, breathin' on me, and my one mistake is turnin' my head to escape his breath.

"*You look at me, girl, when I'm talkin' to ya!*"

My head jerks to the right under the crack of his hand, and white stars dance in the air. Beyond, there's a lake of blackness. I fight it with all my bein'.

In the Hundred Acre Wood, I could always see them comin' before they appeared. Nessa, a pink peekaboo through breathless greenery. Mama, a lemon yellow zing of insulted bushes and low-hangin' branches whippin' across her store-bought ski jacket.

Between the white stars, the lemon yellow flashes, but it don't zing. It sneaks off in the direction it came, at a quick but silent clip.

"Mama!"

But the scream lodges itself deep in my throat like a rabbit's knuckle-bone.

With one sweepin' gesture, our dinner flies to the forest floor, and he uses his free hand to rip off my jeans and undergarments. He hauls me by my ponytail backward onto the table, the metal edge digging into my calf. As the white stars fade, I see him fumblin' with his zipper. He forces my legs apart, his breath quickenin', his weight crushin'. I feel white lightnin' rip through my stomach.

That's the last thing I remember before goin' dark.

It's Jenessa's screams that rouse me. The leaves are a sea, rockin' me. I grab hold of a low-hangin' branch and scramble to my feet.

He has Nessa on the table now. She's naked from the waist down, her dress pushed up to her chin.

In the dyin' firelight, he don't see me crawl to the camper. I should've had it on me all along. An ember pops in the background. Two or three ticks on a watch pass, if that, and that fast, I know what I have to do.

I pull my shotgun from its pegs and inch back down the camper's rickety wooden steps, my mind animal keen.

He struggles with Nessa, his hand clamped over her mouth, swearin' at the thing hangin' limply between his legs like a tree limb struck by lightnin'.

I give him no warnin', my finger cocked and the trigger pulled by a hatred floodin' me bigger than the creek swollen with ten spring rains.

I aim for the heart.

At the last minute, he turns toward me, and I blow a hole through his upper arm. The slug passes clear through his hide, thunkin' into the hickory behind him.

"Stay down, Nessa!"

"You fuckin' bitch!"

He shoves Jenessa away and she crashes to the ground. I hear my voice, clear and true, betrayin' nothin' of my intentions. But boy, do I have me some intentions.

"Go in the camper, Jenessa, and lock the door behind you. Don't you dare come out until I come get you myself, you hear?"

She's a frozen heap on the ground, but I know she can hear me. I have no choice but to yell at her.

"GO! Get your skinny ass in that camper NOW!"

In that moment, it's like I've prodded her with a white-hot poker. She scrambles to her feet, wailin', but she don't make a sound. I stand in front of them, half-naked, but I don't feel shame. I'm a mountain lion landin' on the back of a whitetail buck. I'm the rapids rippin' the river to shreds, pretty to watch but able to kill.

I see it in his eyes, fightin' to sober up quick: He thinks I'm crazy. He must have me confused with Mama. I've never been like Mama.

Once I hear the lock click, I turn to him.

"I'm comin' back for your sister, bitch. For both of you. And I'll keep comin' back, if you catch my drift."

He don't think I'll do it. My mouth slips into a crocodile smile. His stench lingers on my skin as his stickiness runs down my legs. I cock my shotgun. He runs.

He's off tramplin' bushes, gettin' thwacked in the face by low-hangin' branches. He cuts a careless, sloppy trail. It's perfect for trackin' an animal.

I only have time to shove my feet into sneakers and grab the flashlight from a crate under the table before settin' off after him, trackin'

him deeper and deeper into our Hundred Acre Wood. Soon, a heaven
of stars map his trail. I see the violin constellation, the one I don't know
by its real name. More than once, its brightest star has been my point of
navigation, leadin' me back to the camper if I've wandered too far.

The man is makin' decent time, if all be told, only he don't know he's
travelin' farther into Obed. I follow stealthily, thankin' Saint Joseph for
all those years of practice huntin' our own food. I'm a sure shot, exerci-
sin' a precision that comes from those things we do over and over again,
day in, day out.

When I get close enough, I hear Mama's voice in my head, her
words slurred but true.

"We get what we deserve, Carey. Sometimes we're the getters, and
sometimes we're the givers."

I squeeze the flashlight, glad to have it. By the light of the moon, I see
him bent over at the waist, palms on his thighs, breathin' hard. When I
snap a twig, he ups and dominates the clearin', swackin' and stabbin' the
night with a broken branch while turnin' in circles.

Lookin' for me. He's naked from the waist up. He's tied his sweat-
stained T-shirt tight around his upper arm, I reckon to stop the bleedin'.

When I'm close enough to smell him, I shoot straight toward his form,
aimin' at heart height. His mouth forms a scream that never comes. He
collapses to the ground.

I circle him, careful not to get too close. I sweep the flashlight over his
chest, his face. I see no signs of breathin'. I feel nothin'—no triumph, no
remorse. B'ness. Although my body shakes against my wishes, and I let
it. He'll make a bear or a pack of coyotes a right fine meal.

On my wrist, I'm wearin' Mama's watch, like I always do, the one
she taught me time on. The one I'd used to teach Jenessa. Checkin' it, I
see it's taken more than forty-five minutes to get back to the camper, and
it's a lucky thing. No one wants a corpse rottin' close to their camper.
He's too heavy to drag or carry, and diggin' graves is an act of respect.

The river sees everythin' and is cold to the marrow, but I peel off my T-shirt and wade in up to my chin, the moonlight blue on my bare skin. I hold the shotgun over my head; I can't get myself to put it down. The river cools off the swollen parts, baptizin' me back into skin and bone and savin' me into a new Carey, a Carey who, tonight, let go of childish things.

I shake so hard, my teeth clatter against each other. I'm standin' nek-kid in the winter water, and I can't do it for long. I command myself to put the jeans back on, crumpled atop the wanwood leafmeal. I only have two pair, and I need 'em both at night.

My gait is thick and wobbly, my girl parts split like a wild turkey's wishbone. I reckon Mama would say I'm a woman now. I lean over into a bush and retch and retch. Then, I pull a clean T-shirt off the line and fumble with the arm holes.

Afterward, I pretend I'm fingerin' Dvorak's Romance for Violin, usin' the music to steady my breathin'. When that don't work, I repeat the lines in my head, from beginnin' to end and back again, only this time, I insert my own name.

Carey, are you grievin'
Over Goldengrove unleavin'?
Leaves, like the things of man, you
With your fresh thoughts care for, can you?
Ah! as the heart grows older
It will come to such sights colder
By and by, nor spare a sigh
Though worlds of wanwood leafmeal lie;
And yet you will weep and know why.
Now no matter, child, the name:
Sorrow's springs are the same.
Nor mouth had, no nor mind, expressed

What heart heard of, ghost guessed:
It is the blight man was born for,
It is Carey you mourn for.

Against the walnut's rough bark, the hatred slides down my face and my sobs are shardlike and stranglin'. I pick up my pee coat and slide it on after pickin' off chips of leafmeal stuck to the matted collar. I sit my butt right down on top of the metal table, reclaimin' it.

Accordin' to the watch, it takes twenty minutes for the violent shudderin' to stop. That's when I get up, knock on the camper door.

"Ness? It's safe, baby."

No response. I cuss under my breath, catchin' sight of the camper window, screenless and unlocked. I squeeze my head through.

I find Ness in the circle of my flashlight, her thumb stuck in her mouth and the cot's thin blanket wrappin' her up in a cocoon. Her legs are drawn up to her chest and she rocks back and forth, back and forth. She sees right through me, and it's like she don't hear me, neither. She don't make one peep.

I scramble through the window and scoop her up in my arms and out the door. When we reach the river, I strip her bare. One dunk, that's all she can handle, and then I wrap her back up in the blanket and sit her in my lap in front of the fire.

We watch her dress, the T-shirt, and our underwear curl into the flames, all reminders torched to ash in less than a minute. Her blond ringlets hang limply, all the light gone out of 'em. Droplets of creek water sit on her eyelashes, and she blinks them down her cheeks. When she's warm again, I help her put on jeans and her sweatshirt, tyin' the hood snug.

"He won't be comin' back, Nessa. You don't have to worry."

I reposition my legs beneath her, restin' a hand on my shotgun.

Not a peep.

"I took care of it. I had to. Please say somethin'?"

I jump at the touch of my father's hand on my shoulder.

"We're here, Carey."

I blink at him, seeing someone else.

"We're here," he repeats.

He pulls onto the scenic overlook and shuts off the truck, then comes around to my side and reaches out a hand to help me down. I make pretend I don't see it, skin and warmth, not foreign or strange like it should be. But I don't deserve it. I don't deserve the help.

"Here."

He reaches into the truck.

"Put on your hat and mittens."

I take my time, even though, at the sight of my trees, my heart leaps with joy. Will they recognize me, this girl of faux ermine and bedazzled jeans?

He follows behind me. I know the way home like I know the sky at night. It's as if no time has passed.

When we reach our clearing, I stop, unsure for a moment. The fire pit is a charred black-and-gray circle, almost indistinguishable from the surrounding snow. The camper sags in its same old place, but looking much smaller and shabbier than I remember.

I rush ahead through the brush, leaving him alone for a good ten minutes as I make my way to the hollow tree. Scooping out the accumulation of snow, the metal glints through, and I pluck it out. I reckon the string still smells like Mama. I take a sniff.

"Carey?" He yells through the tiny window. "I'm already inside."

Up close, I see the front lock of the camper's been busted and the door handle juts at an odd angle. In the doorway, my eyes water as the fumes sting my nose. I reckon the fire isn't that old. I stare at the ruins.

And then I remember. Frantic, I pull up the floor panel over the front left wheel, and it's still there—Mama's watch—passed down by my gran.

I used to pretend watches were like outside hearts, caring about our lives. I used to hold up the watch and say to Jenessa, "Even though she's gone, her heart is still with us."

Jenessa never met our Gran. She died during my third year in the woods. I used to wring my hands, imagining her driving by my parents' old house, or back at her own, pushing aside the curtains to peep out the picture glass, watching for cookie girl. Waiting for me.

The second hand tick, tick, ticks. It's like an omen, the fact that it still works. My father takes it from me. Recognition floods his face.

"I'd as soon bust anything of Mama's under my heel," I admit, "but one day, Jenessa might want something from her gran. She learned time on that watch."

He tucks it into his pocket for safekeeping. I glance at the delicate watch on my wrist, the one Melissa gave me. Funny how we can't hold on to time, even when it's strapped to our wrists.

I survey the skeletal remains of the rest of my poetry books, burned to a crisp. I thought I'd be taking them back with me, the stack sliding back and forth across the backseat as we drove. Something for me to read in prison. Instead, the sight of them hurts so hard, I can't breathe.

My father clears the snow from the rickety stairs, using the rake that's missing two teeth. I watch him, his red scarf a streak of color against the gray surroundings, this man who doesn't fit in here at all. Willing my feet to move, I gather wood, branches and kindling, and he uses the matches from his cigarettes to light the fire.

It's time.

I swallow hard, raising my eyes and then lowering them. It's not so much what the man did to me. It's what I did to him.

The savage in humanity.

Funny how a person knows what shame is, even when you don't have a name for it. No matter. It feels the same.

"Something happened out here, didn't it?" he asks, lighting a cigarette.

"Yes, sir." *Please, Saint Joseph.* "I did something wicked wrong."

I look straight into his eyes, gathering myself into the baptized Carey, shoulders back, ready to put a finish on things.

"Tell me."

"I was the real thirteen, and Jenessa was five. . . ."

I pause, wavering.

"Go on."

"We were eatin' dinner by the fire. A man came out of nowhere, lookin' for Mama. He said she owed him money for drugs."

His jaw sets. The cigarette burns down toward his fingers, but he doesn't smoke it.

"He was on the meth. Drunk on moonshine, too."

My father eyes are so sad. Pained.

He already knows.

"He took off my jeans and he hurt me," I whisper. "I couldn't push him off."

I look away, but not before I note the tears slipping down his cheeks.

"I fell asleep in the middle of it."

"Passed out," he says gruffly. "It happens to people when they're seriously hurt or shocked."

I nod in agreement, filing the phrase away for future use.

"Where was Jenessa?"

His words cling thick as tree sap, hoping against hope.

But I can't give it to him.

"She was sittin' right there, like you are now."

I flinch when he stands up suddenly, turning away from me. He swears under his breath, kicking the ground with his boots, his hands in fists.

"She saw what happened?" he asks.

I talk to his back.

"Yes, sir. When I woke up, he was gettin' ready to hurt her like he hurt me. So I snuck into the camper and got my shotgun."

He spins around and finds my eyes. I nod. He heard right.

"I shot him in the shoulder. I was aimin' for the heart, but he moved. I told Ness to lock herself in the camper and not come out until I gave the say-so."

He watches me with eyes I can't read. No matter.

I pause. "He promised he'd come back to hurt us. He said he'd keep comin' back."

I kick dirt, leaves, and snow onto the fire until it sputters and dies, then motion for him to follow. I retrace the trail we trekked that night, not surprised I remember the way, as these woods were my whole world. The trail leaves off and the undergrowth thickens, the tree branches blocking the sunlight. I move by instinct, noting the terrain and the sound of the creek, the babbling water first to my right, then over my shoulder.

In the light, it takes only thirty minutes to reach the spot. I know it's the place because of the tire graveyard. We both tripped over the discarded tires that night. I slide down the bank of the ravine. *The body will be just like the bear carcass we found last year. A heap of bleached bones and telltale hide.*

My father slides down behind me, his breath heavy with exertion. He stands next to me, surveying the area.

We kick around.

"Here," I call.

Side by side, we stare at the hump under the cover of leaves and a dusting of snow. I push the end of it with my toe.

A jawbone falls away, stopping against a rock. Some teeth are missing; others are rotted. *Meth*, I think.

This time, it's my father who turns and retches.

I chant to myself.

Ness will be okay. Ness will be okay. That's all that matters. Ness will be okay.

My body shakes. I can't make it stop. My father holds me against him, warming me like he'd warmed Shorty. I close my eyes, making a memory.

Then: "I reckon you won't be wantin' me no more, sir." I shove out from under his arm, ready to accept my punishment. "But Ness had nothin' to do with this. I put her in the camper, and took care of b'ness."

"Listen to me, Carey. Look at me."

I wrench my eyes from his boots.

"It's called *self-defense*, you hear me? You had a right to protect yourself and your sister."

His eyes shift to the mound, but I'm woods-smart; I can see he's shocked. I can feel the distance, falling cool between us. I stand frozen like Jenessa, bean spoon bouncing off the leaves. His voice fills the woods from far, far away as I remember what I spent the last year desperate to forget.

"Carey?"

And then he looks like him again. Looking at me.

He believes me.

He extends his hand.

But hands hurt too much. Again, I pretend I don't see.

It's almost dusk when we reach the camper. He sits on a stump, the one I used to sit on when I played for Nessa, the notes weaving through the firelight, the music adding its own color to the yellow, orange, red.

He lights a cigarette, the tip glowing like a star that's fallen to earth. Finally, as the shadows grow long, he turns to me.

"And that's when Jenessa stopped talking," he says, but it's not a question.

"Yes, sir. What happens in the woods stays in the woods."

He inhales, then exhales a trail of smoke.

"We're going to need to tell the police. Fill out a report. We'll have to take them back to the body."

"I understand, sir."

"I want to be honest with you, Carey. I don't know what might happen. I'll do all I can to help you."

"Saint Joseph's son said, 'The truth will set you free.' I reckon it's true."

"It's a good start. And I want you to tell them everything. You hear me? Everything that was ever done to you. Everything that happened that night. You know why?"

I have no idea.

"You were the victim, Carey. Not him. And sweetie—"

My eyes well, the eyes of the girl from before the woods.

"You have nothing to be ashamed of."

I nod at his boots.

Flooded with feelings I don't have words for, I bend down to fetch the old lantern, which is lying on its side under the picnic table. When I turn the key, the light shines out of my hands.

He waits on the steps while I enter the camper, holding the lantern in front of me and searching for anything salvageable. I never thought I'd cry over this place. I push aside debris, the remains of

Nessa's blankie blackened and hard to the touch. It's gone, all gone—our old life is gone.

"You tell anyone about this and I'll come back and snap both your necks," he grunts, each thrust like a bolt of lightnin' rippin' through my body.

I slip my skin and rise into the inky dark, sit on the arm of one of the white stars, my legs swingin'.

"I might have to hit this again sometime," he says. "I'll give your Mama a discount."

One hundred dollars, I think. One hundred dollars, for breakin' and enterin'. Before the white-star night, that was one of the lucky things. None of those men ever had one hundred dollars.

I've detailed every mole, freckle, and mark on the dark underbelly of the Hundred Acre Wood. Looking through the doorway, my father's eyes are bright, but I don't feel it, none of it. I am ice over the creek. I am as emotionless as a hundred-dollar bill as I close the camper door forever.

Standing in the snow, I reach into my pocket, the key cold against my palm. Using all my might, I fling it far into the trees.

The man didn't know that I knew his name—Josiah Perry—or who he was, his evil, gap-toothed grin a photo negative of the angelic smile that sleeps each night in the bedroom across from mine, Shorty curled up around her like an aura.

A trick baby. A fuck for a fix. The words are as ugly as what Mama did to bring Nessa into the world.

"You're making a big mistake!"

I reckon I'll take the secret of his identity to my grave, but not for my sake. For Nessa's.

When we leave camp, the only thing I take with me besides my g's and Gran's watch is my dad. Until he offers his hand. This time, I take that, too.

The ride home is silent but different. We're both different. Somehow, I'm older. Somehow, he's realer.

If the newness had a sound, it would be the sound of the last puzzle pieces snapping into place, the kind that fit even when you don't want them to.

"May I ask you something, sir?"

He takes his eyes off the road just long enough to glance at me, his face thoughtful but worried. Really, really worried.

"Shoot."

"It seems you like Jenessa and all. I mean, it seems like you really care about her. I know she isn't your blood. But please"—I choke back the tears, the sticky, tangled tears—"you'll keep her, won't you? She doesn't deserve to suffer because of me."

"Keep her? No one's going anywhere."

"But if I go to prison . . . she isn't even yours."

"She's *yours*, Carey. That makes her *ours*. If you'll let her."

I cry silently, my shoulders heaving, and he lets me. It's like he knows that sometimes we're in it alone. I zone out to the trees rushing by, thinning out as we travel farther into civilization. I'm straddling two worlds again. It's so exhausting.

"You have questions, Carey? Ask them."

I've been waiting my entire life. I would've thought the words would be hard, once faced with the actual, real-life chance. But the words fly out sharp as bee stings, my voice warped and ugly.

"Why didn't you come lookin' for me? Why did you let her take me?" I can't control it once I start. "If you didn't want me then, why are you even bothering now?"

My shoulder smacks into the door panel as he swerves down an

off-ramp and into a spacious parking lot. A red neon sign blinks
H WAY DINER TRUCK STOP. Under that: FO D AND FUEL.

"What are you talking about?"

"I know what you did! You beat Mama and me. She had to save
us! You threw us out! Mama told me!"

He punches the dashboard, then flings open the door and
climbs out, slamming it behind him. I curl into a ball in my seat,
sneaking peeks through the rearview mirror as he paces the asphalt
behind the truck. I jump when he comes around and knocks on my
window.

But the anger has smoldered into something stronger. Tougher.
Sadder. I roll down the glass.

"It's time you heard the truth," he says.

He opens my door and turns me toward him, so I'm sitting with
my boots dangling out the opening.

"You really have no idea, do you?"

I think of the cold, the rain . . . the steel I couldn't always be. I
refuse to make this easy for him.

"About what, exactly?"

We wait while an eighteen-wheeler pulls out of a parking space
and ambles toward the on-ramp.

"I never hurt you or your mother."

I shake my head, disbelieving. "Mama said!"

"Well, your mama lied to you! That's your mama. C'mon, a smart
girl like you? Think! You know what she did to you. My whole world
fell apart when she took you!"

I want to believe him. I ache to. But I can't hurt like that again. I
just can't.

"She took us to save us from *you*!" I spit the words, sounding
more like Mama. Less like him.

"She took you because I filed for sole custody. Your mama was sick. I tried to get her help, but she refused. One night, she left you in the car and couldn't remember where she'd left it. It took a day and a half to find you. You were four years old and hysterical. You don't remember?"

I shake my head against the words, screaming inside, not knowing what to believe.

Saint Joseph!

"I moved out of the house, hired a lawyer, and the court awarded me sole custody. Your mom must've found out. She stole you that afternoon."

My father's voice cracks.

"When I went to your baby-sitter's house, you were already gone."

"Clarey," I whisper.

"You remember her? Clare Shipley. A friend of your mama's. She had no idea Joelle was going to run. It was the worst day of my life."

I look at my father, *really look*, and see the broken part of him, broken by Mama, like she'd broken all of us. I remember what Mrs. Haskell said. She had no reason to lie.

Kidnapped.

Ryan's flyer, making paper noises in the wind.

"Everyone was looking for you." His eyes are slanted at the tips, just like the girl's in the flyer. "I registered you with the National Center for Missing and Exploited Children, and put up posters for years. I even went on the news a bunch of times."

We didn't have a television in the woods. Would I have seen him if we had?

"That day we found you, it finally made sense. She'd hidden you away in the middle of nowhere, in an eight-and-a-half-thousand-acre forest. Even if someone had seen you, who'd be suspicious of a family gone camping?"

I think of how many people we'd seen when we lived in the Hundred Acre Wood.

A few hikers. Drug dealers. Men who liked kids. No one who could help.

No one, in all those years.

My father turns my face to his, forcing me to look him in the eye.

"Aren't you happy at the farm? Haven't we been good to you?"

His question is like the seed to a planet-size ache. He wants to give me back all that I've lost. I don't know how to let him.

"Life isn't like this! It's not real!"

"What do you mean?"

"No one gets hugs and new clothes and all this good stuff for nothing." I mimic Mama's voice. "'Everythin' gets paid for in one way or another, girl, and flesh is more plentiful around here. Young flesh pays more. So git goin'!'"

Now he knows that, too. But he doesn't flinch.

"This isn't what life is like." My voice breaks. My words aren't saying what I mean, but I don't know how to explain it clearer. I think of Jenessa the way she is now, like a pink-cheeked crocus pushing up through the snow. I want to be wrong more than anything in the world.

"This isn't real," I whisper.

"Says who? Who says what's real? What your mama did was *unreal*. She doesn't have the last word on real. Maybe I do."

My shoulders shake. I make sounds a person could never make on purpose.

"Families aren't like what your mama did to you. Or what she had you do."

I hide my face in my arms and sob.

"I can't erase those years, Carey, and God knows I'd give my life to make yours and Jenessa's whole again. I can't give you back all the time she stole from us. That's the hardest thing to reconcile."

Tears slide down his cheeks, their path determined by the lines and wrinkles in his face. My tears continue to fall, but for all of us—him, Ness, myself, and even Gran.

"All I can hope is that the lean years made you stronger, and that you'll get through this like you got through that. But no matter what happens, you and Jenessa always have a home with me."

I break down completely, and when he reaches for me, I let him. He holds me to him and we cry together, holding on for dear life. I breathe in the smoky smell of his sheepskin coat, rough against my cheek. The *h* word fans its wings into a *D*.

Dad.

I close my eyes, trying to remember him from before. It's so hard.

"I can't remember much from before the woods," I say, hiccuping through my tears. "Not you, not living indoors, not tap water or light switches or bubble baths. Not even Christmas."

He holds me tighter, his stubbly chin resting on my head.

"Give it time. It'll come back when you're ready."

He rocks me back and forth, back and forth, as long as I need it. Then: "So, any more secrets?"

"Ryan Shipley." My words are muffled by his coat. "He's my best friend."

"I reckon he is. You were like two peas in a pod once upon a time." He chuckles. "You'd better bring him by the house, then. Been a few years since I've seen that boy."

"Yes, sir."

It's true: Ryan's my best friend. But what I don't say is that I love him. From the tips of my chunky hair to the wiggle in my clean toes, I love him. My stomach squirms like worms (in a good way) just thinking about him. And I reckon when love's in short supply, you know it all the more when it finds you.

"See," my dad says, grinning.

"What?"

"You remember some things."

"Some things I don't want to remember."

"That'd be normal, I guess. But some things you need to remember. Or how else will you know who you are?"

I turn to him. I have to say it out loud. *For the girl in the woods.*

"My name is Carey Violet Benskin. My mama kidnapped me when I was four years old."

"You have no idea how many people were looking for you, sweetheart."

"And I was just over yonder, in the woods," I say wistfully.

"Might as well have been a whole 'nother world," he replies.

This is our world, now, our own special bubble. He drives with one hand on the wheel, his other arm around me. I snuggle against him, flesh, blood, and bone, our combined breath fogging the side windows.

I think of the writing on the camper wall, just above the baseboard, scrawled by my six-year-old self. I saw it when I retrieved Gran's watch; up until then, I'd forgotten all about it. *If you find me, take me home,* I'd written. Like I knew, somehow, this day was coming.

I don't remember Melissa greeting us in the driveway, nor my dad carrying me up the stairs to my room, taking off my coat and shoes, hat and mittens before slipping me under the covers and leaving me to a dreamless sleep.

I just know when I wake to the roosters crowing and the sun warming my cheeks, everything has changed.

I told.

And it's only the beginning.

Epilogue

I'll never forget my woods.

The trees remain my witnesses, living proof that Ness and I existed, growing a whole forest of shimmering memories, even if we were one day meant to leave the Hundred Acre Wood behind. I reckon my heart is veiny and green because I carry the woods with me. And maybe, just maybe, they carry me.

When I was little and lonely, before Jenessa bedazzled my world, I used to believe that if I thought about it long and hard enough, my toes would wiggle, then itch, then worm their way into the earth, corkscrewing around old pop-tops, and through clots of bedrock to root me there forever, because it was the only place I belonged.

But last night in the woods, my heart turned real when I let my dad into it. I could feel my heart break to let the love in, break into something bigger. Yet fear for the future filled my stomach like the tiny pebbles the sparrows nibble on.

And I wanted to stay within the arms of my trees and keep the life I've always known.

And I wanted to leave because even amongst my trees, I didn't fit in, anymore.

And I was so surprised.

Most of all, I'd told someone—I'd said the important words.

The civilized words. And when I did, it was like Nessa said them, too. Backwoods words and peach cobbler words and puffer coat trimmed in faux ermine words, words for the woods and words for second chances, a life's worth of words more plentiful than the colors in Nessa's jumbo crayon box.

But that was last night, a night as large as Saturn. This morning, my cheeks are still sticky with yesterday's tears, but that's okay, I reckon. Like Mama says, a person has to do what a person has to do, even if they think they can't do it, because they can, if they have to.

I shift in bed, my body toasted-marshmallow warm and burnt around the edges. It's the wood smoke, the scent of last night's fire. With my eyes closed, I can still feel the warmth of my dad's hand pressed against mine, and I make a fist to hold it in, hoping love doesn't trickle between fingers like the Obed River.

Love leaves all sorts of evidence behind.

I know this now.

I smile at the shimmering memory of Jenessa's phoebe in the rusted cage.

"What's its name," I ask her.

"Phoebe," she says, like how could I not know?

"What if it's a boy?"

"Phoebe."

"Of course."

I remember how the bird didn't want to come out at first, shy about its leg, the length slightly crooked, but mended right good. Ness didn't care one tidbit, because she smiled love all over that bird. Its crooked leg made it hers.

My crookedness makes me hers, too.

I reckon that's just the way it is.

I lean over until I can reach the nightstand drawer, and I pull out the creamy square of cardboard for the first time. The bed squeaks beneath me and I want to get my violin out and play the squeak, let the music carry me away over the trees. My dad's trees.

Instead, I play the phone, little bleeps in my ear each time I punch in one of the numbers penciled on the back of the card. I call the number that says *home,* and I take a deep breath. It's 6:30 in the morning, but Mrs. Haskell picks up on the second ring.

"Mrs. Haskell?"

"Carey? Is that you?"

"How did you know?" I ask. All of a sudden, I don't know what to say. Not even in my head.

"Is everything okay, hon?"

She sounds raspy, like she needs water. I'd get her a glass, if I could.

"No," I say, my voice shaking. "But it will be."

And just like I did with my dad yesterday, I tell her my story. Jenessa's story, too. And today's tears wash away yesterday's. I reckon that's how it works in the civilized world.

An hour later, I tie on my robe and peek through Jenessa's door. There she is, spooning with Shorty, who arches his back and stretches out his legs like taffy at the sound of my voice. "Hi, old man," I whisper, smiling at him as I pull the quilt back over my sleeping sister. Shorty's toes flex, then go slack. "You go back to sleep, you hear?" I tell him, pulling the quilt up over him, too, because I know what it's like to be old. Maybe not on the outside, but on the in.

At least Shorty doesn't have to know what I did. But everyone else will. At school. In town. Delaney. *Ryan Shipley.*

I tiptoe out of Nessa's room, only to spy Delaney hiding in the shadows of the landing. I'm envious of what she's wearing—her smoky blue, ruffled Victoria's Secret nightgown that makes her look like a pre-Raphaelite angel from one of Pixie's art books—as she eavesdrops on the conversation going on in the kitchen below.

"I can't believe what Joelle put those children through. My God. If Jenessa hadn't had Carey looking out for her . . ." Melissa's voice trails off, and it's easy to imagine the look on her face, even if it hurts inside, knowing why. Just like it hurt to see my dad's face yesterday, when I showed him the bones.

"Carey acted in self-defense," my dad tells her. "I'm sure the police will see it that way. I called this morning. The sheriff will be in after Sunday services."

"She must be a wreck. That poor child."

"Actually, Mel, it's the damndest thing. I think she's relieved," my dad says.

"What an awful burden to carry." Melissa's words splash between clanking plates and soapy silverware and running water.

"I dare say she saved their lives. Oh no, Mel, don't cry—"

The clatter stops, and I know them well enough to know what they're doing. Holding each other. Swaying slightly back and forth in a sadness dance, right there in the middle of the linoleum.

"You bring her home, Charles, you hear me?" Melissa's words are muffled, probably by my dad's clean flannel shirt. "I want my girls home. *All* my girls, remember?"

My dad sighs. "I called Rubrick last night, and he'll meet us at the precinct. He's willing to represent Carey in whatever capacity is necessary."

"Your old friend Henry? But he's a criminal attorney."

"He also does juvenile."

"Like that's a comfort," Melissa says, her voice tight.

I shift my weight, and a board squeaks beneath me. Delaney

whirls around. Catches me watching her. We study each other, the tiny opening between us still there.

"Holy shit, Blackburn. I guess you did use your rifle."

"Shotgun," I tell her, not knowing what else to say.

"Okay, lousy joke. Just—I'm so sorry, Carey. Maybe it sounds lame, coming from me—"

"No." I smile at her, just a corner of a smile, but a smile nonetheless. "It's *complicated,*" I say knowingly, and we lock eyes, just two girls at opposite ends of a future bridge. "But I'm going to fix it."

Then I brush past her, my loose hair a curtain of leaves and branches and vines to hide me. That's what I wish, anyway, as I hurry down the staircase.

"I had no idea it was as bad as it was," she calls after me, "or I wouldn't have been such a witch."

And I think, *Why* would *she know?* I'm glad she doesn't know. I'm glad she doesn't know about the wrong hands and the bitter cold and the hurts that brand one's soul. I'm glad she had food and a bed, bedazzled jeans and a dishwasher. I'm really and truly glad. Because that's what it means to be sisters. She just doesn't know it yet. She didn't have Jenessa, like I do.

But she does, now.

Saint Joseph, as you probably know, I'm not a coward anymore. I'll do whatever it takes to keep Jenessa here with Dad and Mel. Even if they take me away, she'll be safe here.

You can tell when people are safe. You can tell when people are real. Sometimes it takes time to clear away the overgrowth of the past, like untraining one of those dogs that salivates at the sound of a bell. But if you wait out the fear, if you stay to find out, sometimes, just sometimes, you might get your miracle.

Nessa deserves a chance. The chance I never got.

She'll get it here, because love is spelled h-o-m-e.

Jenessa has a home. A Barbie with a clean nose. Another sister to watch out for her if they won't let me come back. And she's talking again.

Thank you, Saint Joseph.

Two men, one in a blue uniform, the other in a white button-down dress shirt and smart black trousers, sit at a long table across from my father, Mr. Rubrick, and me.

"That's Officer Bentley and I'm Detective Wood," the man in the dress shirt says, extending his hand.

Wood. Like a kindred spirit.

All the men shake hands, and when everyone resettles, the detective turns to me.

"We're going to record your statement. Whenever you're ready," he says, pushing a button on a machine I don't recognize.

I wipe my moist palms on the legs of my jeans, the bedazzled bumps rough like bark beneath my hands. "I'm willing to tell you everything that happened, under one condition," I say.

I say it in my strongest woods voice, because I'm still in charge. Of this, of my life, of the truth—I'm in charge. I wring my hands beneath the table.

"And that condition is?" Detective Wood asks.

"That you leave my sister out of this. She's only six, and it has nothing to do with her. I don't want her having to talk about it and getting *re-traum-a-tized*. Our case worker, Mrs. Haskell, agrees. I spoke with her on the phone this morning. She's writing up a report."

The officers confer in whispers. Finally, they turn to us.

"You have our word, Carey."

I swallow down the butterflies and sit up straight, all dignified-like, as Mama taught me. I take a deep breath and I avoid their eyes as I tell my story, detailing every scar and bruise on the dark under-belly of the Hundred Acre Wood. When I look up, Mr. Rubrick's eyes are bright; my father's are, too. But I don't feel it, none of it. I am ice over the creek. I am as emotionless as a hundred dollar bill. The hurt is two oceans wide and five oceans deep, at least. But to drown in it would mean drowning Nessa, too.

I tell them about the drugs, the men, all of it.

The white-star night.

My words hang in the air, bloated and strange. I stare at Mr. Rubrick's shiny Sunday shoes. I'd bet I could see my face in them if I tried. I reckon I should be ashamed, as I tell them *b'ness is b'ness*, a job a job, beans in our belly, and a coat for my sister. I tell them I didn't like the things the men made me do; that somehow, I knew it was wrong. But I did what I had to do for my sister. I did what I had to do, to save her.

I jut my chin like Jenessa does when she's not one acorn's worth of sorry. "I don't regret shooting him, sir." I ignore the tears that slide down my cheeks. "And I'd do it all over again if it meant keep-ing my sister safe."

They wait as I pull myself together. I take the tissues my dad hands me, and blow my nose in a goose honk, but I don't care.

"If you think you can continue, we do have some questions for you. This man—do you know his name?" Detective Wood says.

They hold their breath like they're hoping I know, but they don't want to say so. In my mind, I see his drunken, gap-toothed grin. "Josiah Perry."

I say his name like he's one of the wood roaches scuttling be-neath rotting leaves. Again, the officers exchange glances, their eyes buzzing.

"Wait here a minute, Carey. If it's okay with Mr. Rubrick, I'd like you to do a photo lineup," Officer Bentley says.

I don't know anything about photo lineups. Mr. Rubrick nods his consent and, after the officers leave, he turns to my dad and me.

"It's not cut-and-dried self-defense, Charlie, but it fits the definition. You did a great job, Carey. This may go better than we thought."

My father lets out a long exhale, as if he's been holding his breath the whole time. I catch his eye. He doesn't have the words, but his eyes do. I see pain-fear-worry-relief-sorrow. I see me in the mirror of what he sees, and the me he sees is another me, another One Who Is New.

My strong daughter, my dad's eyes say. *My brave, strong daughter.*

It's like the memory card game Melissa plays with Jenessa, the cards laid down in five rows of five. Only, these pictures aren't of bunnies and chickens for the player to seek a matching card. These are pictures of men, some scraggly, some twitchy, some unshaven, some scowling. Some with stains on their shirts, like spaghetti sauce or underarm rings. Some just haven't bothered washing. Men like the ones in the woods.

"Do you recognize the man from any of these photographs? If so, you can pick up the photo and put it aside," Detective Wood says to me.

I don't even hesitate, picking out Perry, leering up at us from the glossy paper. I'm glad there's only one of him.

"That's what we thought," the detective says. "Josiah Perry is wanted for breaking and entering, distribution of an illegal substance and rape of a minor. He's a registered sex offender."

I return to the photos, pulling men out one by one. There are three more photos by the time I'm through. They all stare at me.

"Do you recognize these men, too?" The officer asks.

I nod. "These men paid Mama for time with me."

My dad sucks in his breath, but I can't look at him; not like in the days before I knew what shame was. Shame coats my skin like the oil spill coated the feathers of all those birds on television. They couldn't fly like that. No one could.

Mr. Rubrick rakes his fingers through his hair. And just like that, I jump up, run over to the garbage can, and let the tea Melissa made me before I left gush up and over the dumped cigarette butts, the balled-up tissues, the Styrofoam peanuts I know of from one of Melissa's deliveries. My dad rushes over, but I shake off his hand.

I can't take it another minute more. I have to know.

"Am I going to prison?"

I'm surprised when the detective smiles at me, his eyes turning sad at the edges.

"I don't think so. It would be difficult finding anyone willing to press charges. You can go home with your dad. We'll write up a report, and take it from there. We know how to get in touch. Wait a minute—you're not planning on skipping town, are you?"

It's a joke. I know that much. I look at my dad. Think of the *h* word, and shake my head. "I'm stayin' put, sir."

"Good girl."

Mr. Rubrick hands the officers a card like Mrs. Haskell's. "Here's my contact information."

"I can take you out to the remains," my dad offers, and this time, he doesn't wince.

There's one more thing. One big, important thing.

"Sirs?"

I lean across the table and slide the pages of the report over to my side. With my pen, I cross out ~~Blackburn~~ and replace it with BENSKIN in neat, capital letters. The officers look at the paper, and then at me.

"Are you sure," the detective says, "that you want to use that name? The media will be all over it, and sooner rather than later. I'm surprised they haven't found out about you already."

"We circled the wagons around Carey and Jenessa," my father answers. "We wanted to give the girls time to adjust."

"Time's up," Officer Bentley says with a pained look. "But if you need us, we're here."

He turns back to me. "One last time, young lady. Are you sure that's the name you want to use?"

"My name is Carey Violet Benskin. I'm sure."

"We'll be careful to use the proper name on all our reports then," the detective says.

"My mama kidnapped me when I was four years old," I tell them, my voice ringing out clear and strong.

"I know, sweetheart. And now you're home."

"Home," I repeat, nodding.

I don't feel a smitch of awkwardness when I fall into my dad's arms. He holds me as I crumble, and long after everyone else has left, he's still holding me, swaying back and forth, his arms as strong as a hickory's in a hurricane.

I'm going home.

I hold on to my dad hurricane-tight.

When we pull into the driveway, Jenessa is right there waiting in the mudroom, her face pressed up against the wavy glass of our front door. She throws the door open and flings herself at me, hugging me hard.

"You're not going to jail?"

"Nope," I say, combing through her silky curls with my fingers. I pry her arms from around my waist, squat down on the porch, and cup her chin, so we're eye to eye. "They know he tried to hurt us. They said it wasn't our fault."

"They know," she says, her bottom lip quivering. She falls into my eyes until she's sure she's seen the truth.

"They know, and it's going to be okay. I promise. I'm not going anywhere," I say, "if you're not there with me."

And that's the truth, too.

I let Ness lead me up to my room, her hand so tiny in mine. She plops down on my braided rug and regards me solemnly, her eyes unblinking. "Shorty would bite him if he ever came back. Don't worry, Carey."

Upon hearing his name, Shorty raises his head from his place at the foot of my bed. Ness smiles one of her pinkest smiles, *And if you could see her now, you'd know just what I mean, Mama.*

You'd know you did the right thing by giving us up to Dad. Jenessa deserves a real home. So do you, Mama.

I hope one day you find it.

"Do you want a French braid for school, like Melissa did mine?" I ask.

Nessa nods, happily positioning herself beneath my flying hands.

"Wait until my teacher hears me talk today, Carey. I'm going to read out loud in class just like the other kids."

"You'll do great," I tell her, my fingers weaving sections of hair over and under. "Close your eyes."

I jump up and grab the can of hairspray, spritzing her hair to hold the baby-fine ends in place. She seems older already, less like the baby in the woods I used to cuddle. My heart hurts and soars at the same time, like the best violin pieces.

After she finds her shoes, she takes me by the hand. "Say good-bye to Shorty."

We crouch carefully on each side of the stitched-together hound. Jenessa leans down and kisses the apple of his head. The quilt lurches as his tail wags underneath.

"Now, you."

I lean down and kiss his nose. She grins, leaving me there. I listen to her clomp down the stairs in her pink crocodile shoes, as Melissa calls them.

Crocodile shoes. Imagine that.

"Mom! Can I have a toaster strudel?" Jenessa yells, and I smile at the sound of her voice, clear and true.

My father calls to me. "Carey, do you have a minute?"

I make my way downstairs, sliding into a chair across from him at the table, my stomach jumping.

"I need to warn you, sweetie—the press has been tipped off. I got the call from Mr. Rubrick this morning."

> Out upon the wharfs they came,
> Knight and Burgher, Lord and Dame,
> And around the prow they read her name,
> The Lady of Shalott.

"They can't bother you on school grounds, so you should be fine as far as school goes. Mr. Rubrick said the story will break on the morning news. You're going to need this," he says as he hands me a sleek cell phone just like Delaney's, "and you can call me or Melissa or Mrs. Haskell whenever you need to. If the kids are too much, we may have to pull you out of school and teach you at home."

I take the phone, but the situation takes all of the shine out of it. "Why do people care so much, anyway?" I say, my eyes welling with tears. "I'm just a stranger to them."

"Look at me, Carey."

I look.

"See, that's the thing. You're not a stranger in their minds. I know it seems odd to you, but your kidnapping struck a chord with so many people. They feel as if they know you." My dad pauses, blinking back his own tears. "So many children never make it back. They admire you, because you're a survivor."

"A *survivor*," I repeat, hearing the word in my head with a capital *S*. I know he wouldn't say it if it weren't true.

"Two officers will be in the parking lot, mornings and afternoons. Your mom or I will pick you up, just to be safe. We'll meet in the office at two-fifteen. Okay?"

I nod. I love the sound of the *mom* word, too, if you spell it M-e-l-i-s-s-a.

On the way to school, no one can get a word in edgewise. Jenessa chitters like a magpie, chewing our ears off the whole way. We can't help but smile—Delaney, too—and they're those real smiles, the kind a person can't fake. I still can't get over Nessa. It's like she's making up for lost time. My father pulls up in front of Nessa's school, and Delaney helps my sister out of the truck, catching her under the arms and swinging her down to the pavement.

"I'm still going to worry about you," my dad says once they're gone, jiggling my shoulder. "I'm not going to stop worrying about you or looking out for you, just because you're home."

I watch Delaney, with Jenessa's hand clasped firmly in hers, lead my sister through the door of her Montessori school. No one messes with Delaney. Not even the little kids. The parking lot is half full, and people go about their business like yesterday never happened.

For them, it didn't.

Once again, the woods are an ache, a lump in my throat I can't swallow down. Everything's changing all over again. Everyone walks too fast, talks too fast. It feels like people are moving into my woods, cutting down my trees, threatening me with endless sky.

I turn to my dad. "I reckon I don't want everyone knowing my business," I say, my cheeks hot. "Some parts are private."

"I understand that, honey. You don't have to talk to anyone about anything you don't want to talk about. I'd be lying to you if I said this was going to be easy, but you have us—your family—and we *will* help you through this."

I think of him and Nessa at breakfast, asking Ness's Magic 8-Ball the goofiest questions: will Peter Rabbit eat toast and jam with us in the breakfast nook? Would Shorty chase the Cat in the Hat? Can Jenessa have a hippopotamus for Christmas?

"Do you really think it's going to be all right?"

There are twenty answers swimming inside a Magic 8-Ball. My father picks one.

"It is decidedly so," he says, winking at me.

It's mind-boggling, no matter how many times I go over it. One day, as we minded our own business, sitting on stumps around the campfire, the world outside rumbled and shook and made room for Jenessa and me.

I'd thought it was the end of everything.

Instead, it was only the beginning.

I'm standing in front of my locker at school, when someone bumps into me. "Watch it, Benskin," she says under her breath.

I spin toward the voice, my eyes widening when I see who it is. Delaney grins awkwardly, before she reaches out and gives my braid a gentle tug. *Maybe, just maybe*, I think, *the shuffle fox and the waddle badger aren't so different after all.*

"Me and the girls, we've got your back," she says, smiling a smile not usually reserved for me.

I reckon I know the feeling when I smile the same smile back.

"Thanks, Delly."

I wave to Pixie down the hall, where she wobbles on her high heels as she digs through her locker. She waves back, making kissy faces. *Ryan,* she mouths. I laugh, and so does she. I mouth back, *I need to talk to you, later.* She nods, knowing from my face that it's important.

"Hey, CC!"

His whole face lights up when he sees me, and it steals my breath every time. No one has ever looked at me that way, looked at me like I'm Margaret's spring. I wait for him as he sprints down the hallway, out of breath by the time he reaches me.

"I tried to call you this weekend. Your dad said you were busy, out looking for a dog?"

"Not just any dog," I reply, as I snap my locker shut. "I was out looking for Shorty. My sister's dog got loose and his collar got hung up on the old fence line. We couldn't find him, and he almost froze to death."

His eyes are campfire warm, while his forehead creases with concern. I reckon I've always known his expressions, his clouds and his suns, the storms we shared and the ones we didn't—until we did, again.

"Is he okay?"

"He will be."

"How about you? Are you okay?"

I expect him to look away, but he doesn't. His eyes hold mine, steady and true. "Your story was on the news this morning."

"Already?"

Holding on to his eyes when I feel coated in shame is like holding on to a baby in a funnel cloud. But I make myself do it. Especially for him.

"Yes, it was." His voice is softer than faux ermine. "I'm so sorry, Carey."

I scowl at him. "I reckon the worst thing you could do is feel sorry for me, Ryan Shipley."

"Hold on. I didn't mean it like that. Never like that," he assures me.

"Good. Because you can't get weird on me," I say, letting him see me, the real me, tears and all. "Not you of all people," I add.

"I was clueless, though, wasn't I?" he asks, catching one of my tears on the tip of his finger. "I didn't think past the kidnapping. Or I wouldn't have pushed you into things you might not have been ready for, like some idiot guy—"

"Ryan."

I reach for him and he meets me halfway, his hand wrapping around mine. "All you've been is kind to me," I say, giving his hand a squeeze. "And I reckon there are things I'd rather you hear from me. Not the newspapers or the television." I quake inside at the thought. "But later, okay?"

"Okay. But I want you to know that there's nothing you can tell me that would change how I feel about you, Ceec. So how about giving me a peck on the cheek?"

"I'd rather have a kiss," I say, suddenly brave. "A real kiss."

"Are you sure? I mean—"

"I know the difference, Ryan," I say, and going by his face, I know he knows what I mean. *It was on the news this morning. The whole world knows, now.* "I know the difference. So I reckon you need to hush up and kiss me," I say, leaning in to meet him.

But all we can do is laugh against each others' mouths.

"Mrs. Hadley's out sick," he finally says with a devilish grin, "and you have the sub who doesn't take attendance. How about ditching English and coming with me?"

It's not even a question. "Where to?"

"A surprise, m'lady. And bring your violin."

"As if I could leave it behind. It doesn't fit in my locker, and it's too valuable to leave in homeroom."

I grab it with my free hand, never letting go of Ryan's hand for a second.

"Where are we going, again?"

"You'll see. Close your eyes."

"Seriously?"

"Just do it."

I cling to him as he leads me down the hallway, a dangerous endeavor even with eyes wide open. I hear a door push open and creak shut behind us.

"Open your eyes!"

Even with my inexperience, I know where we are: in a room where people play music. An old, boxy piano stands off to the right, and lines of metal chairs snake around the room in wiggly rows.

I laugh. I don't need to ask. I set my case on one of the chairs and remove my violin and bow. I walk over to Ryan, who's perched on the piano bench, the piano keys exposed.

"Let's do *Winter* this time," he says, "in keeping with the weather."

fee bee! feeeeee beeeeee!

Our gazes turn to the yellow-bellied bird arcing over our heads. The bird alights on the windowsill, pumping its tail and settling in as if for a front row seat.

"No way—that bird's *indoors*," Ryan says, shaking his head. "Do you think it'll find its way out of here?"

I don't need to think. I know. "I reckon that bird can take care of itself. You'd be surprised how resourceful critters can be."

Like Jenessa and me.

As if marking my words, we watch the phoebe dart through an open window, disappearing in a blur of wings.

"Ready?" Ryan's fingers hover over the keys.

I nod, my bow poised.

The room fills with Vivaldi's *Winter*, the crisp, sparkling notes dusting everything fresh and new. Our instruments blend together until there's no separation, no space between us, no end, and no beginning.

"Put it into the music," Mama used to say. "The anger, sadness, worries—there are notes for all of it."

There are notes for happiness, too, if you listen past the ache. Light-filled notes that wing and soar, that fly by night like the Violin constellation, serenading you home. I know, because I've been listening for the happiness notes all my life, like a far-off music I could almost hear but never capture, not even with my violin.

And I know why, now. After Melissa, my dad, Ryan, Pixie . . . even Delaney.

It's because happiness is a song that plays *you* when you share it with the people who matter the most. And that's when you hear it in the most important place: your heart, which is an organ, after all.

Thank you, Saint Joseph.

Thank you for knowing the song all along.

Acknowledgments

A book is a living, breathing thing. It spends the first chapters of its life curled up in the mind, symbiotic with its creator as it grows fat and round. And then the book is born. If you're lucky like me, by the time you turn the pages for the first time, your book will have been cradled by many sets of careful, talented, and capable hands.

To my amazing agent, Mandy Hubbard, thank you for too many things to list, and most of all, for believing in this book. I'm so glad our stars aligned, and I feel lucky for it every day. Bob Diforio, you've been a kind and guiding light through the entire process. Words don't suffice.

For my editor, Jennifer Weis, and assistant editor, Mollie Traver, much appreciation for steering me through this process with precision and enthusiasm, and for honoring me with a true collaboration. My copy editor, Carol Edwards, made the novel sing with her deft touch. My deepest gratitude to everyone at St. Martin's who had a hand in this book from start to finish. It truly takes a village.

Tasha Harlow, my fellow fearless flower, and Cate Peace, thank you for first reads and eagle eyes and pom-poms flying. Big thanks to all my writing friends across the Internet—speznas, caw caws, heart-shaped pupils, and lucky black cats to all of you.

To the agents and editors who cared along the way, and who go out of their way to help aspiring authors find their way, I owe you a debt of gratitude. For the love of books, go we.

For Piggy, who never hesitated to leave the warm spot on the bed to "come help with the book" in his loving terrier way, keeping me company from my lap as I pounded the keys into the wee hours of the morning, you and me, buddy. You and me.

To my husband, Jack, goes my love. Your unwavering encouragement and support have been the truest gifts. Thank you for believing that anything is possible . . . even castles in the air . . . especially castles in the air.

Turn the page for a sneak peek at
Emily Murdoch's next novel

Available Winter 2015

1

Back

He rocks me in arms as thick as the branches of a Texas ebony blackbead, his crooning gentler than the feet of a caterpillar tickling my palm. My forehead is on fire, that's how it feels, and I want my mom, but she won't come.

"You're a big girl now, Rabbit," he says, continuing to rock me in the same gentle way. "It's only the flu. You'll be okay soon enough."

I don't believe him, but I want to, so I settle myself against his chest, hacking and croupy as he uses a cupped hand to smack my back, helping me cough up all the gunk into his handerchief. There's a whistle in my throat with each exhale. Now both my head and my chest are on fire.

"Take some of this," he says. "The warmth will do you good."

I obey all of Kristof's commands. I no longer think to question him; not if I want to survive. Not if I want to see eleven. But the problem is, I'm not sure, anymore. Sometimes I think the alternative is better—any alternative is better—than this life of fear I'm living.

Like being rocked in the arms of a serial killer . . . the same one whose lips now nuzzle my hair, giving rise to the silent scream that could shatter the entirety of Texas, that invokes the flee feelings, *so close, too close*, to his touch, his smell, the smell of want. Of evil.

That's what close means, now. On the inside.

On the outside, I'm Rabbit. Sitting rabbit-still. Screaming rabbit-silent.

"C'mon now. Take it."

Spoonful after spoonful of chicken broth, my stomach in revolt, but I take it anyway. *Numbers have no feelings. Rabbits do.* I count each spoonful in my mind, anything to take me away from here.

From him.

Five . . . six . . . seven . . .

I never know when I'll have the opportunity to eat, again. And if we're ever going to escape, we need to be strong, that's what Hunter says.

So, I close my eyes and make pretend I'm the old Katinka, baking Christmas cookies with Mommy. Flour on the tips of our noses, as I press silver cookie cutters into the dough and lift out noble evergreens and Santa's big head and the Bethlehem star, careful not to round its pointers, the whole lot drowned in red, pink, blue, or yellow sugar sparkles, and sometimes all four colors at once, while mommy protests while tickling me with doughy fingers.

Nine . . . ten . . . eleven spoonfuls, the broth tinged purple by the cup of calf's blood Kristof always adds when Hunter or I get sick.

Hunter.

It's been three days since I've seen Hunter, since I've felt his warm hand search for mine under the table, his three squeezes, *in-it-together*, and then my response, *forever-and-ever* . . . and the last time, I'd flicked his hand away because he squirted my dress with cow's milk, just to make me cry.

I hate the smell of milk dried in the sun. Hunter knows this, because Hunter knows me better than anyone in the whole world.

Hunter's big for twelve . . . but not big enough. *Kristof must've locked him in the cellar.* I wish I could save Hunter some of my broth. *There's no food allowed in the cellar.*

Kristof says that's like eating Doritos in church.

Please don't let it be Velvetina Moo. I'd raised Velvetina Moo from the day she was born, nursing her with a rubber-nippled baby bottle when her mama died during the birthing. *Please don't let it be Velvetina's blood.*

Or Hunter's.

The vomit rises at the thought, but I swallow it down with *sixteen . . . seventeen . . . eighteen* spoonfuls.

"You're doing good, Rabbit," he says, and I nod, always nod. Because I know how Kristof's moods can whirl like dervishes, the switch so fast there's no time to sweet-talk or prepare for the consequences.

Still, I can't help it. "I want my mom," I say, before I can stop myself. I cringe, waiting for the backhand to swoop down, my rabbit mind zigging left, then right.

"You know she needed to be released of her sins. She's gone to a place that everyone goes to one day. She's very, very lucky."

"Thank you," I say, in Rabbit's voice. It's the only way. I know he needs to hear it.

"You're welcome. I'm the only one you have left, you know. I'm the only person who loves you in the whole world," he says, grinning down at me, "but you needn't worry. You're lucky enough to have God for your father."

I nod, but I don't mean it. I'll never mean it, and I don't have to.

What saves me? What keeps me Katinka, even if she's a secret? That his words aren't true. Because Hunter loves me. Hunter loves me for real.

I will my mind to float out of my body like a white balloon bumping against the ceiling. *He can't make me stay.* I pretend I'm the old Katinka, again, obliviously tucked into her trundle bed in her pink and purple bedroom, giant retro flowers growing across the walls, two kelly-green bean bag chairs, one for me, one for a friend. And my new gold lock on the door.

... *twenty-two* ... *twenty-three* ... *twenty-four* ...

"All you need is sleep, Rabbit."

God would know. My eyelashes flutter and close like butterfly wings put away for the night. The spoon clanks against the bowl as he pushes it aside, rising to his feet with me in his arms, barely the weight of a shadow's shadow.

My flannel nightgown is soaked straight through with fever and I shiver, going where he takes me, maybe thinking, maybe just a little, of believing him just for now. No matter what he's done in the past.

That he'll take care of me.

That he really does love me.

Kristof props me up in my white, ruffly bed, his arm around my body to keep me upright, his hand at the small of my back.

"Let's get you more comfortable."

I raise my arms when he instructs me to, and he strips me of my nightgown. I shiver in the cold room, all of ten years old and naked in front of him, but I'm used to it by now, and it's okay. *I'm a balloon bumping against the ceiling. I'm a balloon bumping against the ceiling. I'm a balloon bumping against the ceiling* ...

He doesn't drop a clean nightgown over my arms, letting the flannel slide down my body, hiding me again. This is Rabbit. That would've been Katinka, the girl who would've never been here, who would've never been sitting this way in front of a man. That four-leaf clover girl disappeared a year ago, the day Kristof took us ... and everyone knows four-leaf clovers are rare in the first place.

I know it's the smartest thing I could do, becoming Rabbit. Letting it happen. The world is a wild, tangle-dy place, but it rewards the cunning of little girls.

The devil you know is better than the devil you don't.

Especially when he says he's God.

Kristof drapes a cool rag over my forehead.

"Thank you," I say, before I can stop myself, using the last of my strength to form a smile, even though it's wrong. Wrong, to smile at him. My voice stretches thin as doll's hair in this plain bedroom of white walls, one white night table, one white lamp and one white desk. No pictures hang on the wall; only an antiquated, oval mirror in a whitewashed wooden frame. No special touches. No girl colors. No objects that make it mine, even though it is mine. My room in my new life.

"May I have some food, instead," I plead. "Maybe half a slice of bread?"

I can't remember when I baked the last loaf. I try to think, squinching my eyes tight, only to open them again when I feel his hand on my shoulder.

He smiles easily, raising my hopes for a moment, but when I look, *really look*, his eyes look like doll's eyes, bright and unfocused.

No relief to be found.

This time, he's starving me in the name of Catherine of Sienna. Because he caught me stealing an orange. And now I must be purified. It's been six days, and I think I may have pneumonia. I close my eyes. Pretend myself back in time, but it never works.

"I won't let you die," he says, reading my mind like God always does, the back of his hand brushing my cheek. I flinch before I can stop myself, and we pretend it didn't happen. I'm Rabbit again when I reach out and pull his hand back, butting my head beneath his palm like a kitten after the milking. Rabbit is good at pretending. At pretending she welcomes his touch, or even better, craves it.

"I won't let you die," he repeats, his hands massaging my pointy shoulders. "Not yet, anyway," he adds, his words soft as rain sliding down a Rabbit's face.

For the moment, I've saved my life. I open my eyes. Search his, but I can't see even a moment ahead.

I can't see down.

I can't see deep.

All I see is the nothingness of death and rot. I see what I'm not supposed to see, and inside, I recoil from the sight.

And then the disgust passes, and on the outside? On the outside, I see a man. A man caring for me, crooning church hymns under his breath and brushing the damp bangs off my forehead with fingertips that mean it.

And just then, I feel it; the familar wooziness of the knock-out sleepy pills crushed and mixed into fresh cow's milk, Coca-Cola in miniature glass bottles, TV dinners, pudding cups—the extras, the treats, the food I don't make from scratch each day as is my duty, to feed Kristof and Hunter.

Hunter.

I know what God does after he knocks me out. I'm not supposed to know, but I do.

"Bye," I say to Rabbit, as I let the River of Nothingness carry me downstream. Sometimes the best a girl can do, is leave. Decide what's real by deciding what she will or won't think about. Will or won't be present for. Will or won't bear witness to.

Sometimes it's the only way to say *no.*

You have to let yourself go.

Let your *self* go.

In that sense, the sleepy pills help more than harm.

Kristof's figure blurs around the edges like dandelion fuzz as I watch him set up the lights around me and start the camera rolling. I realize that's why the clean, dry nightgown never comes, and my body is slick with sweat as I wonder what part I'll be playing tonight. *Sick girl? Dying girl? Ravaged, skeletal saint?*

I see Mommy in heaven as I slide beneath the River of Nothingness, my lids too heavy to keep consciousness afloat.

She's waving at me from the spongy bank across the water, her arms loaded with daffodils.

"I love daffodils," I sing out, my strokes strong as I swim to shore, the sun like a big yellow blow dryer as I run to her side, my legs fast and strong like they used to be.

"Of course you do," Mommy says, her arm protective around me, her hand rubbing the small of my back in soothing circles. When I look up at her, she wears the sunlight like a halo. "You're my girl. My flower girl. Wild and free. You and me," she says, as she has since I was born, me that baby all purple and pruney screaming her opinion to the world from day one.

That girl's gone, now. But when Mommy comes, I'm her, again. I'm her girl. *Her* girl.

And even at ten, I know it's a huge price to pay . . . but one I'm willing to pay over and over, to have her back. To pretend it's life *back*, not *forth* . . .

Especially when there's always a *forth*. Especially when Kristof's always in it.

As I match my stride to Mommy's, my last thought is of Hunter. I stop dead in my tracks. Drop her petal-soft hand.

"*Where's Hunter?*" I ask her, my eyes pleading, my voice coming from my soul.

The sky crowds with storm clouds stamping and snorting and reminding me of Kristof's largest cow herd. I shiver in my skin, realizing my nakedness for the first time, and all of a sudden, it's not okay . . . not even in front of her.

And then the clouds pass. I hear the river burping and gurgling with joy. I'm clothed in a dress of sunbeams, and we scooch down to gather the spilled daffodils, smiling at each other, but it doesn't soothe me all the way.

Because even here, I'm still Rabbit, smiling half a smile until Hunter smiles back the other half.

Even here, I'm Rabbit.

And when the pills wear off, Rabbit always wakes up.